To my sister,
Brenda P. Holt:

"Though she be but little, she is fierce."

A Midsummer Night's Dream, Act III, Scene 1

Praise for Toni L.P. Kelner and her
Laura Fleming mysteries

COUNTRY COMES TO TOWN

"This is one you don't want to miss."

—*Mystery Lovers Bookshop News*

"A classic, cozy whodunit."

—*San Jose Mercury News*

TROUBLE LOOKING FOR A PLACE TO HAPPEN

"Lively and lighthearted."

—*Publishers Weekly*

"Charming and chatty . . . Laura and her clan's Southern hospitality will make you feel welcomed."

—*Fort Lauderdale Sun-Sentinel*

DEAD RINGER

"The motive is a surprise and the complications convincing."

—*Murder ad lib*

"Blends romance and violence with long buried secrets, then adds a dash of humor for a mystery that goes down smoother than a glass of sweet iced tea."

—Margaret Maron, Edgar award–winning author of BOOTLEGGER'S DAUGHTER

DOWN HOME MURDER

"A wonderful book, a terrific character driven storytelling triumph. It is an exceptional piece of work. Highly recommended."

—*I Love a Mystery*

"Kelner has written a tightly woven tale of family quarrels, jealousies, secrets and loyalties. Laura Fleming is interesting, likable and a delight to read."

—*The Armchair Detective*

"Toni L.P. Kelner serves up a mystery as Southern as grits and sausage biscuits with a heroine who is as brave as she is likable."

—Carolyn G. Hart, author of YANKEE DOODLE DEAD

Books by Toni L.P. Kelner

DOWN HOME MURDER

DEAD RINGER

TROUBLE LOOKING FOR A PLACE TO HAPPEN

COUNTRY COMES TO TOWN

TIGHT AS A TICK

DEATH OF A DAMN YANKEE

Published by Kensington Publishing Corporation

A LAURA FLEMING MYSTERY

TIGHT AS A TICK

Toni L.P. Kelner

KENSINGTON BOOKS
Kensington Publishing Corp.
http://www.kensingtonbooks.com

KENSINGTON BOOKS are published by

Kensington Publishing Corp.
850 Third Avenue
New York, NY 10022

First Kensington Hardcover Printing: January, 1998
First Kensington Paperback Printing: August, 1999
10 9 8 7 6 5 4 3 2 1

Printed in the United States of America

ACKNOWLEDGMENTS

I want to thank:

- Stephen P. Kelner, Jr., for doing everything he could to help me finish this book. He encouraged me, took care of Maggie so I could work, edited the manuscript at every step of the process, and laughed at all the right places.
- Peggy R. Perry, William E. Perry, and Warren K. Schnabel, Jr., for telling me what it's like to work at a flea market and for giving me more great stories than I could fit into one book.
- John W. Holt for supplying Carney Alexander.
- Elizabeth F. Shaw for proofreading, baby-sitting, and reminding me that not everybody speaks Southern.
- Robin P. Schnabel for sharing the experience of getting a hummingbird tattoo.
- Troy Soos for last-minute baby-sitting and creating the Byerly Bobbins.
- Connie P. Spencer for last-minute proofreading while on vacation.
- Magdalene W. Kelner for taking long naps.

Chapter 1

I wasn't there when they found Carney Alexander's body, but my great-aunt Maggie was, and like many Southerners, she has a gift for storytelling. Between her description and my getting a chance to see the place later, I had no problem imagining it.

The Tight as a Tick Flea Market was busy that Sunday, Aunt Maggie said. There were lots of people coming by her booth to look at Carnival glass plates, Fenton vases, and Occupied Japan figurines. But it wasn't too busy for Aunt Maggie to notice that Carney hadn't shown up at the booth where he sold collector knives. That wasn't like Carney. He usually got there at the crack of dawn, even earlier than Aunt Maggie.

Around ten-thirty, Bender Cawthorne came by to collect the day's rent, which he was supposed to do first thing in the morning. But Aunt Maggie said that Bender usually drank so much on Saturday night that ten-thirty was first thing in the morning for him. Aunt Maggie asked him where Rusty was. The half-chow, half-German shepherd was the only creature on earth who could stand to live with Bender. Bender explained that Rusty was at Dr. Josie's.

The people living near the flea market lot had been complaining that every puppy born for the past few years looked just like Rusty. Bender's brother Evan, who actually owned the lot, didn't like it when the neighbors complained, and he'd insisted that Bender get Rusty fixed. Bender had done what he was told, but he didn't see what the fuss was about. Rusty was an awful good dog, and those lady dogs could have done a lot worse.

Aunt Maggie told Bender he was probably right. Rusty was the smartest dog she'd ever seen, except for his taste in human companions, but she didn't tell Bender that. Anyway, after she paid her rent, Bender saw that Carney wasn't there.

He asked Aunt Maggie if she knew where he was, but when she told him that she didn't, he went to collect rent from the rest of the inside dealers. Aunt Maggie said he asked everybody near enough for her to hear if they'd talked to Carney, but neither China Upton, who sold country crafts, nor Obed the Donut Man had heard a word. Tattoo Bob said he'd been concentrating so hard on the dragon he was inking across a man's shoulder that he hadn't even noticed that Carney was missing.

In Aunt Maggie's opinion, if Bender had had a lick of sense, he'd have known something was wrong. Carney had been a dealer at the flea market for four years, almost as long as Aunt Maggie, and in all that time, he'd never missed a weekend. But then again, if Bender had a lick of sense, he'd have been doing something with his life other than running a flea market on his brother's property, and he'd be living someplace other than a beat-up house trailer in the back of the lot.

Bender didn't even think to check around Carney's booth to see if anything looked out of place, or to go get Carney's phone number and call him. He just scratched his head and went to collect rent in the other buildings.

Aunt Maggie admitted that maybe she should have done something herself, but she didn't even have a chance to take a bathroom break until nearly four o'clock. After that, there was a steady stream of business until Bender locked up at five. She didn't think about Carney again until the end of the day.

Once the customers were out of the building, Aunt Maggie straightened up her tables and set out fresh stock to fill the gaps from where things had sold during the day. China was doing the same thing while Bob cleaned his needles and Obed washed his pans and utensils. China finished before anybody else, and when she walked by on her way out, Aunt Maggie asked her if she knew anything about Carney.

She said she didn't, and when Bob and Obed joined them a minute or two later, they didn't either. It was Aunt Maggie who suggested that they look around his booth to see if everything looked all right, and though the others agreed, they acted like they felt funny about it. So they let Aunt Maggie go back behind Carney's table.

The sheet Carney used to cover up his display cases was still in place, and Aunt Maggie shook her head over its condition. Lots of dealers use old sheets to keep the dust off, but Carney's sheet went beyond being old. It was nothing more than a rag, and filthy dirty to boot. It was so nasty that Aunt Maggie didn't see the blood right away. There were dark brown stains along the edge touching the floor.

Aunt Maggie said that there was a smell, too, which she hadn't noticed before. Of course, with donuts and pork skins frying all day, she wouldn't have. Now that she did, she thought she knew what she was smelling. Anybody else would have left that sheet where it was, and called Bender or the police, but not Aunt Maggie. She just took a deep breath, grabbed hold of the sheet, and whipped it off. There was Carney, folded up under the table like a ventriloquist's dummy in a suitcase. Aunt Maggie didn't see the knife buried in his back, but she did see the blood. There was way too much of it for Carney to be alive.

Chapter 2

I wasn't thinking about blood when I got to Aunt Nora's house the next Friday evening. Well, I was thinking about my own flesh and blood, which is what Aunt Nora calls us Burnettes, but that's usually a peaceful thing to think about. Only it wasn't at all peaceful when we arrived.

Aunt Nora's middle son, Thaddeous, could have warned us about what to expect when he picked us up at the Hickory Regional Airport, or during the drive to Byerly, but he was too busy asking us about his girlfriend Michelle. He'd met Michelle while in Boston visiting me the previous January, and they'd fallen for each other hard enough that she was planning to move down to North Carolina as soon as she could get a job in Byerly. For now they were separated, and my husband Richard's month-long trip to England was still recent enough that I could be sympathetic. Besides which, Thaddeous had had so many unsuccessful love affairs that the whole family was relieved that this one seemed to be working out.

So I dutifully recounted all of Michelle's messages to Thaddeous, and assured him that she wasn't having second thoughts about him or moving to Byerly. Then I gave him the thick letter that Michelle had made me promise to deliver.

Once we got to Aunt Nora and Uncle Buddy's house, Thaddeous said we should go on in while he transferred our suitcases to Aunt Maggie's Dodge Caravan, since we'd be staying with her. Why he didn't warn us then, I don't know, but I guess he was thinking about the letter. I knew he wouldn't be coming inside until he'd read it through at least twice.

I braced myself for a bombardment of hugs as soon as we opened the front door, because that's what usually happens when I come home, but this time they didn't even notice we were there. There was too much going on already.

Thaddeous's older brother Augustus was sprawled on the couch looking angry, which surprised me. After all, Augustus's homecoming was the reason Richard and I were there, and I'd thought it would be a happy one. Aunt Nora had been beside herself when she found out he was coming home after four years in the army, especially so close to his birthday, and had immediately started planning the biggest celebration she could manage.

Augustus wasn't the only one mad. Though Uncle Buddy didn't look mad, he had that blank expression on his face that means he's mad. Since he was pointedly not looking at Augustus, I was pretty sure that they were mad at each other.

Aunt Nora and Uncle Buddy's youngest son, Willis, was sitting next to Uncle Buddy, not saying a word. Of course he rarely says a word, so that didn't prove much.

Aunt Daphine and her daughter Vasti and son-in-law Arthur were over in the corner, talking quietly. Since Vasti isn't much on being quiet, I could hear her side of the conversation, which consisted of things like, "What on earth is the matter with him?" and, "I hope he's happy."

Aunt Maggie was picking up Aunt Nora's knickknacks so she could check for identifying marks on the bottom. Professional interest, no doubt, since she's a flea market dealer.

Nobody had noticed us yet, so I said, "Are we at the right party?"

Everybody jerked in our direction, and some of them smiled, but Vasti said, "Laurie Anne, does this look like a party to you?"

"Not yet," I said. "There aren't enough people here." As many as there were, it still wasn't all of us Burnettes. We were missing Aunt Ruby Lee and Uncle Roger, with Clifford, Earl, and Ilene; Aunt Nellie and Uncle Ruben and the triplets, Idelle, Odelle, and Carlelle; and Aunt Edna with her son Linwood, daughter-in-law Sue, and their kids. Plus there were usually various sweethearts around, like Clifford's girlfriend Liz, Aunt Edna's beau Caleb, and Ilene's new boyfriend Trey. "Are we early?"

"Yeah, you're early," Uncle Buddy said. "About a week early."

"Is that Laurie Anne and Richard?" Aunt Nora called out, and without waiting for an answer, she burst out of the kitchen. "Why didn't somebody tell me y'all were here?"

Finally I got the hug I'd been expecting. Once she was through, Aunt Daphine was right behind her, with Vasti, Arthur, Willis, and Uncle Buddy coming next. With a roll call like that hugging onto me and Richard, you wouldn't have expected anybody to notice that Augustus hadn't joined in, but Aunt Nora did.

"Augustus, aren't you going to hug Laurie Anne's neck?" she asked.

Since when did anybody in my family have to be invited

to hug somebody else's neck? "If he doesn't, I'm going to chase him down and hug him anyway," I said, trying to make a joke out of it.

"Hey there, cousin," he said with a little smile, and came on over. His hug was enthusiastic enough to reassure me; at least it was until Uncle Buddy spoke.

"You may as well apologize to her while you're at it," he said, "and to Richard, too."

Augustus stiffened and stepped back, not seeming to notice Richard's outstretched hand. Then he walked up the stairs without saying a word.

"Well, I never," Vasti said indignantly, hands on her hips. "After all this, the *least* he could do is explain to Laurie Anne and Richard. If he's got an explanation, that is, because goodness knows he hasn't given one to anybody else."

"What in the Sam Hill is going on?" I asked.

"Oh, Laurie Anne, I am so sorry," Aunt Nora said, and hugged me again. "I don't know how it happened, but I know Augustus didn't mean to do it. He must have just forgotten to call and tell you, what with the excitement of being home and all."

"Forgot to call and tell me what?"

"Did Thaddeous not tell you?" she asked.

I shook my head.

Vasti said, "He was probably too embarrassed. I know I am, and Augustus is just my cousin, not my brother. Sometimes I am so glad I'm an only child."

There are times when we're all glad Vasti is an only child. Not that my cousin, with her bouncy brown curls and high heels to match every outfit, isn't charming in her own way, but having one of her around has always been a gracious plenty.

"Could somebody tell us what it is that we were supposed to have been told?" Richard said.

"We had to move the party," Aunt Nora said, looking miserable. "Vasti said there were too many people to crowd in here, and it'd be better if we had it at the church hall."

"Y'all said it was a good idea," Vasti said defensively.

Aunt Nora said, "I know we did, Vasti. I'm not blaming you. It's just that the church hall was already reserved for a Girl Scout sleep-over tonight, so we decided to reschedule. Augustus's birthday isn't until Wednesday, so we figured that later would be just as good."

"So the party is tomorrow?" I said, but I wasn't hopeful. Aunt Nora wouldn't be looking so unhappy if we were only one day off.

She shook her head. "No, it's next Saturday. I meant to call, but—"

"Don't you go taking the blame, Nora," Uncle Buddy said. "Augustus was supposed to call right after we found out. There'd have been plenty of time for Laurie Anne to change her plans if he'd called like he said he would."

"It just slipped his mind, I guess," Aunt Nora said, but she didn't sound convinced. "I should have checked with him—"

"A grown man shouldn't need his mama to check up on him." Uncle Buddy raised his voice, most likely to make sure that Augustus could hear him all the way upstairs. "And he should be man enough to apologize for his mistake."

"Laurie Anne and Richard will just have to stay until next Saturday," Vasti said.

That was easy for her to say. She wasn't the one who'd already planned a week on Cape Cod when Aunt Nora came up with the party idea. It was August, so Richard had the time off from teaching at Boston College anyway, but my vacation days were nearly used up. I'd had to shorten the Cape Cod trip to be able to come to North Carolina at all, and we were planning to leave early Sunday to head straight for the Cape.

Fortunately, Aunt Daphine understood. "They can't up and change their plans like that, Vasti. I bet they've already got their hotel set up and their plane tickets bought."

"We did plan around the party being tonight," I said.

Aunt Nora nodded, still looking mournful. "I wouldn't expect y'all to change your plans. After I realized y'all hadn't been told—"

There was an ominous rumble from Uncle Buddy.

Aunt Nora went on. "I tried to move the party back to tonight, but Roger and Ruby Lee had already set up a road trip, and they took Ilene and the boys with them. They won't be back until next week."

"The triplets have gone to Myrtle Beach," Aunt Daphine said. "They offered to cancel, but they'd already put in for their vacation at the mill, and they couldn't change it. Edna and Caleb went to a grocers' convention in Charlotte, and Linwood and Sue decided to go along and take the kids to Carowinds."

Aunt Nora waved her hands around helplessly. "There just wasn't anything we could do, Laurie Anne. I wanted us all to be together so bad. It would have been the first time since before Paw died."

I looked at her standing there, her eyes wet with tears. Then I looked at Richard, and shrugged, meaning that maybe we should stay. He shrugged back, which meant that maybe we should, but did I want to? I nodded to say that I did want to, and he nodded to say that it was okay with him.

To those who couldn't read our shrugs and nods, I said, "You know, Richard and I can go to the Cape anytime. It's only a couple hours' drive from Boston." Of course, we'd reserved a cottage right on the beach nearly a year ago, and paid a deposit, but there was no reason to tell them that. "And we can get our plane tickets changed." Michelle, who worked at my company when she wasn't being Thaddeous's girlfriend, had arranged the tickets for us and had warned me that they were nonrefundable and couldn't be changed for anything short of a hurricane, but maybe she could trade them in for a couple of seats back to Boston on a Greyhound bus. "There's no reason we can't stay until the party."

"Do you mean it?" Aunt Nora said.

"Are you sure?" Aunt Daphine asked suspiciously.

"We wouldn't miss it for anything," Richard said firmly.

I was going to have to do something extra special for my husband to make up for this sacrifice. Not that Byerly isn't nice, but visiting family in a small North Carolina mill town just isn't the same as lounging in a beach-front cottage. So much for the new bathing suit I'd bought, and I didn't think I'd be likely to wear the slinky nightgown either, not when we'd be staying at Aunt Maggie's house.

Come to think of it, I'd better make sure that it was going to be all right to stay there for the whole week. Aunt Maggie had stayed in the background, but now I turned to her. And blinked.

"Aunt Maggie?" I said, then wished I hadn't made it sound like a question. It's just that she didn't look like herself. At least, her hair didn't. I've always liked the way Aunt Maggie leaves her hair salt-and-pepper colored. I never thought she'd dye it, especially not like that. "You look good," I finally said, wondering if it was possible to tell a white lie about shoe-polish-black hair.

"I look like a darned fool. Daphine and Vasti have been after me for I don't know how long to dye my hair, but up until last week, I had enough sense not to listen to them. But I found a box of hair color in a lot I bought at auction and thought I'd give it a try, just to hush them up." She ran her fingers through her hair like she was trying to rub the color off. "This is what happens when you listen to your relatives."

From behind her, I saw Aunt Daphine roll her eyes, and I tried not to grin. I asked, "Is it all right if Richard and I stay with you until next week?"

"Of course it is. As a matter of fact, I've got something I want y'all to do."

"Just name it," Richard said, and I tried not to wince, wishing he hadn't been so quick to volunteer. With Aunt Maggie, there was no telling what she had in mind.

She must have guessed what I was thinking, because she said, "Don't worry, I don't want you to paint the house or clean the attic or anything like that. I just want you to do what you're best at."

"You've got a computer you need me to fix?" I asked. Though Aunt Maggie had never shown much interest in my programming, if she'd picked up a PC somewhere cheap, I could see her wanting me to set it up for her.

But she snorted. "I wouldn't know what to do with one if I had it. No, I want you to solve me a murder."

Chapter 3

Before I could ask Aunt Maggie what murder she was talking about, Aunt Nora called us to dinner. "We'll talk about it later," was all Aunt Maggie would say as we went into the dining room.

I suppose Aunt Maggie's annoucement should have affected my appetite, but it wasn't the first time my family had sent me after a killer. Admittedly, I'd gone after the first one on my own, but after that, my family had come to expect it of me. Since I hadn't heard of a death in the family or of anybody in the family getting arrested, I wasn't as worried as I might have been otherwise.

Besides which, Aunt Nora is one of the best cooks in the known universe. She doesn't cook anything fancy, but what she can do with chicken and dumplings is fancy enough for me, especially with collard greens and biscuits on the side. As for dessert, Aunt Daphine may not cook as well as Aunt Nora, but nobody can match her apple pie. She'd brought two of them to make sure there was plenty for everybody, which there was, but just barely. There's a reason that people in Boston get hungry when I tell them about my trips to North Carolina.

Aunt Daphine was sitting next to me, and she said, "Laurie Anne, you know I didn't mean for Aunt Maggie to do that to her hair. I wanted her to come down to the shop so I could fix it for her."

"I know," I said.

"But no, she couldn't do that. Instead she uses some box of hair color that's probably as old as she is, and then blames me when it comes out looking like that."

"I know."

"I could bleach it and put in some decent-looking color but she won't let me. She says she's going to let it grow out. Can you imagine what it's going to look like in two months?"

I tried, I really tried, but I just couldn't. "Will you do me a favor and send me a picture?"

That broke her up, which made me start laughing. Augustus, who was sitting across from me, joined in heartily, and I hadn't even realized that he was listening. In fact, he kept laughing after Aunt Daphine and I stopped.

When he finally quit snickering, I said, "Augustus, tell me about Germany. Was it as beautiful as it looks in the postcards?"

He smiled slowly, and I couldn't help noticing how much he looked like Paw, our late grandfather. Normally that would have been a compliment. Paw had been a slight man with light blue eyes, a good chin, and a smile that hardly ever went away. Augustus had the same features, but his eyes were distant and his smile didn't seem to be aimed at me, or at anybody else in the room. He looked worn, stretched thin in a way Paw hadn't been except in times of bad trouble.

He said, "It was about like you'd expect. Everything was real old. Sometimes I swear I could just feel the age seeping into me. There were some good places to party, though. Some real good places."

He stopped, and I waited for a minute, expecting details, a funny story or two, something. But he didn't seem to have anything else to say. "Where all did you go?" I asked.

He thought it over, chewing slowly. "Worms, of course. That's where I was stationed most of the time. Little place, but they got a big old church there. I went inside it once."

From across the table, Richard asked, "Isn't that the cathedral where Martin Luther posted the Diet of Worms?"

"A diet of worms?" Vasti said. "Who would eat that?"

I think she was kidding.

As for Augustus, he nodded, but didn't say anything else.

I said, "You went to Paris, too, didn't you? What was it like? Is the food as good as they say it is?"

"It was all right. I don't remember much about the food."

"Is Paris where you got that smelly-good-em you're wearing?" Arthur asked.

Now that Arthur mentioned it, Augustus was kind of fragrant. I'd noticed it when we sat down, but I'd blamed it on Vasti, who never thinks that less is more, especially not when putting on perfume. Tonight Augustus smelled nicer than she did.

Vasti must have thought so, too, because she said, "You could have brought me some French perfume."

All Augustus said was, "I didn't do much shopping."

Richard caught my eye, and I shrugged, this time meaning that I didn't have any idea of what was wrong with Augustus. The last time we'd seen him, he'd been chattering a mile a minute about all the sights he wanted to see in Europe. He'd spent months reading up on European history, art, and food. Now he acted like it was no big deal. Of course, it had been a few years since I'd seen him. Though both he and I had been home to visit since then, we'd never been there at the same time. I'd have thought Aunt Nora would have told me that he'd changed so much, but maybe it had happened so gradually that she hadn't noticed.

I tried again to draw him out. "It must be strange to be out of the army after all these years. Do you think you're going to miss it much?"

He just shook his head and took another bite of his food.

"What are your plans now?"

"I haven't got any."

"Why didn't you reenlist?" Vasti asked. "It's not like you've got a job here."

"He can have himself a job at the mill any time he wants," Thaddeous said heartily. "All he has to do is come by."

"I just might do that," Augustus said. "Maybe next week."

But I heard Uncle Buddy mutter, "He's been saying that ever since he got back."

"Augustus is taking some time to catch his breath," Aunt Nora said. "Jet lag and all."

"Jet lag is a killer," I said. "It took Richard forever to get over his when he got back from England." Richard nodded, but both he and I knew that it had taken him no more than a week to get back to normal. Augustus had been back nearly a month. Something was wrong, and no matter what Aunt Nora said, she thought so, too.

Probably to change the subject, Aunt Nora said, "Are you feeling all right, Richard?"

"As far as I know. Do I look sick?" he said.

Richard's dark brown hair was as disheveled as ever,

but he looked good to me, especially those eyes of his, which were enough to make any woman fall in love with him.

"Not at all, it's just I haven't heard you say anything from Shakespeare since you've been here."

Richard looked sheepish as I said, "He's giving it up for a while. We were out with some friends, and Richard laughed at them for talking shop. He said they don't know how to draw the line between work and real life. Then our friend Libby said he had no room to talk because he couldn't quit quoting Shakespeare if his life depended on it, and everybody else agreed with her. Richard wanted to prove them wrong, so he's vowed not to say anything Shakespearean until classes start up again."

"How would they know if he did it when they're not around?" Thaddeous wanted to know.

"They trust him, for one," I said. "And I'm watching him, for another. There's money riding on this, and I get a cut if he loses."

Everybody laughed while Richard tried to look injured. "Apparently some people find the habit annoying, though I can't see why."

"It's not a bit annoying," Aunt Nora said, which was awfully nice of her. "It's just that sometimes it's hard for us to make out what you're talking about."

Thaddeous asked, "How long has this been going on?"

"One week, six days, and eighteen hours," Richard said glumly. "Which means that I've got two weeks, two days, and fourteen hours to go."

Everybody laughed again, except for Aunt Maggie, who was shaking her head like she couldn't figure out what was so funny. I've always thought that deep down Aunt Maggie is amused by me and Richard, but it must be real deep down, because she sure doesn't let it show.

Changing the subject again, Aunt Maggie said, "Arthur, I spoke to Evan Cawthorne the other day, and he wants to know if y'all have done anything about the town line yet."

"He knows I'm doing everything I can," Arthur said. "I want to buy that property as much as he wants to sell it, but that map is nowhere to be found."

"What map is that?" I asked.

"The map that shows where the border between Byerly and Rocky Shoals is," Aunt Maggie said. "You know Tight as a Tick Flea Market where I set up?"

I nodded.

"Evan Cawthorne is the man who owns the lot, and Arthur wants to buy it."

"For a secret business deal," Vasti said. "I can't tell you any details right now."

I already knew what her secret was, and from the expressions on faces around the table, everybody else did, too. Vasti isn't very good at keeping secrets. She was talking about Arthur's plan to relocate his car dealership. Since there's not a lot of public transportation in North Carolina, and none in Byerly, cars are mighty important. Arthur's business was booming, and he needed space to expand.

Aunt Maggie went on. "Evan wants to sell, but he can't until they figure out which town the land is in."

"I thought the flea market was in Byerly," Richard said.

"Part of it is," Aunt Maggie agreed, "but part of it's in Rocky Shoals. The lot is right on top of the town line. According to Byerly maps, most of it's in Byerly, but according to Rocky Shoals maps, most of it's in Rocky Shoals."

"Our map predates the Rocky Shoals map by a month, so that should settle it," Arthur said indignantly. "But the Rocky Shoals town clerk noticed that our map is a hand-drawn copy, and they insist on seeing the original."

"What happened to the original?" I asked.

"It's been misplaced," Arthur said.

Vasti said, "Can you imagine that? Is that any way to run a city? Thank goodness Arthur is on the city council to make sure things are done right."

Aunt Maggie looked skeptical, but all she said was, "Evan's probably got a place in his bank account waiting for that money so he can watch the interest grow. I never saw anybody so close with his money as Evan Cawthorne."

"You can't blame him for being careful," Aunt Nora said. "If I'd spent my childhood never knowing where my next meal was coming from, I'd be thrifty, too."

"Thrifty?" Aunt Maggie snorted. "Evan Cawthorne is as tight as a tick, and you know it. Where do you think he got the name for the flea market?" Aunt Maggie turned back to Arthur. "What do you want me to tell him?"

Arthur mumbled something about what he'd like to tell him, and Vasti said, "I'd think Mr. Cawthorne would have more important things to worry about right now, what with that man getting killed over there. I hear he bled—"

Uncle Buddy said, "Not at the table. That kind of talk upsets Nora."

Actually, it was Uncle Buddy who had the queasy stomach, but even Vasti knew better than to point that out. I wished he'd let her keep talking because that was probably the murder Aunt Maggie had mentioned earlier. Since we couldn't talk about that, we talked about the rest of the family.

Aunt Edna and Caleb were still getting along like gang-busters, but there was some debate as to whether or not Linwood was going to break them up. Caleb was the first man Edna had dated since the death of her husband, and Linwood wasn't happy about it.

"They never get any time alone," Aunt Nora said. "Here they decided to go to that convention, and Linwood just had to tag along. If having him and Sue and those four kids of theirs along doesn't discourage Caleb, it must be love."

Uncle Roger and Aunt Ruby Lee were constantly busy because Roger's Ramblers kept getting more and more popular. Uncle Roger's road trips and the carousing that went along with them had broken up their first marriage, but when they remarried, Aunt Ruby Lee decided to go along and manage the group so Uncle Roger could concentrate on the music. To everybody's surprise, she was turning out to be one heck of a manager. As Aunt Nora explained, "The club owners see those big blue eyes and all that blond hair—"

"And her—" Augustus started, and knowing how buxom Aunt Ruby Lee is, I thought I knew what he was about to say.

But Aunt Nora cut him off. "And her figure, and they think they're going to be able to pull the wool over her eyes. But before they know it, they've promised her twice as much money as they meant to, and free drinks for the band. I don't know how she does it. She's starting to set up dates for the kids' band, too."

Aunt Ruby Lee's three children had started their own band. "Have they settled on a name?" I asked.

"Not yet," Thaddeous said. "Right now they're going by the Carolina Cowboys, but they don't like it much."

"I have a wonderful name for them, but they won't use

it," Vasti said. "I think they should call themselves the Byerly Buckaroos."

I could see why they wouldn't. The Byerly Buckaroos sounded like a kid's cartoon show to me. That brought us to Aunt Nellie and Uncle Ruben, and I asked why they weren't there with the rest of us.

Aunt Daphine said, "They're cleaning out their store. They got the landlord to let them out of the lease, but they have to get everything out of there tonight."

"Already?" I asked. "What happened? I thought a video rental place would go over great in Byerly."

"It would have if they'd had anything anybody wanted to see," Thaddeous said. "They got a good deal on a bunch of tapes, and it didn't occur to them that the reason they were so cheap was because most of them were movies nobody had ever heard of. Half of them wouldn't even run on a regular VCR."

"They didn't buy Beta tapes, did they?" I asked.

Thaddeous nodded.

Even when Aunt Nellie and Uncle Ruben had a good idea, they still managed to wrest defeat from the jaws of victory.

"How are the triplets?" I asked.

"Still chasing everything in pants," Vasti said with a sniff.

I thought about reminding her how man-crazy she'd been before marrying Arthur, but decided to be nice. "They aren't still stuck on Slim Grady, are they?" Slim played guitar for the Ramblers, and last summer, Carlelle, Idelle, and Odelle had all set their caps for him, which had caused no end of trouble.

"Lord, no," Aunt Nora said. "They've gone through two

or three fellows each since then. Now they're down at the beach looking for new ones."

"I don't think those three are ever going to settle down and raise a family," Vasti said. "Which reminds me, Arthur. We have to be sure and get home early. You saw the calendar today, didn't you?"

Arthur turned beet red, and I didn't blame him. The whole family knew that he and Vasti were trying to have a baby, but we really didn't need to know the particulars.

Vasti said, "What about you, Richard? Isn't your clock ticking?"

She was referring to his biological clock, which I know he knew, but he assumed an innocent expression, held up his watch hand, and said, "It's digital—doesn't tick."

While Vasti was trying to come up with an answer, Aunt Nora shooed us away from the table. I offered to help clean up, but she never lets me. The only one she would let help was Aunt Daphine, and that was so they could gossip.

Richard and I went to sit in the living room with everybody else, but Vasti hadn't been kidding when she said she wanted to get home early. She didn't even sit down—just pulled on Arthur's arm and said, "We have to get going, honey. We don't want to miss our chance." His face went red again.

I'd expected to spend the evening visiting, but Aunt Maggie said, "I think we'll be getting on home, too. I've got some business to discuss with Laurie Anne and Richard, and I'd just as soon do it in private." She looked directly at Vasti when she said it. Telling Vasti something is like announcing it over a bad loudspeaker. Everybody around hears it, but the details get garbled.

We didn't leave right away, of course. Goodbyes in

Byerly are long, drawn-out affairs, even when the people involved are going to see each other again the next day. With Richard and me just in town for a visit, it took even longer, and required many hugs, promises to spend lots of time together, and a few tears from Aunt Nora. I'm not sure why she was crying, but Aunt Nora doesn't really enjoy a family event unless she gets a chance to cry about something.

So it was more than half an hour later that Arthur, Vasti, Aunt Maggie, Richard, and I finally got out the door. Then, despite her claiming to be in a hurry, Vasti had to tell me a half a dozen tidbits of gossip about people I barely knew and tell me how pale I looked. I was going to remind her that the weather in Boston doesn't make it easy to get a tan, but Richard spoke up first to tell her that it was the contrast between my soft brown hair and deep brown eyes that made my skin look so fair. That hushed her up long enough for us to jump into the car with Aunt Maggie.

Chapter 4

"If Vasti does get pregnant," I said as we drove away, "I bet the baby comes late."

"And is born talking," Aunt Maggie added.

"Poor Arthur," Richard said. "Having to perform on schedule must be tough."

"Especially with the whole family knowing what they're doing," Aunt Maggie said. "In my day, things like that were kept private."

"Speaking of private matters," Richard said, "what's this about a murder? Can I assume that the death at the flea market is the one you're concerned with?"

"Of course it is. How many murders do you think we have in Byerly?"

He didn't answer, and I knew what he was thinking without any shrugs or nods. For the past few years, there'd been a murder pretty much every time we'd come to Byerly. I was surprised they'd still let us into town.

Aunt Maggie said, "I'd just as soon wait till we get to the house to get into it so I don't get interrupted in the middle."

That was fine with me. I wanted a minute to catch my breath. As much as I love my family, being around them wears me out, especially after a half day at work, two frenzied hours of packing, and the flight from Boston.

Besides, I always enjoy the drive to Aunt Maggie's house. It's not all that scenic, but there's something special about coming home and seeing all the places I'd grown up around. Of course, there are changes every time I come back, but at night they don't show so much.

I'd lived half my life in the Burnette home place because Paw took me in when my parents died. When he died, Aunt Maggie inherited it, but I still feel very close to Paw when I'm there.

It's not a fancy house or even particularly pretty, but it is friendly looking, like a threadbare old bathrobe that feels better than anything else you own. In the dark, I could just barely tell the difference between the parts that had been the original wood frame farmhouse and the pieces that later generations added on.

Richard and I always stay in my old bedroom, and we took our stuff upstairs as soon as we got inside. Then we went down to the den in the basement, where Aunt Maggie had bottles of Coke waiting for us.

Richard and I sat down on the couch, still covered in a bright floral pattern that refuses to fade. Aunt Maggie sat in the battered brown recliner facing us.

"Here," she said, handing us a pad and a ballpoint pen. "I figured you'd want to take notes."

Richard took the pad, but I was starting to get peeved. Aunt Maggie was assuming that we were going to do what she wanted before we even knew what it was all about. I said, "I don't remember saying that we'd be doing anything we'd need notes for."

"I figured that since you were going to be in town anyway, you'd want something to do," she said.

"I think we could find enough to do to fill a week." Shoot, if we only allotted two hours per relative, we'd barely have enough time to sleep. "Why would we want to spend our vacation chasing a murderer? We didn't even know the man who was killed, did we?"

"No, you didn't, but you've got a good reason to find his killer."

"Why?"

"Because I'm asking you to."

I started to argue with her, but instead I took a swallow of my Coke. Aunt Maggie is one of the most independent people I've ever met. I couldn't think of the last time she'd asked anybody for help. Even at her age, she'd tried to paint the house by herself last year. Fortunately, Aunt Nora drove by and saw her at it, and got her boys to come take over. If catching this murderer meant that much to her, I wasn't going to turn her down without a darned good reason.

I said, "All right, Aunt Maggie, we'll do what we can."

"Absolutely," Richard chimed in.

"I appreciate it."

Then I asked, "Did you know the man who was killed?"

"Carney? I knew him for years. He started selling at the flea market a month or two after I did. His booth was right across from mine."

"Were y'all close?" I thought maybe I knew why this was so important to her. I hadn't heard about her dating anybody since the night she went dancing with Big Bill Walters, but if anybody in my family could keep a romance secret, it was Aunt Maggie. Then she knocked that idea right out of my head.

"No closer than I had to be. I never did care for Carney."

"Is the person the police think killed him a friend of yours?"

"The police don't have any idea of who killed him, and at the rate they're going, I don't think they ever will."

"Really? Junior usually knows what she's doing." Junior Norton is Byerly's police chief, and I'd never dream of getting in her way unless family was involved.

"It's not Junior who's in charge," Aunt Maggie said. "Laurie Anne, why don't you let me tell it from the beginning? Then you can ask questions."

"Yes, ma'am."

"All right. This is what happened." She lowered her voice like she used to when she told us kids ghost stories, which was appropriate, because what she said was spooky enough for a ghost story. The idea of all of those people walking by when there was a dead man so close they could have touched him really gave me the creeps.

"What did y'all do?" I asked after Aunt Maggie described finding Carney's body.

"Bob ran to the pay phone at the snack bar, and Obed took off for Bender's trailer to tell him."

"They left you and the other woman alone with the body?" Richard asked.

"Why wouldn't they? Do you think I got the vapors?" She gave Richard a look, and he looked embarrassed, as well he might. Arnold Schwarzenegger is more likely to get vapors than Aunt Maggie.

She went on. "We knew that Carney couldn't do us any harm, and it was plain that he'd been dead for a while, so whoever it was that killed him was long gone." Then she added, "Unless it was one of us there, but that's for y'all to figure out. Anyway, Bob called the police, Obed found Bender, and Bender called his brother Evan."

"Evan owns the lot, right?" I said.

"Right. So we had two sets of police running around like chickens with their heads cut off, plus Bender and Evan Cawthorne getting in everybody's way."

"Why two sets of police?" Richard asked.

"You remember what I said at supper about the town line being in dispute? Well, the body was found smack dab in the middle of the part that both cities are claiming. I swear, if I'd known that, I'd have rolled the body to one side or the other so they wouldn't have anything to fight over."

I started to point out how much damage that would have done to the physical evidence, but I was reasonably sure that she was kidding. Instead I said, "I'm surprised there was a problem. Junior and Chief Monroe usually get along all right." Junior and Lloyd Monroe, Rocky Shoals's police chief, have very different styles, but they also have a lot of respect for one another.

"I told you that Junior isn't involved, and neither is Lloyd Monroe. They're both in Fort Lauderdale for a police convention. Mark Pope is in charge of the Byerly police, and some gal named Belva Tucker is running the show in Rocky Shoals."

"Do they not get along?" I asked.

"About as good as Lee got along with Grant," Aunt Maggie said. "Mark got there first, with Trey Norton." Trey is Junior's little brother and part-time deputy, and my cousin Ilene's full-time boyfriend. "Mark told Trey to secure the scene, whatever that means. As far as I can tell, all he did was string yellow tape all around the building so nobody would come in or out, which was locking the barn door after the horse got away, considering how many people had trooped through there. Trey hadn't got all his tape up when in comes Belva Tucker with her roll of tape. Belva and Mark spent a good half an hour arguing over whose body it was. Finally I said that no matter whose body it was, Dr. Connelly was going to be the one looking at it."

"Dr. Connelly is the county medical examiner," I explained to Richard. He also runs a medical lab, because fortunately, the county doesn't have enough deaths to keep him busy.

"It took another five minutes for them to decide who was going to call him. Evan Cawthorne showed up right after that, fuming about everything. I think he was afraid that his insurance rates would go up, because the only thing he gets that steamed up about is money."

"Because he's tight as a tick," Richard said, proud of himself for using a new phrase.

"Mark and Belva ignored him as best they could, and asked us dealers what had happened," Aunt Maggie continued. "Only we couldn't hardly answer for them talking over each other. Finally they lined us up, and Mark started on one end and Belva started on the other. That meant that we got asked the same questions twice, but by that time we were so glad that they were doing *something* other than fuss at each other that we didn't care.

"We didn't know exactly when Carney had gotten there, but it must have been before seven, because that's what time I got there. Bender said he didn't notice anything earlier, which means that he was probably tight as a tick. As usual."

Richard looked puzzled. "What difference did Bender being cheap make?"

"She didn't say he was cheap; she said he was drunk," I pointed out.

"As drunk as a skunk," Aunt Maggie agreed.

"I thought *tight as a tick* meant tight-fisted," he said.

"It does," I explained, "but it also means drunk. You tell which it is by context."

"What does being a tick have to do with being cheap or drunk?" Richard asked.

I'd never thought about it before, but I said, "Well, a tick is a bloodsucker, like a cheapskate is, and a tick lives by drinking, like a drunk does."

Aunt Maggie cleared her throat noisily. Obviously she wasn't in the mood for a language lesson. "Anyway, for all Mark's and Belva's arguing and securing the scene, that's all either police department knows."

"What about Dr. Connelly?" I asked.

"He was the one who found the knife in Carney's back. He said he couldn't say so officially before the autopsy, but it sure looked like he'd been stabbed to death. There were marks on Carney's hands and arms that Dr. Connelly said were defensive wounds, meaning that he tried to fight off his killer. As for when he was killed, Connelly said it was probably early that morning, which made sense. I saw Carney drive off when the market closed the night before."

"Was anything taken from his booth?" Richard asked.

"Only the knife."

"The knife he was killed with?" I asked.

Aunt Maggie nodded. "A big one, with a confederate flag on it. Obed thought it looked familiar when Dr. Connelly found it, and Mark went through Carney's display cases until he found the place it came from. I forget whether it's Mark or Belva who's going to get it checked for prints. Naturally they argued over that, too."

"If they're having so much trouble," I said, "why don't they call in the state police? They've got experience with murders."

Aunt Maggie said, "Not in this lifetime—that's the only thing they agreed on. I guess they hate the state troopers even more than they hate each other. Anyway, even though they were acting so silly, I wasn't too worried because I figured that as soon as Junior and Lloyd Monroe heard, they'd come running back to take over. But they aren't coming back until the conference is over."

"At which point the trail will be stone cold," I said.

"That's why I want you and Richard to take care of it."

"No offense, Aunt Maggie," I said, "but why do you care? You said you didn't like Carney."

She looked away. "I don't want my customers scared off."

"It seems to me like this would attract business," I objected. "You know how morbid folks are."

"I don't want that kind of business." Before I could point out that she was contradicting herself, she added, "Besides, I'm nervous to go out there with a murderer on the loose. Who knows who he'll come after next?"

I looked at Richard, and he raised one eyebrow. Whatever Aunt Maggie's real reason was, it sure as heck wasn't being scared. I don't think my great-aunt would be scared of anything short of a volcano erupting, and I don't think she'd admit to being scared of that. "Okay, what can you tell us about Carney?"

"Like I said, he'd been selling out there nearly as long

as I have. His specialty was knives: pocket knives and Bowie knives and all kinds of collector knives."

"Did he live here in Byerly?"

"I don't think so. Seems like I heard him talking about Rocky Shoals. Or maybe it was Granite Falls."

She was real helpful. "The flea market is only open on the weekends. What did he do the rest of the time?"

"How would I know?"

"Was he married?"

"I don't think so. He never mentioned a wife, and he flirted with China Upton every chance he got."

"Did he have any family around? Or close friends?"

She just shrugged.

Obviously, working at a flea market wasn't like working at an office. By the end of the first week at my job, I'd known the marital status, number of kids, and hobbies of all my immediate co-workers. I tried a different tack. "What kind of man was he?"

"Not much of a man, if you ask me. Lazy as all get-out—I never saw him lift a finger to help anybody. Nosy, too, and he had a mean streak a mile wide. If you did the littlest thing to bother him, even if it was an accident, he'd go out of his way to stir up trouble for you. I don't think he was strictly honest, either. I've heard stories about him selling phony knives."

"How can a knife be phony?" I asked. "It either has a blade or it doesn't."

"It's phony if you think you're buying a collector knife when you're not. There's a lot of knives out there. Some of them are worth money and some aren't worth using as letter openers. Bowie knives are real collectibles, but they're also easy to fake."

Lazy, nosy, mean, and dishonest. I was starting to wonder how Carney had stayed alive as long as he had. Paw used to say that everybody has a good side, but Aunt Maggie wasn't telling me anything about Carney's. "What else?" I asked her.

She had to think for a minute. "I can't imagine what difference it makes, but Carney was always making jokes."

"Dirty jokes?" That would fit in with what we'd heard about him so far.

"Not always. Mostly he made plays on words, and he liked puns."

"That figures. Puns are the lowest form of humor."

"Shakespeare used many puns," Richard said huffily.

"That's right," I agreed. "Why don't you give us a sample?"

"Nice try," was all he said.

Aunt Maggie looked like she was about to clear her throat again, so I said, "What kind of puns?"

"Silly stuff," she said. "He'd ask Bob if he was drawing in business, because he draws tattoos. He said China's business was so-so, because she sews most of her merchandise, and he called her sachets potpourri." She pronounced the first syllable as if it rhymed with rot. "He was always coming up with things like that."

Before I could ask any more questions, Aunt Maggie looked at the clock on the wall. "As late as it's getting, why don't we save this until tomorrow? It'll be easier to explain things when the people involved are handy."

"What people?" I said.

"The other dealers at the flea market. I figure it was probably one of us who did it." She sounded awfully matter-of-fact considering she'd just told us how scared she was.

“Then I guess the flea market would be the best place to start,” I said. “What time should we meet you there?”

“Meet me? Y’all are coming with me. I’ve got my clock set for five-thirty, so you two better get to bed if you want to get any sleep tonight.” And darned if she didn’t grin.

Chapter 5

Once I got over my initial horror at getting up that early on my vacation, I had to admit that it would be easier for us to talk to people if we were with Aunt Maggie. At least that's what I said to Richard as we went upstairs. I wasn't sure that I'd convinced him, but then again, I wasn't sure that I'd convinced myself, either.

"Are you sure you don't mind doing this?" I asked. "It's bad enough that you're missing your trip to Cape Cod—this goes above and beyond the call of duty."

"I could have said 'no' if I'd wanted to."

"I know, but you only said 'yes' because it's my family asking."

"That's not true. First off, when I married you, I married them, too. 'What's mine is yours, and what is yours is mine.' "

"And your money is mine!" I crowed. "That's Shakespeare!"

He shook his head, grinning widely. "Actually, it's Plautus."

"It is not. I know I've heard you quote that before; I just can't remember the play."

"Oh, I'll admit that Shakespeare borrowed the line in *Measure for Measure*, but Plautus said it first."

"Richard Fleming, I do believe that you've discovered a way around the bet."

"The bet only says I can't quote the Bard. I can still quote other people."

"Since when did you get so sneaky?"

"Necessity is the mother of invention."

I groaned. It was going to be a long two weeks, two days, and assorted hours.

"Anyway, as I was saying, I have my own reasons for agreeing to spend the week in Byerly. First off, they're my family, too. So of course I think we should stay for Augustus's party."

"You're sweet," I said, giving him a quick kiss.

"Second, like Aunt Maggie said, we may as well do something useful while we're in town. Aunt Maggie needs us, and I couldn't turn her down any more than you could."

"I do love you," I said, and gave him a longer kiss.

"And third, you have no idea how much I'm looking forward to your making it up to me."

This time, he kissed me, and it lasted longer than the other two kisses put together.

When I got a chance to draw a breath, I said, "Maybe I should start paying you back right away." I reached into my suitcase and pulled out the new nightgown I'd bought to surprise him with at the beach. "Why don't I slip this on?"

"It's lovely, but I don't think you'll be needing it for a while."

"Is that so?"

He was right. It would just have been in the way during what happened next.

Chapter 6

What with the time spent making things up to Richard, I didn't get much sleep that night. When Aunt Maggie came knocking on the bedroom door the next morning, it almost hurt to open my eyes. I looked at the clock by the side of the bed and realized why. It wasn't morning yet. As far as I'm concerned, five-thirty is still nighttime.

"I'm awake," I mumbled, fairly sure that I was telling the truth. Richard slumbered on peacefully, and I thought about trying to talk him into showering first so I could get ten minutes more of sleep. But since I was still making up for that trip to Cape Cod, I went first.

When the two of us trudged downstairs, Aunt Maggie was standing by the front door rattling the enormous set of keys she always carries. "If I'd known y'all were going to take this long, I'd have woken you up sooner."

I thanked the Lord for small favors as we followed her outside. It was still dark, but as we drove through the empty streets and onto the highway, I thought I saw the faint glow of dawn. It turned out to be the lights from Hardee's.

"Y'all want something to eat?" Aunt Maggie said as we got off of the highway and pulled around to the drive-thru.

I might have been half-asleep, but when I smelled sausage cooking, my stomach growled to let me know it was ready and raring to go. "I'll take a couple of sausage biscuits and some coffee."

"Richard?"

He didn't answer.

I looked into the back seat, and saw that even though he was sitting upright, he was sound asleep. He'd learned that trick in graduate school, and though he'd tried to teach it to me, it wouldn't take.

"Get him a couple of sausage biscuits, too," I said, and Aunt Maggie ordered for us.

A Northern friend of mine once asked me how to make a sausage biscuit, and couldn't figure out why I laughed. The man was a physicist and didn't know how to slice a biscuit in half and stick in a sausage patty. Massachusetts has some fine universities, but they don't teach everything.

A few more miles down the road, it started getting light for real. Or maybe the coffee and sausage biscuits were having their desired effect.

There were actually people moving around when we got to the flea market. A line of cars was parked alongside and between the three long buildings, and folks were busy setting up tables and laying out merchandise ranging from stacks of T-shirts to boxes of trading cards to piles of stuff I didn't recognize. I felt better when I saw that some of them looked as bleary-eyed as I felt, and that large amounts of coffee were being consumed.

Aunt Maggie said, "Aren't you glad I don't have an outside spot, or we'd have had to get up early to set up."

"What do you call this?" I said, and then saw she was grinning. "Aunt Maggie, I think you're enjoying this."

"I did like seeing the expression on your face," she admitted.

Aunt Maggie drove around to the back of the largest building, which had a sign marking it as Building One. I knew from previous trips out there that it wasn't much of a building, just walls made of cinder blocks, a corrugated tin roof, and a concrete floor. Still, it provided shade, electricity, and running water, which was more than the outside dealers got.

We parked in front of a metal door with the words *DEALERS ONLY* badly painted in red paint. Richard was still asleep in the back seat, so I leaned over and said, "We're here."

He instantly opened his eyes, and looked as wide awake as if he'd had ten hours of sleep. That was another trick he'd learned in graduate school, and once again, I wished he could teach it to me. "Do I smell biscuits?"

I handed him the bag and his coffee, and we climbed out of the car.

"Do dealers have assigned parking spaces?" I asked Aunt Maggie. There were several other cars and trucks parked back there, but nobody else had taken the prime parking spot at the door. Like most Bostonians, I consider parking a precious commodity, and I don't even own a car.

"Nope, first come, first served. We must have gotten this place because it's where Carney always parked, and it looks like this is where he died. I expect that's why nobody else parked here."

Hearing that woke me up more thoroughly than the coffee and biscuits had. "I thought you found him inside."

"That's where the killer hid the body, but he killed him out here. It looks like Carney got out of his van and started to open the door to go in. All of us inside dealers have keys because we got tired of having to drag Bender out of bed to come let us in. Anyway, Carney was opening the door when somebody jumped him."

"Does anybody other than the dealers have keys?" Richard asked.

"Knowing Bender, he's probably given them to half the people in the state, but the front door was jimmied, so it doesn't matter. Like I was saying, Carney was at the door when he was attacked. There were cuts on his arms from where he tried to defend himself, and a nasty belly wound, but he died from being stabbed in the back. They think he was trying to unlock the door to his van when the killer finished him off. Then he dragged Carney inside and put him under the table of his own booth, right inside the door."

"Was the van left here?"

"No, the killer drove it over to the church parking lot," she said, pointing to a steepled building on the other side of the flea market. "He parked it way in the back, and it wasn't until after we found Carney that the preacher reported it. There was blood along the driver's side, and they found blood on the ground here, so that's how they figured out what happened. The van's keys were missing, but there were fresh scratches next to the door lock from where Carney tried to get in."

Aunt Maggie scuffed her sneaker in the red clay that covers so much of the area around Byerly. "Mark and Belva shoveled up most of the bloody parts, and Bender cleaned up the rest. I wouldn't have thought it'd show so much in this clay, but it did once we knew what to look for. Didn't look like blood—just dark stains, like an oil leak."

Despite the offhand way Aunt Maggie was talking about

it, Carney's death had been a violent one. To stab a man over and over like that was a brutal way to kill somebody.

I tried to imagine the attack. It had happened earlier in the day, so it would have been darker than it was now, with no other cars nearby.

"Weren't there any outside dealers around?" I asked Aunt Maggie. "You said they come earlier than the inside dealers. Didn't any of them see or hear anything?" Surely Carney would have hollered for help, or cried out in pain.

But Aunt Maggie said, "There weren't any that day. It rained overnight, and was supposed to rain on and off all that day, so none of the outdoor people bothered to set up."

Something still seemed wrong with the picture. "Aunt Maggie, did Carney have problems walking?"

"Not that I ever noticed. Why?"

"Why didn't he run away? If I'd tried to fight somebody off and couldn't, I wouldn't have wasted time trying to get inside a locked van."

"How do you know what you'd do?" Aunt Maggie snapped. "Has anybody ever chased you with a knife?"

Actually, I had been chased a time or two, but I was too surprised by her outburst to say so. Maybe this murder was bothering her more than she wanted to admit. Aunt Maggie was bossy and occasionally sarcastic—make that frequently sarcastic—but she almost never snapped.

Before I could come up with an answer, I heard the wail of a siren coming toward us.

Chapter 7

The sound seemed to warble, and I realized that I was hearing two different sirens.

"What in the Sam Hill?" Aunt Maggie said.

Two police cars came screeching around opposite sides of the building, and they both stopped right behind Aunt Maggie's car, stirring up identical clouds of red dust.

The car to the right was the familiar blue-and-white Byerly cruiser, and I recognized deputies Mark Pope and Trey Norton getting out. The car on the left was black and white with "Rocky Shoals Police" lettered on the hood. I didn't know the heavy-set woman with tight, sandy-blond curls hopping out of the driver's side, but I guessed that she was Deputy Belva Tucker.

"Who's been killed now?" Aunt Maggie asked Mark.

"Nobody," he said. It's a shame Mark is a cop. With his nondescript face and figure, he'd have made a great crook. Even his voice was nondescript as he said "Excuse me, ma'am," before opening the door.

Belva Tucker was right on his heels, and they disappeared inside, leaving Trey to follow. At least, he would have followed if Aunt Maggie hadn't stepped into his path.

"Hold it right there," she said. "What's going on?"

Trey, a tall fellow whose brown forelock won't stay out of his face, said, "There's been a break-in, Miz Burnette. The call we got didn't say whether or not there's anything missing, but there's been some damage. I better get inside."

"Right after us," Aunt Maggie said, going into the building herself.

Trey looked like he wasn't sure if he should let her go in or not, so Richard and I took advantage of his confusion to follow her.

"God bless a milk cow!" Aunt Maggie said, running her fingers through her hair.

That part of the building is long and narrow, just wide enough to hold a line of booths down each side with enough space left over for an aisle for the customers to walk down. Each booth is a rectangle marked off with white painted lines on the floor. There are two long folding tables along the front, where the customers walk by, and shorter ones on each end. A gap between the front tables and the side ones leaves just enough room for the dealer to get in and out of the booth. At least, that's what it's supposed to look like.

The way it looked then, the lines on the floor were the only way I could tell where one booth ended and the next began. There were wads of paper, boxes, plastic bags, and scraps of brightly colored fabric everywhere. When Aunt Maggie took a step, her sneakers crunched on broken glass. A big part of what she sells is glassware, and I knew she was wondering if she was grinding her own stock into dust.

There were maybe a dozen people milling around. Belva had a notepad out and was questioning a scrawny man in faded blue jeans and a white T-shirt that was worn so thin that if it had been mine, I'd have used it for a dust rag. He was nearly bald, with just a fringe of hair around his head, but that fringe had been left to grow long enough to hang in his face. When he opened his mouth to answer Belva, I could see that he was missing a couple of teeth. Standing between the two of them, looking up as if worried about what was going on, was a magnificent red dog with chow in his bloodline.

Meanwhile, Mark was nodding and listening as the man next to him talked. At first glance, the man looked as different as could be from the man with Belva. Instead of wearing clothes that should have been thrown out, he was dressed in a crisp blue Izod golf shirt and starched khakis. His dark hair was neatly combed, and as far as I could tell, he had all his teeth.

But there was definitely a family resemblance between the two men, something about the nose and the shape of the mouth. They looked like nothing so much as the opposite sides of a before-and-after ad. From what Aunt Maggie had said the night before, they had to be Bender and Evan Cawthorne.

I didn't know the other people, but I guessed that they were other dealers. A woman was picking up pieces of gingham, and a stocky man with dark brown hair and muscular arms was straightening bottles that had been knocked over.

From behind us, I heard a throat clearing and a polite "Excuse me." We stepped aside and Trey came on in. When Mark saw him, he called out, "Tell those people to stop interfering with the evidence, and find someplace they can go to get out of the way."

Belva looked annoyed, probably because she hadn't brought a flunky of her own.

Bender Cawthorne said, "The snack bar isn't messed up. People can go over there."

There was general agreement, and the deputies started herding people toward the snack bar at the front of the building. Richard and I were going that way, too, but Aunt Maggie had other ideas.

"I'm going to check out my booth," she said.

Richard and I looked at each other, shrugged, and followed her.

The booth immediately to the left of the door was blocked with yellow tape that said, "CRIME SCENE—DO NOT PASS," but if anything, it was even more damaged than the other booths. Every box seemed to have been turned over, with knives of all description scattered across the floor. The broken display cases were probably the source of the glass on the floor.

"That was Carney's booth," Aunt Maggie said.

"They sure did a number on it," I remarked.

"Looks like a tornado hit it," she agreed. "Of course, Carney kept it pretty messy. I don't know how he ever found anything in there." She went on to her booth, which was across the aisle from Carney's.

"Lord love a duck," she sighed, her hands on her hips as she surveyed the damage.

Half of Aunt Maggie's booth was devoted to paperback books, and it looked like somebody had run his arm down each row of books, knocking them off the table to make puddles of books on the floor. Then the table had been pushed over on top of them.

The other half of the booth was filled with all kinds of knickknacks: vases and ring holders, porcelain statues and Bugs Bunny mugs, mismatched saucers and mixing bowls, blue glass candlesticks and flower frogs. Not one piece was left upright, and I couldn't tell how many had been broken.

Even Aunt Maggie's worktable had been overturned, with the electric fan and reference books that were usually on top shoved into a corner.

The only thing left undisturbed were the three signs on the wall. Over the book section was a sign that said, "Don't Buy Books New—Buy Them from the Book Lady." The one over the knickknacks said, "The only one who cares about what your grandmother had is your grandfather." And over the place where Aunt Maggie usually stood to keep an eye on customers was a sign that said, "In God We Trust, All Others Pay Cash."

Aunt Maggie bent down to pick up a blue iridescent shard of glass. "I just bought this platter last week."

I put my arm around her, feeling awkward. Aunt Maggie isn't the hugging type, but these were extreme circumstances. "It doesn't look too bad."

She took a deep breath. "I suppose it could have been worse. Most of my best pieces are packed up to go to auction, so they're probably all right. I just hate to think how long it's going to take to clean it all up." She reached for a vase that was laying on its side.

"We better leave everything until the police have had a chance to look," I warned.

"I don't know what good that'll do," she said, but she pulled her hand back.

Trey walked up then. "Miz Burnette, Mark wants me to tell you—"

Aunt Maggie turned and gave him the look that Southern women use when words aren't enough.

Trey blanched, but managed to stammer the rest of his

message. "He wanted me to *ask* you if you'd come over to the snack bar so he and Deputy Tucker can talk to everybody at once."

She headed in that direction, but she said, "A fat lot of good their talking has done so far. First Carney gets killed, and now this." I wasn't sure from her tone of voice which event bothered her more.

Calling it a snack bar was exaggerating a bit. It was just a hole in the wall with a warped counter that showed a kitchen big enough for one person. Surrounding it were half a dozen ramshackle, formica-topped tables that played the part of dining area.

The other dealers were scattered around the tables with Styrofoam cups of coffee and disgruntled expressions. I noticed that nobody was putting their elbows on the tables, which was a good thing. If they had, they might have stuck—the tables didn't look like they'd been wiped in a month.

Trey joined the other deputies, who were talking to Evan Cawthorne in a room with a sign on the door that said, "Flea Market Office." The door was open, but when Belva saw Aunt Maggie, Richard, and me nearby, she firmly closed it.

Since we couldn't hear anything through the door, the three of us went to sit at an empty table. Richard said, "Would you like some coffee?" He still had his Hardee's bag, but his coffee must have been cold by then.

"I sure would," Aunt Maggie said. "It's going to be a long day."

He headed for the counter, where Bender Cawthorne was manning the coffeemaker. His dog was in the kitchen with him, but since Rusty looked cleaner than Bender, I saw no reason to complain.

Aunt Maggie was looking so disgusted that I thought I

should distract her. "Are these folks ones you think might have had something to do with Carney's death?" I asked in a low voice.

"This is most of them. Obed isn't here yet."

"Why don't you tell me who's who."

She nodded at a young blonde in blue jeans and a black Harley-Davidson T-shirt. "That's Tammy Pruitt. The man next to her is J.B. Doughty, her live-in." J.B. looked like he was a few years older than Tammy, or maybe he'd just lived a harder life. He had dark hair and a bushy mustache, and was wearing a black leather vest with a Harley emblem on the back. "They sell Harley-Davidson stuff. Shirts, jackets, belt buckles, even stuffed pigs they call Harley hogs."

That explained their clothes. J.B. looked like he'd be right at home in a biker gang.

Aunt Maggie said, "I don't know why they're here. They set up outside."

"Who's that?" I said, looking at the woman I'd seen picking pieces of cloth up off the floor.

"China Upton. She sells country crafts—pillows and stuffed geese and such."

I wondered if China made the things she sold. Her red-and-white gingham blouse and the denim wrap-around skirt with matching ruffles looked handmade.

"The fellow at the table with China is Bob Tyndall. You remember Bob, don't you, Laurie Anne? He notarized those papers for us after your granddaddy died."

"I thought he looked familiar." How could I have forgotten? It's not often that you meet a tattoo artist who's a notary public on the side.

"That scrawny little fellow by himself is Thatcher Broods. He was one of Carney's point men."

"His what?"

"That's what Carney called them. Carney had a whole bunch of fellows who'd bring him stuff. He'd buy from them, then sell it out here. Thatcher found a lot of the pieces Carney used to repair knives."

I could tell from her voice that she disapproved. "Is something wrong with that?"

"Not necessarily. Lots of dealers sell items that have been repaired. It's fine as long as they tell the customers that it's reconditioned."

"But Carney didn't tell people."

She shrugged. "I don't know for sure, but it seems to me that he sold more 'mint condition' knives than he bought."

Thatcher didn't look like he was more than seventeen or eighteen, despite his old-fashioned name. He had that angular look some boys get at that age, all elbows with a prominent Adam's apple. His long brown hair was pulled back in a ponytail, which made his face look even more bony. "If he's not a dealer, then he's not a suspect, right?"

"Not necessarily. Even though Thatcher's not a dealer, he's always out here. He comes early to cherry-pick the outside dealers and sell what he can to Carney."

"Cherry-pick?"

She shook her head at my ignorance. "A lot of the outside dealers aren't professionals. They're just folks trying to clean out their houses, and they come out here instead of having a yard sale so they won't have people tromping all over their yards. Most of them don't have any idea of which pieces are valuable and which are junk. A Hull pheasant planter will be marked three dollars, but they'll want fifty for a set of dishes you can get brand-new at Wal-Mart for forty-five. So a lot of dealers like to get here ahead of the customers to see if there's anything worth buying outside. I do it myself when I get here early enough." The look she gave me reminded me that it was Richard and me that had slowed her down.

"Was Thatcher here the day Carney was killed?"

"I think so. It seems like I remember him coming by with some pieces to sell. In fact, I know he did because he said Carney owed him some money, and he was right put out that he wasn't around. I think Thatcher is trying to build up enough stock to become a dealer himself. He's crazy about knives."

I wondered if a knife aficionado would be more likely to kill somebody with a knife, or too respectful of the collector value to want to mess one up. Would he use a really good knife, or a just a cheap one?

Aunt Maggie nodded at two women. "You know those two, don't you?"

"All too well." Mavis Dermott and Mary Maude Foy were hard to miss. I think their hair started out black, but it hasn't been naturally black for a long time, and nature had never given anybody hair *that* black. It looked like Aunt Maggie's did now, but Aunt Maggie's hair had been an accident, and they did theirs that way on purpose.

The hair was bad enough, but they made it worse by layering on foundation and powder that was three shades lighter than their real skin color. I could tell because they never blended the makeup along the edges, meaning that there was a line circling their faces. Of course, with all that, they had to wear bright red lipstick.

I knew from long experience that their personalities were just as attractive. "You must love having them around," I said.

Aunt Maggie just grunted.

Richard finally got back with our coffee.

I asked, "What took you so long?"

"I thought I'd take the opportunity to see what I could find out from Bender. From the horse's mouth, as it were."

"Horse's mouth?" Aunt Maggie said. "Talking to Bender is more like getting it from the horse's—"

She didn't get a chance to finish because Belva and Mark asked everybody to quiet down. I wondered how they were going to handle the next part, since it was obvious that neither of them wanted to give the other one a chance to speak first. They must have decided to let Evan Cawthorne speak for them as a compromise.

Evan cleared his throat loudly. "Let me start by expressing my sincere apologies for any losses y'all may have suffered. Thankfully, the damage was minor."

"Minor?" Bob Tyndall called out. "I lost half a dozen bottles of my best inks—do you know how much it's going to cost to replace them?"

Evan held his hands out in what I supposed was a calming gesture. "I'm not trying to minimize your losses—"

"It's all my fault," Bender said as he came out from behind the snack bar. "I'd been extra careful all week because of what happened to Carney, but I had to take Rusty to the vet yesterday. We were only gone for a little while, but they must have broken in then. I can't tell you how sorry I am."

He looked so pitiful that I guess Bob couldn't stand it. "Hell, Bender, I'm not blaming you or Rusty. I just want to know who's going to pay for my ink." He turned back to Evan. "Have you got insurance to take care of this?"

Evan put on a regretful expression, but I didn't quite

believe it. "I also apologize for my brother's failure to be on duty, and of course I carry insurance on the property, but I'm afraid your losses aren't covered."

"The hell you say!" Bob shouted.

"If you'll recall, the contract you signed when you became an inside dealer states that while Cawthorne, Inc., provides reasonable security measures, I am not liable for any loss due to theft or vandalism."

Bob started to say something else, but Aunt Maggie said, "Give it up, Bob. You signed that paper the same as the rest of us." She glared at Evan. "It ain't right, but it's legal."

Evan cleared his throat again. "Let me say that in recognition of these unfortunate events, I will not be collecting rent for today."

There were some noises of appreciation at that, but Aunt Maggie couldn't resist pointing out, "That's mighty good of you, considering the fact that we're not going to be able to do any business today."

"That's not necessarily true," Evan countered. "I looked around, and I don't think it's going to take long to clean up. I intend to open Building One for business at eleven o'clock."

There was a fair amount of reaction to that, ranging from Aunt Maggie saying, "That's easy for you to say," to China Upton saying, "I'm sure we can get the worst of it straightened up if we work together."

After everybody had had a chance to grumble, Evan continued. "While I have you here, I have a couple of announcements. Thatcher Broods has made arrangements with the late Carney Alexander's sister to take over his business. I think we can all agree that Carney would be glad to see his work carried out."

That sounded a bit highfalutin for the business in question, but I reminded myself that flea market dealers took their work just as seriously as anybody else. Aunt Maggie sure didn't put up with people making fun of *her* business.

Evan went on. "Of course, Thatcher understands that he won't inherit Carney's location because other dealers have been waiting for some time. J.B. Doughty and Tammy Pruitt will be moving into Carney's old spot."

"What are you trying to pull, Cawthorne?" Mary Maude thundered. "Me and my sister have been setting up here longer than them two."

"Check the dates," J.B. thundered back. "We put our name on the waiting list a good two weeks before y'all."

Evan tried his best calming gesture, but it didn't do any good. Both J.B. and Mary Maude stood up so they could try to stare the other down.

Then Belva said, "People, I've got something to say that's more important than your bickering. Do I have to remind y'all that there's a criminal investigation going on here?"

"It doesn't look like much of an of investigation to me," Mary Maude muttered.

Belva ignored her. "I've got a theory about this break-in, but I want to check out the evidence before I say more."

"What about you, Mark?" Aunt Maggie said. "Do you have a theory?"

"Miz Burnette, I've always believed that it's a waste of time to theorize until *after* I look at the evidence." He smirked at Belva, whose face got a little red.

Glaring at one another, the two of them headed back to the area that had been most damaged, with Trey trailing along behind.

That left Evan Cawthorne standing alone, but not for long. Mary Maude and Mavis converged on him, and I'd have felt sorry for him if he'd had the decency to insure the place properly.

"Remind me what Bender's excuse was," Aunt Maggie said. "Where was he when he was supposed to be guarding this place?"

Richard had started eating a sausage biscuit, but paused to say, "He went for a follow-up visit to Dr. Josie. I assume that this was because of Rusty's recent operation, but Bender was so uncomfortable talking about it that it was hard to tell. Apparently he was worried that Rusty wasn't 'acting like himself,' but Dr. Josie assured him that everything is fine. Bender said they were only gone two or three hours, but that was enough time for whoever it was to get in and do the damage. Neither he nor Rusty noticed anything until Bob Tyndall arrived this morning, saw the mess, and went to Bender's trailer to get him up."

"Two or three hours?" I said. "What on earth took so long? Dr. Josie's place is only ten minutes from here."

"If you take Jackson Road back from there, you go right past Dooley's Bar," Aunt Maggie commented. "I bet Bender took a side trip and doesn't want to admit it."

"I thought I detected a hint of eau de stale beer," Richard said.

"If he was drunk, somebody could have broken in while he was here and he wouldn't have heard a thing," I said.

But Aunt Maggie shook her head. "Nope, it had to have happened while they were gone or Rusty would have noticed. Bender is supposed keep an eye on the place during the week to make sure nobody messes with our merchandise, but Rusty really guards the place. That dog is the only reason Bender can hold on to this job."

"Surely Evan wouldn't fire his own brother," I said.

"Yes, he would."

Obviously the Cawthornes weren't like the Burnettes. I asked, "How many dealers are there out here?"

"Maybe a couple dozen in Building One. I'm not sure about Buildings Two and Three."

"Did they break into either of those buildings?"

"Just this one, according to Bender," Richard said between bites. "They jimmied the front door, just like last week. Bender admitted that it wouldn't have been hard because he had only jury-rigged it until Evan got a new lock installed."

I looked around at the booths closest to the snack bar. Clearly somebody had thrown a few pieces around and kicked over some boxes, but there was nowhere near as much damage as there was around Aunt Maggie's booth. "If they came in up here, why is the worst mess in the back of the building?"

"I see where you're going, Laurie Anne," Aunt Maggie said. "Last week Carney gets murdered—this week the place is broken into and his booth is the hardest hit."

"There's no way this could be a coincidence." I didn't think the police would miss the connection, either, which meant that Richard and I might be off the hook. Surely this new evidence would help them solve Carney's murder themselves, and we'd be able to relax for the rest of the week. Maybe we could join the triplets in Myrtle Beach. It wasn't Cape Cod, but it could be a lot of fun.

I was trying to decide if we could borrow a car or if we'd need to rent one when the delegation of deputies returned.

Mark opened his mouth, but Belva spoke first. "Okay, folks, I think I've seen all I need to. It looks like it was a bunch of kids looking for a place to get drunk and party."

"That's your big theory?" Aunt Maggie said. "A bunch of kids? How did a bunch of kids know that Bender wasn't here?"

"They were lucky," Belva said with a shrug.

"They were neat, too. Has anybody seen any beer cans on the ground?" Aunt Maggie looked around, but nobody spoke up.

Belva got a little red in the face again, but said, "That's an excellent observation. The kids must have been on drugs."

"What about Carney's murder?" Aunt Maggie persisted. "Are you saying that you don't think the break-in was connected with the killing?"

Belva looked pleased with herself. "As a matter of fact, I think the kids broke in last week, too. Carney got here before they could do any damage, and they panicked, stabbed him, and ran. That would explain the violence of the attack. Drug-related crimes are often the nastiest."

The last part sounded like it had come from a policeman's magazine. I didn't imagine that Rocky Shoals had that big a problem with drug-crazed killers on the rampage.

Aunt Maggie sighed loudly. "Mark, tell me you've got a better theory than that."

"Like I said before, Miz Burnette, I don't think theories mean a whole lot. What I need is facts, and it's a known fact that most break-ins are robberies. I want you people to check your inventory and let me know what's missing. I'll keep an eye out at the pawnshops, and once something shows up, proper procedures will lead the way."

"We don't know that anything is missing," Aunt Maggie said. "And how is a robbery connected to Carney's death?"

"I don't have any evidence that they are connected," Mark said.

"Of course they're connected!" Belva snapped. "It's as plain as the nose on your face."

"I don't see any evidence of that," he repeated.

They glared at each other until Evan said, "I'm confident the police will be able to handle this matter. If it's all right with the deputies, I'd suggest that we all get our booths ready to open."

I was surprised that Aunt Maggie didn't say anything else. Maybe she figured it wasn't worth the trouble. She led the way back to her booth and stared at the mess for a full five minutes before she finally said, "It's a good thing y'all are here, because as far as I can tell, Mark and Belva couldn't figure out how to work a paper bag."

It struck me then that Myrtle Beach had more in common with Cape Cod than I'd previously thought. That was the fact that I wasn't likely to see either place any time soon.

Chapter 8

Aunt Maggie put Richard and me to work sorting the paperback books strewn across the floor. At first I thought she meant to divide them up like you see books in stores: Mysteries, Science Fiction, Romance, and so on. But Aunt Maggie had her own system, with categories like Oprah books, Dean Koontz, Danielle Steel, Stephen King, Nice Romances, and Adult Romances.

All around us, other dealers were busy putting their booths back together: Tattoo Bob Tyndall sweeping up broken ink bottles, Thatcher Broods putting knives into their proper boxes, China Upton fluffing up pillows. I wondered if they were all satisfied that Belva and Mark knew what they were doing. I sure wasn't.

Richard must have been thinking the same thing because he said, "I wish Junior was in town."

"Me, too. Belva's jumped to the wrong conclusion, and Mark can't come to any conclusion. It was obviously an inside job."

"Why are you so sure?"

"First off, what Aunt Maggie said about Rusty being such a good watch dog. If he'd been here last night, he'd have heard the break-in, and if he'd been here last week, he'd have heard Carney being attacked. Only one of the dealers would have known that he wasn't going to be here."

"Not necessarily. Couldn't Bender have told a friend? Or maybe he was overheard at the bar."

"We can ask Aunt Maggie about Bender's friends later," I said, "but I don't think somebody who overheard a conversation would realize how important Rusty is. If I heard that a building was guarded by a man and a dog, I wouldn't assume that the dog was the brains of the outfit."

"Okay, maybe it was just a coincidence that the killer picked days when Rusty was gone."

"That's a pretty big coincidence."

"They do happen."

"True, but I still can't swallow the coincidence of a thief being at Carney's booth just as Carney showed up. And we'd have to either accept the coincidence of a sneak thief stuffing Carney's body under his own booth, or explain how the thief knew which one was Carney's."

"Excellent points," he said.

"We'd also have to explain why Carney's booth was the most heavily damaged in the break-in. I think somebody came to Carney's booth first, maybe to look for something. He messed up the booth while searching, then messed up other booths to cover his tracks."

"What was he looking for?"

"That I don't know. I'll ask Aunt Maggie if she's got any ideas." She picked that moment to drop a handful of broken crockery into a metal garbage can, and then kicked the can. "But I think I'll wait a little while."

"I take it that you and she discussed all these coincidences while I was talking to Bender."

"Actually, no. Aunt Maggie has her own reason for thinking somebody here at the flea market killed Carney, something she isn't telling us."

"Like?"

I shrugged. "I don't know. I do know that she's got some reason for wanting Carney's murderer caught, and she isn't telling us that, either. I don't think it's too much of a stretch to assume that the two reasons are connected somehow."

I knew Aunt Maggie trusted us, or she wouldn't have asked us to help in the first place, so why wouldn't she tell us everything?

Once Richard and I got the books straightened out, we helped her arrange knickknacks. Breakage wasn't as bad as we'd thought at first. It looked like enough pieces had been broken to make a mess, and the rest were just knocked over to make it look bad. Still, some expensive pieces had been ruined, and every time Aunt Maggie found another broken dish or a bowl that had been chipped, she got madder and madder. After a few attempts to cheer her up, Richard and I decided it would be better not to talk to her until she calmed down.

Though Aunt Maggie doesn't sell toys, she did have a few old dolls with china heads. The problem was that when I set them up, I had four dolls and only three heads. We looked through the jumble on the table, and then Richard crawled under the table to check under there. A minute later, I heard him solemnly say, "Alas, poor Yorick, I knew him well."

When he came out from under the table, doll head in hand, I cried, "Gotcha!" But instead of looking crestfallen or mad at himself, Richard was grinning like the cat who swallowed the canary. "That's a quote!"

He shook his head.

"It is so! *Hamlet.*"

"Not quite." He pulled out a paperback from his pocket, and naturally, it was a copy of *Hamlet.* "Check out Act V, Scene 1."

I thumbed through until I found the place where Hamlet encounters the grave diggers, and read the line out loud. " 'Alas, poor Yorick! I knew him, Horatio . . .' "

"The line I spoke appears nowhere in Shakespeare," Richard said.

"That's cheating," I said indignantly. "Everybody thinks that's the quote."

"I can't be held accountable for what people think."

I gave him my sternest look, but he was right and he knew it. "Okay, you didn't quote Shakespeare. But you can only get away with that once. The 'alas, poor Yorick' part *is* a quote."

"I'll be more careful next time," he said, but he was still grinning, even after I bopped him on the rear end with his book.

Aunt Maggie was watching us with that look she gets when she thinks we're being silly, and I figured that if she was paying attention to us, her temper must have cooled down and it might be safe to ask her some questions.

I turned to her. "Aunt Maggie, did it look like Carney's booth was searched the day he was killed?"

"Like I said before, his booth was always so jumbled up that I don't know that I would have noticed. Why?"

"Because we think the break-in was a cover for the killer to come back and look for something."

"Something that would tell us who it was?" she asked.

I thought about it, but shook my head. "No, it's been too long for that. If there'd been anything incriminating, the police would have found it nearly a week ago. Why would he risk coming to look for it now?"

"So what was he looking for?" Aunt Maggie wanted to know.

"Beats me. Did Carney have anything valuable?"

"I suppose one of his knives could have been worth more than he thought," she said, "but if that's so, Thatcher will figure it out. Besides, if Carney had something marked for less than it was worth, why not just buy it? Carney never would have known the difference."

"Did he have anything that somebody really wanted, but couldn't afford?" I asked.

"He did have that Elvis knife. Shaw Stevens said Carney had it marked twice what it was worth, but Carney wouldn't come down on it. He figured Shaw wouldn't be able to resist forever."

Carney had probably been right. Shaw is a devoted follower of the presumably late King of Rock and Roll. I said, "Couldn't Shaw have bought it if he'd really wanted it?"

"That wasn't the point. He just didn't want to get gypped."

"Then he's not likely to have killed Carney over it," I said.

"I guess not. The only other person I can think of who wanted something Carney had was Thatcher. He started working as one of Carney's point men a couple of years ago, and he was always wanting Carney to let him do more, maybe take some of Carney's extra stock to one of the knife and gun shows. He even offered to buy in as a partner, but Carney wasn't interested because he knew a good thing when he saw it. Thatcher always found the best knives, and Carney bought them dirt cheap. He knew Thatcher didn't have enough money to start his own business, so he kept him dangling. Of course, now Thatcher gets it all."

Was a flea market business worth killing for? Maybe it would be to Thatcher. Becoming a knife dealer didn't excite me much, but then again, Thatcher probably wouldn't be all that excited about computer programming. We all turned to look at him. He was skinny, but that didn't mean that he wasn't strong enough to have stabbed Carney.

I've heard that people can tell when they're being watched, and maybe they can, because he looked up at us. Then he grinned, clearly happy to be in charge of his own business at last.

Wanting to be polite, we all grinned back, then looked away.

"He sure doesn't act like he has anything on his conscience," Aunt Maggie said. Richard didn't say anything, but I could tell that he was resisting saying something Shakespearean.

I said, "So either he's innocent, or he has no conscience." With all those knives handy, I sure hoped it was the first choice.

Chapter 9

While we'd been straightening Aunt Maggie's booth, Mark and Belva must have been finishing up their business. They walked by right then, heading for the door.

"Mark," Aunt Maggie called out, "I'd like to talk to you."

"I'm on my way out, Miz Burnette," he said, speeding up. "Another call just came in."

"That's all right. Maybe Deputy Tucker would like to hear what I've got to say."

Needless to say, Mark couldn't stand the thought of Belva learning something he didn't know, just like she couldn't stand the thought of him learning something she didn't know. Both deputies came over.

"Laurie Anne, Richard, and I have been talking this over—"

"Who's Laurie Anne and Richard?" Belva interrupted.

"I'm Laura Fleming and this is my husband Richard," I said. "Miz Burnette is my great-aunt."

"They live in Boston," Mark said, not quite sneering as he said it.

"Anyway," Aunt Maggie said, "we were talking about Carney's murder and this morning's break-in, and we think you two are missing something."

That was probably the least tactful way she could have put it, but Aunt Maggie's never been known for her tact.

She went on. "It's obvious that Carney's murder was an inside job."

"Meaning what, exactly?" Mark asked.

"Meaning that it was one of the dealers who killed him." She explained the coincidences we'd come up with: Rusty being gone both times, the killer either knowing where Carney's booth was or just happening to hide him in that booth, and Carney's booth being the most damaged. "Do you see what I'm getting at?" she asked when she was finished.

"I can't say that I do," Mark said.

"Pope, use your head for something other than a hat rack." Belva remarked.

"I suppose this all fits in with your so-called theory," Mark said.

"At least I've got a theory," she said. "But all this fits in with is the fact that this lady here has a beef with one of the other dealers."

"Excuse me?" Aunt Maggie said, not quite believing it.

"After the way those other two were fighting over the dead man's booth, I guess I shouldn't be surprised. Who'd have thought the flea market business could be so petty?" She shook her head ruefully, then asked, "Which dealer do you want to pin the murder on? Did the tattoo guy's hand slip when he was working on you? Did you get a bad donut?"

I thought Aunt Maggie was going to explode, but somehow she managed to keep her voice under control. "You watch how you talk to me, little girl. I'm not about to put up with any nonsense from you just because you're wearing that uniform. I've been a citizen and a taxpayer since before you quit making messes in your panties."

Belva had the gall to grin at her the way you'd grin at a child having a tantrum. I don't know about Aunt Maggie, but I was about to have a tantrum myself.

I said, "Deputy Tucker, I suggest you call Chief Monroe and ask him if Laura Fleming knows what she's talking about. I'm sure he remembers Tom Honeywell's murder." Then I turned to Mark. "And I can't imagine that you've forgotten Leonard Cooper's murder."

"No, I haven't forgotten," Mark said. "It's not often that citizens take it upon themselves to interfere in a criminal investigation."

"Interfere?" I said. Richard and I had been the ones to figure out who killed Cooper, and Mark knew it.

Belva said, "In Rocky Shoals, we don't put up with civilians sticking their noses in police business."

"We don't in Byerly, either," Mark said firmly. "Now, if y'all have any actual evidence, I'd be glad to hear about it. But if not, I'd advise y'all to let us professionals take care of these matters."

They both turned away, Mark looking solemn and Belva looking amused.

"I'd advise you to be expecting a call from my friend Big Bill Walters," Aunt Maggie called after them.

Mark smirked. "If you were that close a friend, you'd know that he's out of town for the rest of the month." He left before Aunt Maggie could say anything else.

Chapter 10

"I'm so mad I could spit!" Aunt Maggie said.

"You're not the only one," I said. "I never thought Mark was smart; I never realized what a weasel he is. If he weren't a cop—"

"If he's a cop, then I'm the Queen of Sheba," Aunt Maggie said. "I don't care if he does have a badge. And that Belva Tucker is worse. Telling me that I'm trying to settle a feud!"

"She's an idiot," I said. "They're both idiots!" I realized that Richard hadn't spoken. "Don't you think so, Richard?"

"Why did I take that bet?" he asked. "I have never wanted to quote Shakespeare so much in my life. Nobody else can insult the way he did—I'm not even going to try."

I laughed, and even Aunt Maggie half smiled, which broke the mood. We were still angry, but at least we knew that we were on our own. If we were going to find Carney's murderer, we were going to do it without police assistance.

We went back to arranging the booth until Aunt Maggie was satisfied, which took a while. Finally she said, "I guess that'll do."

Then she handed Richard a canvas change apron. "Tie that around your waist." As he obeyed, she said, "Quarters go on the right, dimes in the middle, and nickels on the left. I don't take pennies because I don't want to mess with them—everything is priced to the nickel. Bills go in the middle with the dimes. There's a rubber band in there to keep them together."

She pulled out another apron and tied it around herself. "I've only got one spare apron, Laurie Anne, but we can buy you one from China." Then she took a handful of change from the lock box she'd carried in from the car, and counted it out. "Here's your quarters," she said, putting a bunch into the correct pocket of Richard's apron.

"Why do we need cash aprons?" I asked.

"How were you planning to make change? I tried using the lock box as a cash register, but I took my eyes off of it for a second one day, and somebody ran off with a twenty-dollar bill. The aprons are safer."

"I mean, why do we need to make change to find out about Carney's murder?"

She looked at me like I was a few bricks shy of a load. "You need a cover story, don't you? What were y'all planning to tell people?"

"Aunt Maggie, we haven't had time to figure out what we're going to do," I said.

"I thought y'all were making plans last night. I heard y'all moving around after you went in your room."

I carefully did not look at Richard as I said, "No, we didn't plan anything last night." Before she could ask what we had been doing, I said, "Why don't you tell us what you've got in mind?"

"It seems to me it wouldn't be smart to tell people that you're looking for Carney's murderer. You don't want to warn the murderer to watch out for you, and you don't want him coming after you. I wouldn't even have told the police if I'd realized how dumb they are. Anyway, if you waltz up to people and start asking questions, that's as good as announcing what you're doing over the loudspeaker. This place is bad for rumors, and all it would take is for one person to figure it out. Y'all have to have a cover story."

Her reasoning sounded good to me, and Richard was nodding, too. I did wonder if she wasn't hedging her bets in case we didn't find Carney's killer. She had to work with these people, after all, and they might not be too friendly if they knew she suspected them of murder. "I take it you've got a cover story in mind."

"Y'all can pretend that you're here to learn about the business so you can start selling up North, but you'll have to help me out so people will know you're serious. Besides which, I can't leave the booth alone to go showing you around. Somebody has to mind the store."

I was both glad that Aunt Maggie had worked this out and embarrassed that Richard and I hadn't. After all, we were supposed to be the experts. But that was no reason not to take advantage of Aunt Maggie's idea.

"Okay, what do we need to know to get started?" Though I'd shopped there, I'd never been interested in the inner workings of Tight as a Tick.

"Not much," she said. "The prices are marked, but if somebody wants to bargain you down a reasonable amount, that's fine."

I nodded like I understood, but fortunately Richard is more willing to admit that he doesn't know everything. He asked, "How much is a reasonable amount?"

"It depends. If somebody has twenty-five, thirty dollars worth of stuff, it won't hurt to come down a few dollars. But then there's the ones who offer you a dollar for something that's marked ten. Don't come down so much as a nickel for people like that. They can pay full price or they can take a hike."

"How do you know what prices to mark?" I asked. "Are they in those books?" I was talking about the stack of reference books that were back in place on her worktable. They had titles like *Price Guide to Flea Market Treasures, The Official Lehner's Encyclopedia of U.S. Marks on Pottery, Porcelain, and Clay*, and *Warman's Glass*.

"Those help me figure out what I've got and give me a price range," Aunt Maggie said, "but I can't find every piece in the books."

"Then what do you do?"

"Just make a guess. If I mark it high and it doesn't sell, eventually I'll mark it lower. If I mark it low and it sells real quick, I know to mark the next one that comes along a little higher. You get a feel for it after a while."

Then she showed us where she keeps bags, warning us to only give them out if people asked for them. "People who know flea markets carry their own shopping bags," she said. She also had stacks of old newspapers to wrap breakables in.

"I think that's all you need to know right now," she finally said. "Richard, if you don't mind being on your own for a little while, I thought I'd go introduce Laurie Anne around."

"You're sure you're not just doing this to get free help?" he asked with mock suspicion.

"Richard, if I needed help with this booth, don't you think I'd get somebody who knew what he was doing?"

"Point taken."

She said, "I expect we'll be back before Bender opens the doors, but if not, just do like I told you. Now remember—"

"I know. Everything's marked. Let them bargain a little. If they break it, they buy it. And we don't care if their grandmother had one just like it."

She nodded at him. "You'll do."

Chapter 11

I started to follow Aunt Maggie, but she asked, "Don't you need a notepad?"

Usually Richard takes notes because my handwriting is atrocious, but I didn't want to tell her that, so I said, "I thought I'd better not, since I'm undercover. I don't imagine I'll forget anything important." She seemed satisfied with that.

"This is China Upton's booth." There was a redwood sign propped in the middle of the table with the message "I Was Country When Country Wasn't Cool" burnt onto it. Funny, I'd grown up in what most people consider the country, and I'd never seen so much gingham and so many ribbons in my life.

I'm afraid that China Upton's country was the country people imagine when they live in the city. There were wire baskets filled with plastic eggs, each egg decorated with rickrack. There were gingham geese with deep pockets along the side to hold TV remotes and the latest issue of *TV Guide*, sofa cushions that were more ruffle than cushion, and wooden spoons with cross-stitched mottoes glued onto them.

China's specialty was sachets, little pillows stuffed with

sweet-smelling herbs. They came in gingham, of course, plus denim, velvet, and even a sensible seersucker. Probably all of them smelled good taken one at a time, but the combination was overpowering. My nose and eyes started to itch immediately.

"Good morning, Maggie," China said. Her hair was snow-white, her eyes bright blue, and her smile wide and genuine. Like Aunt Maggie, she was wearing a cash apron, but hers was gingham with ribbons and ruffles.

"Hey there. China, this is my great-niece, Laurie Anne Fleming."

China and I exchanged how-do-you-dos.

"Looks like you've got your booth put back together," Aunt Maggie said.

"Fortunately the vandals didn't do too much harm. They ripped apart some sachets and stomped on my geese, but there's nothing that can't be fixed with a needle and thread or some soap and water. Did you lose much?"

"Just enough to make me mad. A few pieces got broke, and some book covers got torn from being thrown on the floor."

"What is the world coming to when young people break into a place for fun?"

Either China believed Belva's theory or she was an excellent actress.

Aunt Maggie said, "China, if you've got any spare cash aprons, I could use one."

"What color would you like?" she asked, pulling out a box of aprons as ribboned and ruffled as her own.

"Don't you have something plainer?" Catching the hurt look on China's face, Aunt Maggie added, "These are pretty, but you know how dirty money is. They'd be filthy in no time."

"That's all right," China said. "You can throw these right into the washing machine. I checked the material and trim myself, and they won't fade or shrink."

Defeated, Aunt Maggie picked out a red checked one that didn't have quite so much ribbon as the others. She paid for it and said, "Here you go, Laurie Anne."

"Thanks," I said, not at all enthusiastic about wearing it.

"China, Laurie Anne is thinking about setting up a little business on the side, so she's checking out how we do things around here." To me, she added, "You could do all right with this stuff. China sews her own merchandise, and you could do that in your spare time."

Actually, I could barely sew on a button, but I nodded anyway. What China said next confirmed that I wouldn't be going into the country craft business any time soon.

"I even grow the herbs for the sachets. I could give you some seed catalogs, if you'd like."

There was no way I was going to grow herbs. Though the Burnette family had farmed for years and years, the bloodline had thinned out by the time it got to me, leaving both of my thumbs decidedly brown. I said, "My husband and I are going to be doing this together, so we'll have to discuss it before we decide anything."

"It's so much nicer when you can work with somebody," she said, looking sad for a minute. "We do the best we can alone, don't we, Maggie?"

Aunt Maggie nodded politely, but I knew it must have hurt her to do it. She's always said that the best company on earth is herself.

"Does your husband not work with you, Miz Upton?" I said, having noticed her wedding band.

"No, I'm a widow."

"I'm sorry."

"I am, too," she said, but she was smiling when she said it. "Stan has been gone a long time now, so I guess I'm as used to it as I'm going to get."

Aunt Maggie said, "China, Laurie Anne is a little nervous about what happened to Carney, especially after the break-in, but I told her nothing like that has ever happened before."

"Never," China said with a little shiver. "Until last week, the worst we've had was a little shoplifting."

"It's funny not to see Carney over there, isn't it?"

China looked in the direction of his booth, and shivered again. "Poor man."

"He sure was sweet on you," Aunt Maggie said.

This time China didn't so much shiver as shudder. "I hate to speak ill of the dead, but I'm afraid I didn't return his feelings, and he didn't know how to take 'no' for an answer."

"He was pretty pushy," Aunt Maggie agreed. "Always coming over here to talk to you. He never did anything else, did he?" She looked hopeful.

China shook her head. "No, he just talked, but that was bad enough. Stan Junior would never have stood for it if he'd been here."

"Does your son sell out here, too?" While I couldn't picture China killing Carney, I could see a strapping youth wanting to protect his mother.

"No, Stan Junior passed away a couple of years ago."

"I'm sorry," I said again.

"Don't be sorry. Stan Junior was a fine son, and I was

blessed to have him as long as I did. I'm just glad I was there to care for him when he needed me. If you ever have children, you'll know what I mean."

"Yes, ma'am." That led to her asking if I wanted children, a question I don't usually like answering, but since I'd stirred up so many sad memories, talking about future babies seemed like the least I could do.

China sure didn't sound like somebody who'd stab a man to death. Bloodstains don't go with gingham. But I reminded myself that I shouldn't jump to conclusions right away—there'd be plenty of time to jump to conclusions later on.

Aunt Maggie must not have considered China a likely suspect either, because she said, "We better be moving on. I want to show Laurie Anne around before Bender opens up."

As we walked away, I said, "What happened to China's son?"

"She's never said."

"Did Carney ever try to see her away from the flea market?"

"How would I know?"

I was starting to get exasperated. Last night she hadn't known much about the victim, and now she didn't know anything about the suspects. "Aunt Maggie, I don't know these people. If you can't tell me about them, how are Richard and I supposed to solve this?"

"I'm sorry, Laurie Anne," she said, and she did sound sincere. "The only place I see most of them is out here and at the auctions. I don't always know if people are married, or where they live, or if they have kids. I'll tell you about what goes on out here, but that's the best I can do. Is that going to be enough?"

I sighed. "There's no way of knowing until I try." Besides, I had other resources. Aunt Nora knows more about people in Byerly than Bill Gates knows about making money, and Aunt Daphine runs the town's only beauty parlor, where they go through more gossip than hair spray.

"Talking to China didn't do us much good, did it?"

"What did you expect?" I asked. "Even if she did kill Carney, she's not going to just tell us."

"Then how do you figure out who killed somebody? The other times, it looked to me like you just went around and talked to people."

"That's a lot of it," I admitted. "If I ask enough people about the same thing, usually I'll catch somebody in a lie. If somebody's lying, there's usually a reason. So I talk to other people and try to figure out why that person lied and what the truth is." Aunt Maggie looked dubious, and I didn't blame her. It wasn't exactly scientific or systematic. So I echoed what she'd said to me earlier. "After a while, you get a feel for it."

Chapter 12

The booth next to China's was actually a small trailer, the kind where they sell popcorn and hot dogs at carnivals and fairs. I could smell something heavenly cooking, and it wasn't popcorn or hot dogs. The sign over the service window said "The Donut Man," and hand-printed signs taped to the side listed prices for donuts and fried pork skins. I was looking forward to making friends with this dealer.

There was nobody visible through the window, but we could hear clattering and an electric mixer from inside.

"Obed!" Aunt Maggie called out.

A second later a man's head appeared from under the counter, and I do mean from under, as if he'd been hiding down there. He was an older man, with deep-set eyes and thinning gray hair.

"Hey there, Maggie," he said.

"Hey, Obed. I know you heard about the break-in. Did they get you, too?"

"They dumped some of my donut mix onto the floor and threw some of my pots and pans around, but I've got it all squared away now. I 've got my first batch of donuts about ready to come out of the fry vat, if you're interested."

"No, thanks, I didn't come for donuts. I wanted to introduce you to my great-niece, Laurie Anne. She and her husband Richard are helping me out this weekend. Laurie Anne Fleming, this is Obed Hanford."

"Pleased to meet you," he said, and stretched his arm over the counter to shake my hand. It was a stretch, too, because his arm wasn't as long as I expected it to be.

"Laurie Anne and Richard live in Massachusetts, and they're looking into starting something on the side. Have you got any advice about the donut business?"

"There's no better way to make a living. I was on the road as a performer for years, but when the circus stopped running sideshows, I switched over to concessions, and I never looked back."

Aunt Maggie must have been able to tell that I was confused. "Obed's a little person, Laurie Anne."

Obed waved it away. "Little person, nothing. I'm a dwarf, but people decided that it's not politically correct to be a dwarf. I used to tumble, but selling donuts is better—I get to be my own boss. I retired a few years back, and just set up here on the weekends to keep my hand in."

"Are you from around here, Mr. Hanford?" I asked.

"Mama and Daddy traveled with Ringling Brothers, and I was born on the road, so I'm not from anywhere. I ended up here because I thought North Carolina would be a good place to settle down. I got a map of the state, closed my eyes, and pointed. Rocky Shoals is where my finger landed."

"You'll have to come hear some of Obed's stories," Aunt Maggie said.

"Some of them are even true," he added with a chuckle. "When you travel enough, you see pretty much everything."

"Is that right? Then tell me, did you ever see anything

like what happened to Carney last week?" Aunt Maggie said, in a smooth change of subject.

He shook his head. "I've seen killings, but they were always crimes of passion. A roustabout drinks too much and starts a fight that gets out of hand, or a woman finds out that her husband has been teaching some sweet young thing more than bareback riding. I never knew anybody to try to hide a body like that."

Just then, a bell went off inside the trailer. "Excuse me, but I've got to get my next batch in the vat. Stop back by, Laurie Anne, and try out my donuts." He disappeared back inside the trailer, and we walked on.

"You could have warned me about him so I wouldn't make a fool of myself," I said.

"You mean about his height? Tell you the truth, I've known Obed so long that I don't even think about it anymore."

"How tall is he, anyway?"

"He comes to about here," she said, holding her hand to the middle of her chest.

"Then he's out of the running for killing Carney."

"Just because he's little doesn't mean he can't use a knife. He's as strong as an ox—I've seen him lifting bags of flour and sugar that must weigh as much as he does."

"I'm not talking about strength," I said. "I'm talking about height. Dr. Connelly would have known from the angle of the wounds if the knife had come from below."

"That's right," Aunt Maggie said, sounding impressed.

But I had to go and ruin it. "Of course, he said he was a tumbler, so he might have been able to rig something. Heck, for all we know, Carney was pushed down and the killer stabbed him while he was on the ground." Then I thought of something else. "Of course, Obed couldn't have driven Carney's van away."

"Yes, he could have," Aunt Maggie said. "He puts blocks on his car's pedals, and he's got a pillow to sit on. It wouldn't have been any trouble to move them into Carney's van."

"Then he's still a possibility," I said. "Assuming he had a motive for wanting Carney dead, that is."

"He had a motive, all right. First off, they never got along. The first time they met, Carney asked Obed if he'd always been a short-order cook. He made short jokes where Obed could hear, too."

"That's mean," I said.

"Obed just ignored him, because he's used to it. But a while back Carney bought a bag of pork skins from Obed and broke a filling eating one. He wanted Obed to pay his dentist's bill, but it turned out that Carney had bought them the week before and let them get stale. Obed says that if Carney didn't have any more sense than to eat a week-old pork skin, he deserved to lose a filling."

"I take it that Carney didn't agree."

"You got that right. Not long after that, Obed's business started to fall off. He didn't think anything of it at first, but after a while, he did start to wonder. One day, I overheard somebody telling a new dealer that he ought not buy any donuts because Obed's trailer was infested with roaches. He said that somebody had bit into a donut and a roach crawled out. That's not even possible, because Obed fries those donuts too long for a roach to survive. Besides which, I've been in that trailer. Obed keeps it as clean as Nora's kitchen."

"Do you think Carney was the one to make up the story?"

"I know he was. The next day, I saw him talking to a customer who was eating a bag of donuts. I didn't hear what he said, but I saw that man take a half-eaten donut out of his mouth and throw it and the rest of the bag into the trash."

"That's awful."

"That's the kind of man Carney was," she said. "I didn't like to cause trouble, but Obed needed to know what was going on, so I told him. Obed got so mad I thought he was going to bust a blood vessel. He said circus folks knew how to take care of people like Carney."

"What happened?"

"I got him calmed down, and we went to the other dealers to start spreading the real story. A bunch of us made a point of buying donuts or pork skins every day, and waving them under our customers' noses. It wasn't too long before Obed was selling more than ever, but after that, I don't think Obed would have sold Carney a cup of pee if he was on fire."

I laughed, but I still wondered what it was about such an unlikable man as Carney that made Aunt Maggie so determined for me and Richard to solve his murder.

Chapter 13

"Tattoo Bob isn't here," Aunt Maggie said, looking over at his booth. "Let's go talk to some of the outside dealers."

"What about these folks?" I said, nodding at other dealers who were cleaning up from the break-in. "Aren't they suspects?"

"Not the Samples—they weren't here last week. The first week of the month, they set up at the Metrolina Flea Market in Charlotte."

She was talking about a couple whose double-sized booth was filled with pieces of furniture that were either antiques or amazing reproductions. I was afraid to look at anything more closely for fear that I'd fall in love with it.

Aunt Maggie glanced at the other booths, filled with everything from beads for do-it-yourself necklaces, to toys from when I was a little girl, to plastic-wrapped comic books. "I don't know these folks as well, and as far as I know, none of them had anything against Carney."

Since so many people had known motives for wanting Carney dead, I was perfectly willing to start with them. If none of them panned out, I could always check out the other dealers later.

The building's main door was a metal roll-up door, like

in a garage. It was still closed, but there was a regular door next to it, and that's where Aunt Maggie was leading me.

I noticed that the booth right in front was empty, and said, "I thought inside booths were at a premium."

"That's Ronald's spot, but he doesn't leave his things here during the week. Evan put him up here because he really puts on a show—draws the people right in. I bet he's working outside until we open up."

Sure enough, a crowd was gathered around a table set up in front of the building.

"What's he doing?" I asked.

"Making jewelry. Go take a look."

I'm short enough that I had to squeeze my way right up to the table to be able to see. A middle-aged black man was twisting a long piece of copper wire in his hand. Every few minutes, he'd pick up a handful of tools, toss them around, and pick up the one that landed on top. Then he'd use the pair of pliers or vise to work on the piece, which was quickly turning into a bracelet.

All the while, he kept talking to a short woman with brown hair shot with gray. "This will help you with that arthritis. There's nothing like a copper bracelet for arthritis."

As if all that activity and conversation weren't enough, he had a tape player on and was moving his feet to the music, too. I don't think I could have counted to ten with all those people watching, let alone made jewelry while holding a conversation and dancing, but Ronald seemed perfectly at ease.

By then, Aunt Maggie had gotten up beside me. "Hey, Ronald," she said.

"Hey there, Miz Burnette. You didn't lose too much in the break-in, did you?"

"Nothing I can't live without. Bet you're glad you keep your things with you."

"You know I am." He looked at me. "This young lady must be related to you."

I nodded, a little surprised. I'm good at spotting family resemblances, but I'd never seen much similarity between Aunt Maggie and me.

"Laurie Anne is my great-niece," Aunt Maggie said.

Ronald wove in the last piece of copper and used a cloth to polish the bracelet. Then he displayed it with a flourish. "How do you like that?" he asked his customer.

"It's beautiful," she said with a smile.

Ronald held it up to look at it for a few seconds longer, then brought it to his lips and kissed it. "That's because there's a piece of me in there, and I want to thank God for letting me share it," he explained. Then he took the woman's hand and slipped the bracelet onto her wrist. It fit perfectly.

The bearded man next to the woman reached for his wallet. "How much do I owe you?"

Ronald shook his head. "No, sir, that's a present from me to your wife. I couldn't sleep at night if I thought that arthritis was bothering her."

They thanked him profusely before leaving.

Aunt Maggie said, "Ronald, how are you going to make any money if you keep giving away bracelets?"

"God wanted me to, Miz Burnette, and I never argue with God."

"God doesn't want you to starve to death, does He?"

"It'll never happen, Miz Burnette. I'm a blessed person,

and I'm glad to share my blessings with those who can appreciate them."

"Is that why you never made anything for Carney? Him not appreciating it?"

For the first time, Ronald quit smiling. "I tried to tell Carney that all he needed to do was use his gifts instead of trying to bring down other people, but he wouldn't listen." Then he looked at me again. "You've got to use *your* gifts, you know. Can't let them go to waste when they're needed, and your gifts are always going to be needed. Come back later, and I'll make you a ring." Then he turned to a couple with a baby in a stroller who were waiting for his attention.

I blinked. Of course, it was just a coincidence that Ronald had said that just as I was wondering why it was I was looking into Carney's death. Wasn't it? I was still trying to decide as Aunt Maggie and I backed out of the crowd watching him work.

Chapter 14

As Aunt Maggie led the way, I asked, "Did Carney ever do anything to Ronald?"

"Not even Carney was that dumb. Everybody out here loves Ronald." She turned to glare at me. "You better not be saying that he's a suspect."

I raised my hands in surrender. "If you say he's not a suspect, that's fine with me."

"Good." We walked on, and she said, "It figures that we'd have to open late today. This is the best crowd we've had all month. It's either been too hot or raining."

Of course, that pretty much described summer in North Carolina. That day was an exception. The sun was shining brightly, but there was enough of a breeze that it didn't feel hot. More importantly, there wasn't much humidity. Jokes aside, it really is humidity that makes the dog days in Byerly so awful.

Aunt Maggie was probably right about the weather luring folks from their air-conditioned houses, because people were so thick you couldn't stir them with a stick. Fortunately, Aunt Maggie has a way of driving through a crowd that leaves a wake behind her, and I was more than willing to take advantage of that wake. She seemed to know where she was going, too, unlike most of the browsers.

We ended up in front of a dark green van hemmed in on three sides by tables. The fourth side was against Building Two. The area was sunny now, but I could tell that as the day went on and the air got hotter, the building would provide shade. Little things like that identify a professional dealer.

Tammy Pruitt and J.B. Doughty were watching over stacks of T-shirts, belt buckles, beer can huggers, mugs, and all kinds of stuff, every piece marked with the Harley-Davidson logo. I'd never realized how many items went along with the motorcycles. A bumper sticker that caught my eye said it best: "A Harley isn't just a motorcycle—it's a way of life."

There seemed to be plenty of people who shared Tammy and J.B.'s devotion. They were doing good business, and we had to wait awhile before we were noticed. When Tammy did see us, she said, "Hey there, Miz Burnette. What do you think about us being neighbors? Mr. Cawthorne said we can move our stuff inside as soon as Thatcher gets Carney's things packed up."

"He better do it quick," Aunt Maggie said. "Evan Cawthorne's probably charging him rent. I wonder if he's going to try to charge Carney's estate for last Sunday—after all, Carney was there in the booth. It's not Evan's fault that he was dead."

J.B. snickered.

"Laurie Anne, say hello to Tammy and J.B. Tammy, J.B., this is Laurie Anne Fleming. Laurie Anne and her husband are looking into setting themselves up as dealers up in Massachusetts."

"Are you going to sell Harley stuff?" Tammy asked. "We

just love it, don't we, J.B.? We're official dealers, too, none of those cheap knock-offs."

"We haven't decided yet," I said, "but I know Harley-Davidson merchandise is big business these days. One of the malls near me even has a Harley boutique."

"That's what we want to have someday, isn't it, J.B.? Right now, we just sell here on the weekends, but we're getting there. Moving to an inside spot is the first step. We'll be able to set up displays and everything, won't we, J.B.?"

J.B. hadn't said anything, but he nodded amiably whenever it was called for.

"They're getting Carney's spot," Aunt Maggie reminded me with a significant look.

Surely she wasn't implying that a better location could be a motive for murder. I looked at J.B. again, and noticed the leather knife sheath at his belt. Just how good was he with a knife? Then I realized that my prejudices were sneaking up on me. It wasn't like I didn't know any other bikers—my friend Sandy was married in a biker wedding.

Tammy looked a little crestfallen. "I feel bad about getting an inside spot under these circumstances, but we've been on the waiting list for months and months, haven't we, J.B.?"

"The man's dead, Tammy," J.B. said gently. "It can't make any difference to him."

"I suppose not," she said. Then she brightened up. "It's going to be so nice being your neighbor, Miz Burnette, and I know I'm going to gain a ton being so close to Mr. Hanford's donuts. Dulcy can eat a million of them. I know I shouldn't give them to her, but she loves them." To me she added, "Dulcy's my little girl."

"What an unusual name," I said.

She wrinkled her forehead. "It's a family name—my ex-mother-in-law insisted on it. It does kind of grow on you."

"Where is Dulcy?" Aunt Maggie asked.

Tammy looked nervously at J.B. "My ex said he'd have her here an hour ago. He kept her last night and he wanted to keep her all weekend, but Dulcy wanted to come out here. She just loves meeting people. There are such interesting people out here, don't you think, Laurie Anne?"

"Absolutely," I said with complete sincerity.

"You and your husband have to come by later, when it's not so busy," Tammy said. "We'll be able to tell you anything you want to know about the business. Does your husband like Harleys?"

Since Richard thinks that people who drive motorcycles in Boston might as well shoot themselves and get it over with, I couldn't come up with an answer right away. Fortunately, we were interrupted by a tiny blonde in pink throwing herself at Tammy.

"Mama!" The child hugged Tammy in that all-or-nothing way that only little children can hug. Then she jumped back and posed proudly. "Look at me!"

"Aren't you pretty!" Tammy said.

She did look adorable in a pink dress and crisp white pinafore with lacy socks and black Mary Janes, but I had to wonder who would be crazy enough to dress a child like that to go out there. That pinafore was sure to wilt in the afternoon heat, and nothing stains like North Carolina red clay.

A moment later, the answer appeared. Only a woman who'd wear a salmon silk dress with matching high heels to a flea market could have dressed Dulcy that way. Her ash blond hair looked like she'd had it styled for the occasion.

"Grandmother bought it for me," Dulcy said, smoothing the dress.

"Wasn't that nice?" Tammy said, and for the first time since I'd met her, she didn't sound genuine. "Hello, Mrs. Lamar. I thought Roy was bringing Dulcy by."

"Roy had an important social engagement," Mrs. Lamar said. "I'm sure he told you how inconvenient it was going to be for him to drive all this way and still get to the country club on time."

All what way? Mrs. Lamar had to be talking about the Rocky Shoals Country Club, because Byerly doesn't have one, and the Rocky Shoals Country Club couldn't have been more than five minutes away from the flea market.

"Roy didn't say anything to me," Tammy said. "I wish he had. It would have been just as easy for us to swing by and get Dulcy ourselves."

"It's too late for that now. Besides, I wanted to see where my granddaughter spends her weekends." From the expression on her face as she surveyed the area, Mrs. Lamar was not impressed. She picked up a T-shirt, frowned, and put it down like she was afraid it had left dirt on her manicured fingers. "I had no idea people would pay for this type of thing."

Tammy's face froze, but she didn't say anything.

Fortunately, Dulcy hadn't noticed how uncomfortable the situation was becoming. She said, "Hi, Maggie!"

"Dulcy," Tammy said, "you know better than to call grown-ups by their first names. Call her Miz Burnette."

"Don't worry about it, Tammy," Aunt Maggie said. "You know *I* don't put on airs." Her emphasis, and meaning, were plain. "I don't believe we've met," she said to Mrs. Lamar. "I'm Maggie Burnette. This is my great-niece, Laurie Anne Fleming."

"Where are my manners?" Tammy said. "Miz Burnette, this is Annabelle Lamar, my ex-husband's mother."

Mrs. Lamar sniffed like she knew exactly where Tammy's manners were. "Mrs. Roy Lamar, Senior."

"Pleased to meet you, Annabelle," Aunt Maggie said.

"Burnette?" Mrs. Lamar said. "That's a mill family, isn't it?"

Aunt Maggie bristled, and when she bristles, she does it thoroughly. "That's right. Four generations of us Burnettes have worked at Walters Mill, and we're mighty proud of it."

Apparently even Mrs. Lamar knew when to back down. She turned to me. "I suppose you work at the mill, too."

"Actually I'm a programmer. Mostly object-oriented programming for the Mac, but I dabble in Windows, UNIX and whatever operating system that's hot." I knew it was rude to spout techno-babble, but Aunt Maggie wasn't the only one Mrs. Lamar made bristle.

"I see," Mrs. Lamar said. "Tammy, you know I try not to interfere, but I feel I must object to your bringing Dulcy into this environment. Surely it's not healthy for a child to be around . . ." I suspected that she wanted to comment on the people, but didn't quite dare. "The heat can't be good for her," she finally said.

Aunt Maggie said, "Dulcy, do you get too hot out here?"

"It's not too hot," Dulcy said firmly. "I get to play in the dirt!"

"There you go," Aunt Maggie said. "All children like to play in the dirt."

I don't think Mrs. Lamar thought playing in the dirt was

an appropriate activity, but she had enough sense not to contradict Dulcy. "That's fine, dear, but Tammy, surely it's not safe for a child. Just last week, that poor man was—"

"We know what happened," J.B. said, glaring at Mrs. Lamar in a clear warning against speaking about Carney's death around Dulcy. "We can take care of Dulcy."

Mrs. Lamar didn't even look at him. "I'd be more than happy to keep Dulcy on the weekends if you insist on peddling your biker objects. Wouldn't you like to come with me, Dulcy? We could have a lovely lunch together and then shop for more dresses."

Dulcy looked down at her dress. "I like this dress."

"Yes, dear, but you can have other dresses, too."

"I like *this* dress," she repeated. "I don't want another dress."

"Then we could get a lovely new doll, or maybe go meet your father at the country club."

"Daddy's playing golf," Dulcy said with a frown. "I don't like it there. He won't let me play in the sandbox. He says it's a trap."

"It looks like she wants to stay here," J.B. said. "Dulcy, aren't you going to give me a hug?"

"J.B.!" she said with delight, and launched herself again. Mrs. Lamar's face looked like she was sucking lemons. Really sour ones.

She made one last attempt. "But, Dulcy, if you stay out here, you'll get your dress all dirty."

Dulcy looked concerned, and rubbed the little smudges that she'd already gotten on the pinafore.

"That's all right," Tammy said. "I always bring a spare outfit for her. Dulcy, your blue shorts and your Harley T-shirt are in the van. I brought your sandals, too."

"Yay!" Dulcy cried. "I can stay!"

Mrs. Lamar could tell she'd lost, but couldn't resist saying, "If you get tired and want to leave, you tell your mother to call me. I'll come right out and get you." She opened her purse. "Let me give you a quarter for the phone."

"I think I can scrape up a quarter," J.B. said.

Mrs. Lamar snapped her purse shut. "I'm so glad. Dulcy, come hug Grandmother goodbye." Dulcy enthusiastically obeyed. "I think I'll go have lunch with my friend Mr. Humphrey. We were just speaking about you the other day, Dulcy." Even though she was talking to Dulcy, she was looking at Tammy when she said it. "He's awfully interested in how you and your mother are getting along."

Tammy flushed, and J.B. looked thunderous. As soon as she was gone, Tammy said, "I can't stand that woman—"

"Come on, Dulcy," J.B. said. "Let's get you changed out of your dress so you can play in the dirt." J.B. lifted the little girl into the van and partially closed the door behind her. Then he gave Tammy a quick kiss, and in a quiet voice said, "Don't worry," before going to wait on a customer.

Tammy said, "I should have known that Roy was going to dump Dulcy on his mother again. He always does! I don't think he cares a thing about spending time with her. And then Mrs. Lamar goes and buys Dulcy dresses and toys she doesn't need, just to show her how wonderful she is."

"Tammy, Dulcy may not realize what she's doing now, but when she's older, she'll know," Aunt Maggie said. "A child can tell the difference between somebody who loves her and somebody who doesn't."

"Oh, Mrs. Lamar loves Dulcy, I'll give her that. It's just that she thinks she knows how to raise her better than I do. Dulcy is her first granddaughter, and she wants to turn her into a debutante so bad she can taste it."

"Since when do they have debutantes around here?" I asked.

"They will if Mrs. Lamar has anything to say about it. But Dulcy's *my* daughter, and I won't have her growing up to be a snob!"

Aunt Maggie said, "Just keep standing up for yourself, and there's nothing Annabelle can do."

"I wish you were right, Miz Burnette," Tammy said sadly, "but you heard what she said about going to see Mr. Humphrey. He's Roy's lawyer, and he's the reason Roy didn't have to give me any money when we split up. I even lost the savings I had before we got married. Mrs. Lamar wants Roy to try to get custody of Dulcy, I just know it. Roy doesn't want Dulcy getting in the way when he has women over and throws those parties, so if he gets custody, Mrs. Lamar will get to run Dulcy's life."

"She can't do that, can she?" I said, horrified.

"She can if she can make it look like I'm not a fit mother. She says J.B. and I are living in sin, but the only reason we haven't gotten married is because we know she'd try to use that against me." She lowered her voice. "J.B. was in trouble with the law when he was a teenager; but everybody knows he straightened up after that, and he loves Dulcy just like she was his own. Why can't she see that?"

Aunt Maggie said, "I don't know why she's acting so high and mighty. Those boys of hers have been married and divorced so many times that I saw a bumper sticker that said, 'Honk if you were married to a Lamar.' "

Tammy and I both snickered.

"Anyway, if it does go to court," Aunt Maggie said, "any

judge worth his salt will be able to tell that you're a good mama."

"That's sweet of you to say, Miz Burnette. I just hope it doesn't come to that. If only Mrs. Lamar hadn't found out about J.B.'s record. I don't know who told her."

"I'm sure it will work out all right," Aunt Maggie assured. "Right now, we better let you get back to work."

When we were far enough away, I said, "Carney again?"

"Probably. I didn't know J.B. has a record, but now that I know, it explains something. I heard Carney calling J.B. J.D. once, and when J.B. corrected him, Carney grinned like J.B. had said something funny."

"I don't get it."

"J.D., as in juvenile delinquent. I don't know what Carney had against those two, but he must have known about J.B.'s record, and he's the only person I know of mean enough to tell Annabelle."

As sweet as Tammy seemed, she had one of the best motives for killing Carney I'd found so far. Though she said she didn't know who had told her ex-mother-in-law about J.B.'s record, how could we be sure she was telling the truth? Wouldn't a mother kill to protect her child?

There was also J.B. to think about, and not just because he looked rough. Maybe Tammy hadn't known that Carney had been the one to cause trouble, but that didn't mean that J.B. hadn't found out. Tammy said J.B. loved Dulcy like she was his own. Wouldn't a father be just as likely as a mother to kill for his child?

Chapter 15

"Where to next?" I asked Aunt Maggie. "Did Carney pull any nasty tricks on the folks in Buildings Two or Three?"

"I don't know that he did. The folks in Building Three are all fairly new because Evan just added that building in April, and we don't mix much with the folks in Taiwan Alley."

"Taiwan Alley?"

"That's what we call Building Two. The folks over there all carry new merchandise that they pick up surplus or at the dealers' auctions: cheap car radios, and toys that break the first time a child plays with them, and knock-off sweatshirts."

"Stuff that's made in Taiwan?" I guessed.

"You got it. Not a piece in there is worth carrying home, if you ask me."

A class system at the flea market? I didn't know if I should be appalled or amused. Right then, I saw Bender rolling up the main door to Building One.

"We better get back to the booth," Aunt Maggie said. "I've got some special pieces put back for a regular customer, and he usually comes by first thing."

I don't know if any of them were Aunt Maggie's regulars

or not, but quite a few folks went in as soon as the door was open, so there were too many people around for Aunt Maggie and me to talk about Carney as we made our way back to her booth.

Richard was talking to a middle-aged woman in a Charlotte Hornets windbreaker who was holding a large mixing bowl. He said, "Yes, ma'am, fifteen dollars is the correct price."

She looked doubtful. "Could you let me have it for ten?"

"No, ma'am, I couldn't do that."

"How about twelve-fifty?"

He looked thoughtful, but finally nodded, and the woman handed him a twenty-dollar bill.

Aunt Maggie and I came inside the booth, and I wrapped the bowl up while Richard made change.

Once the woman moved on, Richard said, "How did I do?"

"Not bad," Aunt Maggie said. "You probably could have got thirteen out of her, but since I only paid two, I'm not complaining."

Richard looked thoroughly pleased with himself.

A man came up and greeted Aunt Maggie by name, and she spent some time showing him pieces she'd stashed under the table. I wanted to tell Richard about the people I'd met, but more customers came around, and we stayed busy for quite a while.

Working the booth was more interesting than I'd expected it to be. I'd never worked retail, not even in college, so it was my first real experience with the great unwashed. Unfortunately, that was a literal description of some of our customers. Others were dressed extremely well, in clothes that even Mrs. Lamar would have approved of. The one thing they had in common was that they all seemed to be looking for something—I could see it in their eyes.

Despite Aunt Maggie's concern about ghouls coming to gawk at the site of Carney's murder, most people didn't give his booth a second glance once they saw Thatcher wasn't open for business. Apparently a recent murder wasn't as interesting to them as the old dishes or Coca-Cola collectibles or whatever it was they wanted to find.

I loved seeing their triumph when they found it, like when a woman bought two matching teacups. As I wrapped them for her, she explained that she'd been looking for replacements for cups her daughter broke ten years before. Then there was the man who bought an emerald green Graniteware pudding pot, saying that he only collected that color. Other people weren't so specific in what they'd look at. It was like they were hoping something wonderful was waiting for them.

"It's like a treasure hunt without a map," Richard said. "I can see why people find the challenge so hard to resist."

"You better resist. We don't have enough room in our apartment for you to start collecting anything. Our books are collection enough."

"Are y'all going to talk or work?" Aunt Maggie said, ending the conversation.

A while later, I was putting out books to replace a batch I'd sold when I suddenly felt like I was being watched. I looked down into two of the deepest brown eyes I'd ever seen, even darker than Richard's. But Richard had nothing to worry about, because these eyes belonged to Bender's dog, Rusty. He was gorgeous, three feet tall at the shoulders, with thick, red fur and an intelligent expression, but not exactly competition for Richard.

"Hello there," I said to the dog.

"Hey, Rusty," Aunt Maggie said, reaching over the table to pat him. "Let him sniff your hand, Laurie Anne."

I offered him my hand, and Richard did the same.

"Rusty, this is Laurie Anne and Richard. They're working with me," Aunt Maggie said as if she expected him to understand her. "Are you feeling all right after your surgery?"

"Much better," a voice said. For a second I thought Rusty had spoken, but the answer had come from Bender, who was right behind his dog. "Dr. Josie says he's going to be fine, and the operation won't change his personality one bit."

"I'm glad to hear that, Bender," Aunt Maggie said.

"You and me both. I wouldn't want anything to happen to old Rusty here." He rubbed the dog's head lovingly, and I could tell from the way Rusty leaned back against his hand that the affection was returned.

"Bender, this is my great-niece, Laurie Anne Fleming, and her husband, Richard. They're helping me out this weekend. Laurie Anne, Richard, this is Bender Cawthorne."

"I believe we met this morning," Richard said.

"So we did. Terrible business this morning, wasn't it?" He shook his head sadly. Even if I hadn't known that Bender was a drinker, I think I'd have been able to tell from looking at him. He wasn't at all healthy-looking, and his hands shook noticeably.

"I thought Evan said he wasn't going to collect rent today," Aunt Maggie said. "Did he change his mind?"

"No, I'm not here for that. It's just that Evan decided that with all that's been happening, he wanted to check everything. After this morning and what happened to Carney, I can't blame him for that. Anyway, he looked at my paperwork, and he was mighty upset when he saw I haven't been using that receipt book he bought. Evan says he's got to have those receipts for tax records—he's a real stickler about taxes. He got audited once, and hasn't been the same since. So he's coming to give you post-dated receipts for the past few months. He's over with Obed right now."

"Just what I need, more paperwork," Aunt Maggie grumbled.

"He also wanted me to check to see if anything is missing from your booth. The police want it for their report."

"I don't care what the police want," Aunt Maggie said, "but you can tell Evan that I don't think anything was taken, just busted up."

"That's good," Bender said. He must have realized how that sounded, because he added, "I don't mean that it's good that your stuff got busted. I'm just glad it was no worse than it was."

Aunt Maggie patted his arm, much like she had his dog's head. "I know what you mean, Bender."

"I appreciate your being so understanding, Miz Burnette," he said. "Some of the other dealers haven't been, not that I blame them. Some of them want Evan to hire somebody else to watch the place."

"Nobody with any sense blames you for the break-in or for Carney's murder."

"Miz Dermott and Miz Foy sure think it's my fault. I guess they're scared, and I can't blame them for that."

It didn't sound like Bender blamed anybody for much of anything, other than himself.

He looked over at Carney's booth. "I feel awful bad about Carney, Miz Burnette. If I hadn't slept late, maybe I'd have heard something that morning."

"And maybe you'd have gotten yourself killed, too," Aunt Maggie said briskly. "It's a waste of time to wonder what might have happened."

"I guess you're right," he said mournfully.

"It's just bad luck that Rusty wasn't here," Aunt Maggie said, rubbing the dog's head.

Bender said, "He feels bad about it, too. He's been off his feed all week."

I thought it more likely that Rusty was affected by his recent surgery than by guilt over not doing his job, but Aunt Maggie didn't seem to think it was too outlandish.

She stooped down in front of the dog and said, "Rusty, you've got to stop blaming yourself. You hear?"

I decided I was more tired than I'd realized. I could have sworn that the dog nodded.

"Here's Evan," Bender said as his brother bustled over.

"Good afternoon, Miz Burnette."

"Afternoon, Evan," Aunt Maggie said. "I won't say that it's a good one, not after this morning." Then she introduced Richard and me.

"Pleased to meet y'all." Evan said. "I'm sorry your research came in the midst of such unpleasant incidents."

I could see where he might call a break-in unpleasant, but it was awfully mild for a murder. I said, "I have to admit that the family's a little worried about Aunt Maggie being out here alone." I didn't have to see it to know that Aunt Maggie was giving me a look, but I figured I could apologize to her later. "Have the police made any progress?"

"Weren't you here this morning when Deputy Tucker made her announcement? She believes it was a gang that came across Mr. Alexander unexpectedly."

"Belva Tucker doesn't know her head from a hole in the wall," Aunt Maggie said.

"It looked to me like she investigated quite thoroughly," Evan stated. "Do you have information she doesn't have?"

"No, I told her everything I know. She just doesn't have enough sense to believe it."

"Miz Burnette, you don't have a thing to worry about. Bender and I are implementing new security procedures tonight so there won't be any more trouble."

"You can tell your family that you're going to be safe as houses," Bender added. "They can count on me to protect you." Then, as if realizing that that wasn't much of a comfort, he added, "And Rusty, too."

Rusty barked in agreement.

"I appreciate that, Bender." She patted the dog. "You, too, Rusty. I'm going to sleep much easier now." With the last part, she glared at me. It was going to have to be an awful big apology.

"If you ask me, you're far more likely to get into trouble with the IRS than with vandals," Evan said. "Bender tells me that he hasn't been giving you dealers receipts like he's supposed to, and I'm sure you'll want that cleared up."

"To tell you the truth, Evan, that's the last thing on my mind."

He looked shocked. "Miz Burnette, you've got to have records of everything or those people will rob you blind. I swear, I think some years I pay more in taxes than I earn."

Aunt Maggie didn't look impressed. "I keep records."

He nodded approvingly. "I'm glad you're businesslike. Unfortunately, our own records aren't what they should be." He frowned at Bender. "That's going to change, starting right now. Could I see your records so I can copy the information?"

"I suppose," she said with a sigh, "but you'll have to give me a few minutes to find them. I usually have everything in order, but with the break-in—"

"Bender, why don't you give Miz Burnette a hand?"

"I sure will, Evan." Bender and Aunt Maggie started going through boxes we'd just thrown stuff into while cleaning up.

"Mr. Fleming, was it?" Evan said. "Have you decided what kind of merchandise you're going to sell?"

It figured that he'd assume Richard was in charge. As matriarchal as most Southern families are, he should have known better.

I said, "We've been thinking about putting together a market of our own. Have you been in the business long?"

"Actually, Tight as a Tick is only one of my business holdings. I received the land in payment for a debt, and since it was already being used for swap meets and such, I took the opportunity to make some improvements and create a better selling environment."

"Have you found it to be a lucrative business?" Great. I was starting to talk like him.

He waved the idea away. "Though I've made a modest profit, I wouldn't recommend it as a way to make real money. As a matter of fact, I'm planning to sell the Tight as a Tick lot, but there's a dispute over zoning."

"I understand the property straddles the border between Byerly and Rocky Shoals."

"Unfortunately. Normally I consider land an excellent investment, but this time, I wish I'd taken a loss on the debt rather than accept this piece. It's become a bit of an albatross."

"Is managing a flea market that troublesome?" Richard asked.

"You have no idea. Maintenance on the building, security concerns, insurance—the list goes on and on."

"And of course, you've got the dealers to contend with," I said.

"Young lady, you've said a mouthful." He diplomatically added, "Of course, your aunt is no problem whatsoever, but some of the others out here . . . This kind of work attracts an unusual variety of people, and they don't always get along. Some of the squabbles I've had to settle were simply ludicrous."

"Like with Mary Maude Foy and Mavis Dermott this morning?" I asked.

"Exactly."

"Aunt Maggie has told me about some of the problems. Like with that man who was killed."

Evan couldn't resist looking over at Carney's booth, where Thatcher was still working. "There had been complaints about Carney over the past few months. Apparently some of his knives weren't what he claimed they were, and to a collector, authenticity is everything. At first, I was willing to chalk it up to honest mistakes, but it was starting to look like I would have to evict him to protect our reputation."

"You don't suppose his murder had anything to do with that, do you?"

"Surely not," he said, sounding shocked. "The police seem quite certain that they're pursuing the right line of investigation." He rubbed his chin thoughtfully. "Though I suppose it is possible. Perhaps Carney sold a spurious knife to a gang member . . . I'll mention that possibility to Deputy Tucker."

I really hadn't intended to give Belva more ammunition, but before I could ask Evan anything else, Aunt Maggie announced, "Found them!" Richard and I dealt with customers while she conferred with Evan. Then the Cawthorne brothers went on to the next booth, with Rusty following along.

Chapter 16

"Did you see how Aunt Maggie was talking to Rusty?" I whispered to Richard after Evan and Bender had gone. "I never realized she had such a soft spot for dogs."

" 'The greatest pleasure of a dog is that you may make a fool of yourself with him and not only will he not scold you, but he will make a fool of himself, too.' Samuel Butler."

"Since when do you know Samuel Butler?"

"Since I found this in Aunt Maggie's stock." He pulled a paperback dictionary of quotations from his apron.

"You mean you just read it? How can you remember a brand-new quote like that?"

"It's a gift."

"More like a curse."

"You're just jealous."

By one-thirty, those sausage biscuits were a distant memory, and I wanted to talk with Richard about Carney so bad I was about to bust. So I said, "Aunt Maggie, if you don't mind, I thought Richard and I could go get something to eat and compare notes. Will you be all right on your own?"

"Laurie Anne, how many years have I been running this booth on my own?"

"Sorry," I said sheepishly. "I wasn't thinking."

"What you can do is bring me back something to eat, and then spell me so I can eat in peace. I can't remember the last weekend I got to eat my lunch while it was still hot."

I found out what she wanted, and Richard and I headed for the snack bar. The place was doing a booming business, but Richard snagged a table while I got our burgers and fries.

As we ate, I told Richard about my conversations with China and Obed, then described the encounter with Tammy, J.B., and Annabelle Lamar. Needless to say, I kept my voice low.

When I was done, Richard said, "They have an interesting batch of motives. Or rather, they all had the same motive: revenge. Vengeance—"

"Yes?" I said sweetly. "Do go on."

"Don't get mad, get even. I dont know who said it, but it wasn't Shakespeare."

"Getting back to motives, revenge does sound the most likely, unless Carney had something else up his sleeve."

"Sounds like he had a lot up his sleeves. A thoroughly unpleasant character."

"I don't think anybody is at all sorry that he's gone," I said. "Not that that's going to stop us from trying to find his murderer." Richard and I had had this discussion before, when I was looking for the murderer of my ex-boyfriend. It doesn't matter if the victim was a worthless human being or a saint, murder is still murder.

"Did any of them strike you as the murdering type?" he asked.

I shrugged. "J.B. comes the closest to looking the part, but—"

"But we shouldn't judge a book by its cover," he said cheerfully.

Maybe I should have let him stick with Shakespeare. "Anyway, none of them seemed like murderers to me. In fact, I liked everybody, except for Mrs. Lamar. What a witch!"

"Can we make a case against her?"

"I don't think she's been to the flea market before, so that makes her pretty unlikely."

"Laura, look at our suspects. A dwarf, a biker and his old lady, and a seamstress. They all sound unlikely."

"Don't they though?"

"If we follow the old rule of suspecting the least likely person, the killer would be China Upton. Maybe Carney made a pass at her, and she was fighting him off."

"Why would she have used one of his knives? She'd have been more likely to use her sewing scissors, or a seam ripper. Besides, it looks like the murder was premeditated."

"Then the next least likely would be the dwarf. Assuming that he could overcome the physical difficulties, that is."

"I don't even want to think about that," I said. "The worst part is that I haven't met everybody yet. Aunt Maggie said she'd take me to meet the rest before closing time."

Richard finished his last french fry, then said, "Laura, there's something I want to ask you." His tone told me that it wasn't a topic I was going to enjoy. "When we were alone with Evan, you took the lead in the conversation, even though he spoke to me first. Why is that?"

"Because it annoyed me that he assumed you were in charge of our hypothetical flea market business."

"Is that the only reason?"

"I think so. Why?"

"I just wanted to make sure that you weren't forgetting that I've been involved in nearly as many investigations as you have. I admit that I was in England when you found Philip Dennis's killer, but even then, I talked to you on the phone and I thought I'd helped a little."

"You helped a lot," I said emphatically.

"Then, why is it that this time, all I've done is watch the booth while Aunt Maggie shows you around, and then listen while you ask questions?"

"I'm sorry, Richard. I didn't mean to leave you with the grunt work. You and I are a team."

"I'm glad to hear it."

He didn't say anything after that, and after a minute, I asked, "Was there something else bothering you?"

"No. I was just hoping for a more demonstrative apology."

"You want demonstrative? I'll give you demonstrative that'll curl your hair." I started with a big hug, added a long, enthusiastic kiss, and then repeated the process. "See, your hair is curly now."

He ran his hands through it. "You're right." He kindly refrained from mentioning that his hair had been curly to start with. "Though I'd rather see if I can return the favor, I think that we better get back to the booth. I have a hunch Aunt Maggie is a stickler about lunch hours."

Chapter 17

It got busy after lunch, which made the time go by quickly, but I was still getting tired. I'm usually a desk jockey—I'm not used to spending so much time on my feet. Aunt Maggie is used to it, but one thing that happened made me think that she was getting tired, too.

Richard had gone to the bathroom when this one man stood there and fiddled with a platter so long I thought I was going to scream. He looked at it, picked it up, held it up to the light to check for chips, put it down, picked it up again, frowned at the price tag, and put it down again. Then he walked away, but came right back and started the process all over again. Aunt Maggie must have finally had enough of it because she said, "Can I help you?"

He said, "I saw one just like this at another booth, and it was only marked ten dollars. You've got this one marked twenty dollars."

"That's right," Aunt Maggie said.

"It's not worth twenty dollars."

"Then don't buy it."

"Why would that other dealer be selling it for ten if it's worth twenty?"

"Why don't you go ask him?"

"I'll give you ten for it."

"No, you won't."

He frowned at her. "It's not worth any more than that."

"Then I'll keep it."

He frowned some more. "You'll take fifteen, won't you?"

"Not from you. In fact, I wouldn't take twenty from you."

"All right, I'll give you twenty." He reached into his pocket like it hurt him and pulled out two ten-dollar bills.

But Aunt Maggie said, "I just told you I'm not going to sell it to you." She grabbed a sheet of newspaper, wrapped up the platter, and put it in a box underneath the table.

He looked so shocked that it was almost funny. "I said I'd pay you the twenty dollars. You have to sell it to me."

"Mister, I don't *have* to do a doggoned thing." Then she turned deliberately away from him.

He stood there holding out the money for a full minute before wandering away, scratching his head.

"I don't get it," I said to Aunt Maggie. "He was going to give you what you wanted for it."

"Laurie Anne, there's not enough money in the world to make me put up with that much aggravation. What's the point of having your own business if you don't run it to suit yourself?"

After Richard got back, there was a lull, and I was wondering if it would be all right to crawl into Aunt Maggie's car long enough to take a nap when Augustus came in, carrying a cardboard box.

"Hey, Augustus," I said, hoping he was in a better mood than he'd been in the night before. He sure didn't look any better.

"Hey," he said. "Aunt Maggie, Mama wanted me to bring these over. She said she'd already talked to you about them."

Aunt Maggie took the box from him and opened it. "Are these the tapes from Nellie and Ruben's place?"

"The first box, anyway. I've got more in the car."

"Weren't you supposed to bring these over this morning? We're going to be closing up before too much longer."

"I meant to come by sooner, but I forgot."

She sniffed as she looked at the tapes. "There aren't any X-rated ones in here, are there? I don't want to sell anything like that."

He shrugged. "I'm only doing what I was told."

"Just like in the army?" I said with a grin. He didn't grin back.

"Richard, do you mind helping Augustus bring in the rest of those tapes?" Aunt Maggie asked.

"Not at all," he said, and the two of them left.

There still weren't any customers around, so I took advantage of the relative privacy to ask, "Aunt Maggie, does Augustus seem all right to you? I thought he was acting kind of funny at dinner last night."

"I haven't seen that much of him since he's been back, but I hear nobody is real happy with him. When you ask him to do something, he says he will, but then forgets all about it. Look at how he forgot to bring these tapes by this morning, and how he forgot to call you about his own party. And he hasn't done the first thing about finding a job." She shook her head. "Of course, I didn't know him all that well to start with—I never could keep Nora's boys straight."

That was Aunt Maggie all over. Aunt Nora and Uncle Buddy's sons were as unlike one another as three brothers could be. Willis was quiet like his father, Thaddeous was outgoing like his mama, and Augustus had always been the charmer, different from both his parents.

Like me, Augustus had decided early on that he didn't want to stay in Byerly. There was just too much world out there waiting. I'd gone to college, and Augustus had joined the army. I said, "He always said he didn't want to live in Byerly. Maybe he's looking for work elsewhere."

"If he is, I haven't heard anything about it."

A trio of women came over then, stopping us from continuing the conversation, but it didn't stop me from worrying about my cousin.

Richard and Augustus made several trips to bring in all the tapes, keeping Aunt Maggie busy trying to find somewhere to put them all.

"I bet I won't sell any of these," she fussed. "Is that all of them, Augustus?"

He nodded.

"Good.Then why don't you keep Richard company for a while? I want to introduce Laurie Anne to somebody." Before he could answer, she said, "Richard knows what to do. Laurie Anne, give him your apron."

I felt bad about him having to wear that silly-looking thing, but he didn't seem to care one way or another. I also felt bad about leaving Richard at the booth again. "Richard, would you rather go with Aunt Maggie this time?"

"What difference does it make?" Aunt Maggie asked. "You two tell each other everything anyway."

"She's got a point," Richard said with a grin. "You go ahead."

I gave him a quick kiss, and as we walked away, I said, "You know, Aunt Maggie, Carney was such a creep that it's hard to get motivated to solve his murder." I paused, hoping she'd take the hint and explain why she cared so much about his death.

But she just said, "Let's see if Tattoo Bob has time to talk."

Tattoo Bob Tyndall's booth didn't need a sign. The posters of tattoos taped onto the wall showed what he was selling. The front tables were lined with samples of his work, and if somebody couldn't find something they liked among the hundreds displayed, there was a row of binders labelled "Flowers," "Big Cats," "Cars," "Military," "Teams," and every other category I could imagine. The back corner of the booth was blocked off with what looked like cast-off office cubical walls, and I guessed that was where he worked.

Bob was scrubbing away at a kaleidoscope of spilled colors on one of his tables. I always think of tattoo artists as grizzled, sloppy-looking men, but Bob was clean shaven and dressed in white jeans and a dark gray, short-sleeved Oxford shirt.

"Hey, Bob," Aunt Maggie said. She reminded him that we'd met and once again explained what I was doing there. At least, she explained what we wanted people to believe. Then she said, "Laurie Anne, why don't you talk with Bob for a minute? I've got to visit the little girl's room." As earthy as Aunt Maggie usually is, there are some things she won't say outright.

"I hope you didn't lose too much in the break-in," I said after she left.

"They spilled some of my colors, but I can replace them. The thing I was most worried about was my tattoo gun, and it seems all right." Bob looked down at the ink spill. "This stain here has given me an idea for a new design."

"It is colorful," I said, but I couldn't picture myself with a multicolored Rorschach test on my arm.

"Have you and your husband decided what business y'all want to go into?" Bob asked.

"Not yet," I said, "but I don't think it will be tattoos. I can't draw a straight line without a ruler, and my husband can't draw one with a ruler."

"Some gifts you have to be born with," Bob said. "You can practice and you can learn techniques and tricks, but if you don't have that God-given ability to draw, there's nothing you can do about it. I'm just one of the lucky ones."

Looking at the sample designs, I had to agree. "Did you draw all of these?"

He nodded with an air of satisfaction. "I want every client to get just the right design. See this hummingbird? I did this on a lady's ankle last week. She has a husband and four children, but she still has a spark of wildness in her soul, and I wanted her tattoo to show that. Look at the eyes—you can see how that hummingbird wants to fly free."

Darned if I didn't see what he was talking about. "It's gorgeous."

"Of course, some of these are based on other people's work—we artists call those swipes—but I've put my own spin on them. Mermaids are traditional in tattoos, but if you look close at this one, you can see where I've given her gills along her throat and webbing between her fingers. There's no such thing as a mermaid, but if there was, she'd need those things to survive."

"Amazing." I looked over the other mythological creatures that covered that part of the table, lingering over a griffin done in blues and purples.

"Have you got any tattoos, Laurie Anne?"

From anybody else, I'd have thought it was an inept

pick-up line, but in Bob's case, I figured it was professional interest. "I'm afraid not."

"Have you ever thought about getting one?"

"Not really." I tried to think of an inoffensive way to explain why not. "Tattoo artists aren't legal in Massachusetts."

"Here I thought Boston was a sophisticated place. Tattooing is one of the oldest art forms in the world. People get tattoos to show their tribe, their religion, what branch of the service they're in, who they love, and just to look pretty. In Japan they've got museums filled with nothing but tattoos, but in this country, there's still places that have made us artists into outlaws." He sighed heavily.

I tried to figure which category the bare-bosomed warrior women fit into—I didn't think it had anything to do with religion. "I guess some people are scared of the needles. Doesn't it hurt?"

"It hurts some," he admitted, "but that lady with the hummingbird said it hurt more to use her Epilady. I know her ankle ached the next day, but didn't it hurt to get your ears pierced? Doesn't it hurt to walk around in high heels? Ties like to strangle me to death, and I hear wearing panty hose is worse."

I decided not to mention that I've never bled from panty hose. "Have you done tattoos on any of the other dealers?"

"Some of them. Do you know Tammy and J.B.? They've got matching Harley-Davidson logos with each other's name in them. They said they wanted to show their commitment to each other. You can lose a ring, but a tattoo lasts forever."

"Or until they get laser treatment." I said it as a joke, but I could tell from the look on Bob's face that it had been a mistake.

"I don't see how anybody can destroy a work of art like that! If any of my clients ever do such a thing, I hope I never hear about it."

Wanting to redeem myself, I asked, "How about you? How many tattoos do you have?"

"Only half a dozen. I'm particular about the ones I get." I could see colors peeking out from his shirt sleeves, and he pushed up his right sleeve to show me a green and gold oriental dragon twisting across his biceps. "I got this after I quit drinking. The dragon represents the alcoholism—the monster's still part of me, but I'm in control." He pushed up the other sleeve to display a growling tiger. "This represents the victory of mammals over the reptiles, because that's how man evolved."

That sounded like something out of Ayn Rand.

"This one here," he said, pulling up his pants leg, "is a replica of my notary seal. I can't show the others in public."

I was just as glad he didn't offer to show me those, but if he had, I'm sure it would have been for art's sake alone. "What kind of tattoos have you done for the other dealers?"

"I've drawn a few Confederate flags and some skulls with flames around them. Tigers are always popular. I offered to design a donut for Obed Hanford, but he said he doesn't have long enough arms to get them decorated. Your aunt never has let me work on her, either. I thought I could do a picture of one of those jugs she collects, but she said she doesn't stay interested in any one thing long enough to want it on her for the rest of her life."

"What about that man who died? Did he ever get a tattoo?"

Bob looked disgusted. "I wouldn't have wasted one drop of ink on Carney Alexander's worthless hide."

That sounded promising. "I take it that you didn't care for him."

"That's one way of putting it. That skunk tried to trade me one of his knives for a tattoo, but I know a little bit about knives, and the one he was offering wasn't worth a monogram on somebody's ankle, let alone what he wanted." He scanned the designs on the wall, then pointed to one. "That's what he asked me for."

The design was a gorgeous Asian woman wearing an inviting smile and not much else. She did have a fan decorated like a peacock's tail, but the way she was holding it didn't detract from her charms.

"It would have taken me half a day or more to do," Bob said. "It's a tough one, with all those colors in the fan and getting the skin tones right so she comes out looking Oriental instead of jaundiced. I told Carney I'd be losing money, but he pulled out some price guide and showed me a description of the knife. Only I don't believe it was the same knife, so I said that when he sold the knife, he could pay cash for the tattoo. The way he stormed off just showed me that the knife wasn't worth that much money. I knew he was mad, but I didn't have any idea he'd pull the stunt he pulled."

"What did he do?"

"The next week I got a visit from the Board of Health. They'd had an anonymous call from somebody saying that I was using dirty needles!" He waved at half a dozen jars of alcohol and disinfectant. "I wash every needle every night and every morning, and every time I use one during the day. There's no way I could have dirty needles, and they could see that for themselves, but what if they'd been the kind to find something wrong when there's nothing to find? I know their being here scared off a couple of customers.

When a tattoo artist gets a bad reputation, he may as well hang it up. It used to be people were only scared of hepatitis, but with AIDS, you just can't be too careful."

Bob looked over toward Carney's booth. "I knew sure as shooting that Carney called them, even if I couldn't prove it. I'd have been glad to put something on him after that, but I don't think he'd have liked having 'low-down sneak' written on his arm."

He didn't seem to realize that his words could make him a suspect in Carney's murder, which told me that he was either innocent or awfully smart. "Aunt Maggie said you were one of the ones who found his body. That must have been terrible."

"Yes, it was. Even after what he'd done to me, I wouldn't have wished that on him. Being in this line of work, I'm not bothered by the sight of blood, but seeing Carney covered in it was different."

"I can't imagine who could have done something like that," I said. Sometimes you get more answers to the questions you don't ask than to the ones you do. Sure enough, it worked this time.

Bob looked around, then lowered his voice. "I have to admit that I've wondered about Bender Cawthorne."

"Really? What did he have against Carney?"

"Nothing that I know of, but Bender hits the bottle pretty hard, and you never really know what a drunk's going to do. I can tell you that from my own experience." He rubbed the dragon tattoo on his arm. "I've offered to take him to one of my AA meetings, but he won't go."

Could Bender have been drunk enough to kill Carney and smart enough to play dumb later that day? Or could he have forgotten all about it? Alcohol plays tricks on memory.

"Wasn't Carney killed in the morning? Would Bender have been drinking that early?"

Bob said, "I'd never seen him real early in the day until this morning, but I have seen him take a nip of Rebel Yell while he's collecting rent money, and that's usually before noon."

Bender was certainly worth considering. I'd have to see what else I could find out about Bob, too, but I didn't have any other questions for him then. I was about to say goodbye and go track down Aunt Maggie when a design on the wall caught my eye. "Bob, is that who I think it is?"

He grinned like he was pleased that I'd recognized it. "Sure is. Tattoos aren't just about naked women—I do intellectual tattoos for educated people, too."

I said something to him as I left, but I was too worried to pay much attention to what it was. Somehow, I was going to have to keep Richard from seeing that design, or I just knew that I was going to have to spend the rest of his career making sure that none of his colleagues ever saw Shakespeare's face inked onto his body.

Chapter 18

I caught up with Aunt Maggie at the bathroom, and when she said she thought I'd met everybody I needed to, we headed for her booth. When we got within earshot, she put an arm out to stop me. Augustus was talking to a well-dressed couple, and I could tell that Aunt Maggie wanted to listen to him.

The woman was holding a china plaque decorated with the silhouette of a girl looking into a mirror. I'd noticed it before because it was marked fifty dollars, which seemed like a lot, but Aunt Maggie told me that it was Noritake and would have been worth more if it hadn't been chipped.

Augustus said, "That hung in my grandmother's house for as long as I can remember, and when she passed on, she left it to my aunt Eula. But Aunt Eula passed away unexpectedly, and didn't have a chance to decide which one of her daughters to give it to. Now Patsy and Lil have fought since the day they were born, and both of them claimed the plaque. They can't split it, and neither one of them will back down, so they asked me to bring it out here to sell." He laughed, like he was embarrassed. "I didn't mean to go into all that, but it's just that if I lower the price even one dime, I'm going to be hearing about it from Patsy and Lil for the rest of my life." He paused, as if thinking it over. "If you really can't pay fifty, maybe I can make up the difference myself, just to keep them happy."

"We couldn't ask that," the woman said.

The man looked amused by the whole thing, but said, "Of course not." He pulled out two twenties and a ten and handed them to Augustus. "Are you going to be able to make change so your cousins can divide this up?"

Augustus grinned. "Yes, sir, I think I can manage that." He carefully wrapped the piece, put it into a bag, and handed it to them. "You take care of that, now. Grandmama would be mighty upset if anything happened to it after all this time."

The woman looked properly concerned, but the man just gave Augustus a mock salute before they left.

"I wouldn't have believed it if I hadn't heard it," Aunt Maggie said.

Augustus saw us. "You don't mind my selling off that plaque, do you?"

"I hope you wiped the dust off. It's been sitting there for ages."

"Wipe it off?" Augustus said in mock horror. "That dust is what proved how old it was."

"Since when do you have an Aunt Eula?" I said. I don't know much about Uncle Buddy's side of the family, but I know there's no Eula, Patsy, or Lil.

"Don't tell me there's family I've missed," Richard said.

Augustus slapped him on the back. "Don't worry, Richard. We don't have any more Burnettes hiding in the woodwork. I just made them up."

"Right there on the spot?" I was impressed. I usually have to plan my lies ahead of time.

"Where did you learn to sell like that?" Aunt Maggie asked.

"In Germany. I used to hang out at the markets over there. I didn't buy much, but I enjoyed being outside and seeing people. At first, I believed the stories folks told about the things they were selling. The more outlandish it was, the more I believed it. But one day I was sitting on a bench long enough to hear a man try to sell a bowl to two different people, and when he told a different story to each of them, I finally caught on."

"What if those people find out that the plaque didn't come from Aunt Eula's house?" I said.

"So what if they do?" Aunt Maggie asked, "They still got a nice plaque, and it's worth what they paid for it. That man didn't believe Augustus, anyway. It's just part of the game."

"As Anacharsis said, 'A market is a place set apart for men to deceive and get the better of one another,' " Richard added.

"You got it," Augustus said. "Well, now that you two are back, I better get going." He untied that ridiculous apron and handed it to me.

"Come back any time you want," Aunt Maggie said. After he was gone, she said, "That boy could charm the scales off of a snake. He's either going to make a lot of money or end up in jail."

She went to tend to a customer, and I said to Richard, "Now *that's* the Augustus I remember. What happened while we were gone?"

"I'm not sure. He saw a man he knew buying something from China Upton, and went over to say hello. Then he went outside with him for a few minutes. When he got back, he was like you saw him."

"Maybe all he needs is a chance to catch up with old friends."

"Maybe it was what the friend gave him."

"What do you mean?"

"Augustus smelled like he'd been smoking."

"Augustus doesn't smoke."

"I'm not talking about tobacco."

"Pot? Are you sure?"

"The smell is distinctive. It is available in Byerly, isn't it?"

"Are you kidding? All those old tobacco fields are perfect for growing pot—it's all over the place. But I don't think Augustus would ever smoke."

"It makes the way he's been behaving more understandable. You remember how he disappeared before dinner last night? When he came back, his eyes were red and he smelled like perfume. Don't you remember Vasti mentioning it?"

"So he uses after-shave. That doesn't make him a drug addict."

"I didn't say he was an addict. I just said that he tokes. We know people who smoke pot. I've done it a few times myself, and so have you. We even inhaled."

"That's not funny!"

He looked at my face. "Why are you so upset?"

"I don't know," I had to admit. Just last week I'd argued for the legalization of marijuana with a coworker. And like Richard said, we have friends who smoke. So why was I bothered by Augustus smoking? "It's just that what you're saying makes it sound like he's hooked on the stuff. I don't like that, any more than I'd like him being an alcoholic."

"Let's not overreact. For all we know, last night and today are the only times he's smoked."

"Maybe," I said, but from what I knew about pot, it took regular use to explain the behavior changes the family had been seeing in Augustus. Solving a murder was one thing—I didn't think I was up to solving my cousin's problem, too, especially not if his parents got wind of it. Maybe Aunt Nora could deal with it, but I couldn't imagine Uncle Buddy allowing pot in his house.

Chapter 19

I was so glad when Bender used the loudspeaker to announce that the flea market would be closing in fifteen minutes. My feet were killing me, my back hurt from bending over to get things out from under the table, and I was tired of asking questions. In other words, I was worn slap out, and I could tell Richard felt the same way. "Fifteen more minutes," I repeated, like it was a prayer.

Aunt Maggie took pity on us and said, "We may as well close up now." I would have cheered if I'd had the energy, but then she said, "We've still got to get packed up for the auction."

I just stared at her. It was Richard who asked, "What auction?"

"Did I not tell y'all? There's an auction over at Red Clark's barn tonight. He usually sells on the last Saturday of the month, but Vasti talked him into holding a charity auction. We dealers make the same money, but the percentage we usually pay to Red goes to the charity."

"You don't need us to go, do you?" I asked.

"I thought y'all would want to go and talk to people. Most of the dealers are going to be there."

I was about to point out that we'd see all of the dealers

at the flea market the next day, but she added, "Besides, I could use some help loading and unloading."

Richard and I looked at each other and shrugged simultaneously. I said, "We didn't have any plans for tonight, anyway." Other than soaking our feet and rubbing each other's backs, that is.

"Good. Some of your aunts are going to be there, too. Vasti put Nora in charge of the refreshments."

That cheered me up. Aunt Nora can make a sliced cheese sandwich into a meal. Imagining what she might have cooked up for the auction gave me enough energy to wrap up the pieces Aunt Maggie handed me and pack them into boxes. Meanwhile, Richard ferried boxes out to Aunt Maggie's car.

"I've been saving these Morton candlesticks for a woman who asked if I'd ever had a pair," Aunt Maggie said, holding up two brown pottery candlesticks, "but somebody said she's moved, so I think I'll take them to the auction. I'll probably get more money for them that way. Folks get crazy at auctions, especially when they're for charity. Wrap them real careful, Laurie Anne."

"Yes, ma'am." They were so tall that I wanted to make sure I had a big enough box first, so I put them down so I could rummage around. While I had my head under a table, I heard a voice call out, "Miz Burnette, have you got a minute?"

"Just what I need," Aunt Maggie said under her breath. "Laurie Anne, hide those candlesticks."

I was too tired to ask for an explanation. I just grabbed a sheet and covered them up, then looked to see who was coming. It was no wonder that Aunt Maggie was looking less than thrilled. Mavis and Mary Maude were coming our way.

Richard said, "Just one quote about the weird sisters. That's all I ask."

"Surely there's something from Poe or Stephen King you can use," I said.

"Miz Burnette, have you got a minute?" Mavis said again, puffing a little from exertion.

"What can I do for you?" Aunt Maggie asked.

"Have you heard what Evan Cawthorne is going to do?" Mavis asked.

"That depends on what you're talking about."

"We're talking about him giving Carney's spot to Tammy and J.B.!" Mary Maude thundered. Mary Maude usually thunders. "That should be our spot!"

"We did start selling out here before they did," Mavis said.

"I remember y'all came out here one weekend," Aunt Maggie said, "but y'all didn't start coming out regular until after Tammy and J.B."

"What's that got to do with it?" Mary Maude said, still thundering.

"Hush, Sister," Mavis said. "Miz Burnette is right." Mavis and Mary Maude had been caught up in a game of good cop/bad cop for as long as anybody in town could remember. Mavis was always the good cop, but that didn't mean she was a bit more trustworthy than her sister. At least Mary Maude didn't try to fool you into thinking she was on your side.

"It just doesn't seem right," Mavis went on. "I mean, what kind of customers are those two going to bring in with all that biker paraphernalia?"

Aunt Maggie shrugged. "People pay big money for that stuff."

Mavis kept on as if Aunt Maggie hadn't spoken. "Sister and I sell genuine collectibles, things you wouldn't be ashamed to buy. Like you, Miz Burnette. Wouldn't it be better for us to be set up across from each other?"

Aunt Maggie couldn't quite hide her shudder, but all she said was, "It doesn't matter what I think. Evan Cawthorne is in charge, not me."

"But Evan listens to Bender, and Bender does anything you want," Mary Maude said. "What do you do? Bribe him?"

It wasn't worth an answer, so Aunt Maggie didn't give her one. She did give her a strong look, but it was a wasted effort. That kind of thing never works on Mary Maude.

Mavis said, "Maybe I could explain to Evan how hard it is for us to load and unload our merchandise every week. Our things are fragile, so it takes a long time to wrap it all up. You know what I'm talking about, don't you, Miz Burnette? At your age, and all. As hard as it is for us to be toting boxes, it must be even worse for you." Even when she was trying to butter up Aunt Maggie, she couldn't resist poking at her. "Tammy is a young girl, and that man she lives with is as strong as a horse—they don't have aches and pains like Mary Maude and I do. I swear, my arthritis gets so bad that I can hardly move come Monday morning."

"It seems to me that if you two aren't up to it, you should quit selling out here," Aunt Maggie said. "I don't imagine you need the money, what with your inheritance and what Mr. Foy brings in."

I was impressed. Aunt Maggie had managed to get in two digs, one at the sisters' claims to vast wealth and one to the fact that Mary Maude's husband hadn't done a day's work in years. Supposedly he was on disability, but I don't think anybody in Byerly believed that his leg still bothered him. If he'd been hurt at Walters Mill, Big Bill would have made sure that he didn't get away with cheating; but he'd been working for Duke Power when he was injured, and a company that big has plenty of loopholes to slip in and out of.

"Of course we don't need the money," Mary Maude said indignantly. "That's not the point."

"The point is that we've been setting up here almost as long as they have," Mavis said.

" 'Almost' only counts in horseshoes," Aunt Maggie said. "Y'all can go talk to Evan if you want, but you'd be wasting your breath."

Mavis said, "What about Tammy? She seems like a nice enough girl, other than the company she keeps. Maybe you could ask her to switch with us. They can have the next indoor spot."

"I couldn't do that," Aunt Maggie said. Mavis waited for her to go on, but no explanation was forthcoming.

Finally Mavis pinched her face up. "I can see we're wasting our time here. Some people aren't willing to help a neighbor." She turned to go, but Mary Maude was staring at the sheet-covered candlesticks.

"What's that?" she asked.

"New merchandise," I answered, reasonably sure that Aunt Maggie wouldn't mind my saying that much.

"What have you got it covered up for?"

I thought up a couple of excuses, but decided to follow Aunt Maggie's lead. "Because Aunt Maggie told me to."

Mary Maude knew Aunt Maggie wasn't going to explain, so she stomped after Mavis. Then she turned around and stomped back. "I hear there's going to be an auction tonight," she said, "but I don't know where it's going to be."

Since we were packing for the charity auction, I expected Aunt Maggie to tell her about it. Instead she said, "Is that right? We're visiting family tonight."

Mary Maude looked vaguely suspicious, but apparently didn't figure out that Aunt Maggie hadn't answered her. "There must be somebody around here who knows," she said, and of course, stomped away.

"Please tell me that those two are suspects," Richard said once they were safely out of earshot.

Aunt Maggie said, "I suppose it's possible, but Carney never did anything to them that I know of. Maybe they thought they were going to get his booth, but I don't think even those two would kill a man just to get at his booth."

"Darn. I'd really enjoy investigating them." He looked at the candlesticks I'd covered. "Why were we hiding those from them?"

"Because Mary Maude and Mavis don't bother to do research to see what's selling and how much to charge. They snoop around everybody else's booths, and price everything just enough lower that people will buy from them. I don't mind them charging less than me, but I do mind them using my own know-how against me."

"When did they get into the business?" I asked. I'd never known them to do much of anything. Nobody knew exactly how much money they had, but from what they said, they'd inherited enough from their father to live on, if not enough to be happy with. Then again, maybe no amount of money would have made them happy.

"They first came out here to sell some furniture and dishes from their late nephew's estate, but they priced things all out of whack. They overpriced some cheap Taiwan junk because it was new and shiny, and let some nice old pieces go for practically nothing. I got a few things from them myself, and sold them for right much more than I'd paid for them.

"After they'd sold what they could, they looked around and realized how much money they could have made if they'd known what they were doing."

"That must have been aggravating," I said.

"We all go through that when we're new. It makes me right embarrassed to think of the pieces I sold for a tenth of what they're worth. But that's the business. It's not what you have—it's what you know. I learned from my mistakes. I got books and I talked to other dealers. Mary Maude and Mavis just copy everybody else. That first weekend they saw how much old furniture goes for, so they spent a month getting together old bed stands, chests, and tables—anything they could drag out of their attic."

"In the meantime, Tammy and J.B. set up here and got on Evan's waiting list for an inside spot," Richard interjected.

Aunt Maggie nodded. "Mavis and Mary Maude showed up again, expecting to get rich in one weekend, but they hadn't done their homework. They didn't know which pieces were solid and which were veneer, and they hadn't made any repairs, or even bothered to clean anything. There's a difference between antique and old, and between old and junk. Most of what they had was junk, and it didn't sell. After a few weekends, they gave it up.

"By then they'd seen how ball cards were selling, so next they showed up with a bunch of them, but they still hadn't bothered to check out the field. All they had were cards nobody wanted. A few weeks later, they tried something new. I don't know how many different lines they've tried to sell."

"Now they're competing with you," I said.

"They're trying to." It was plain from the look on her face that she wasn't happy about it. "A couple of months ago Mary Maude started checking my prices and listening to me talk to my customers, so it was no big surprise when they showed up with glassware. They want to move in on my suppliers, too, so they're always trying to find out which auctions I go to."

"Which explains why you didn't want to tell them about tonight's auction," Richard said.

"That's right. Even though I'm going there to sell, I'm looking to buy, too, and I don't want to have to bid against them for every lot."

"They're not going to run you out of business, are they?" I asked.

"I don't think so, but they're costing me money. Of course, I can switch over to the books if I have to, but the glassware is more fun, and I hate to waste all I've learned about the markings and all."

"You do know your stuff," I said loyally.

Aunt Maggie looked pleased at that, but all she said was, "We better get a move on if we're going to get to the auction on time."

Chapter 20

Aunt Maggie had planned to go straight to the auction, but we talked her into letting us go back to the house long enough to clean up a little bit. Both Richard and I were dying to get into the shower, but Aunt Maggie only has one bathroom with a tub, and she said there wasn't time for both of us to get in there. We didn't dare suggest the two of us taking a shower together, and when I tried to sweet-talk Richard, he reminded me about the trip to Cape Cod he wasn't getting. So while he showered, I made do with a wet washcloth and clean clothes.

It turned out to be a good thing, because the phone rang not long after we got to the house and Aunt Maggie said it was for me.

"Hello?"

"Laurie Anne? This is Junior."

"Hey, Junior. How's the conference going?"

She didn't ask how I knew she was at a conference, any more than I asked how she knew I was in town. Byerly is like that. "It's pretty interesting. I've met some nice folks, and I'm learning a fair amount. I don't know how much of it I'll be able to use, but you never know."

"How do you like the beaches down there?"

"They're great if you like sand, but you know I didn't call long distance to talk about beaches. I want to talk to you about Carney Alexander's murder. You are looking into it, aren't you?"

"Did you talk to Mark?"

"I didn't need to."

"Aunt Maggie did ask me and Richard to see what we can do. She's nervous about having a killer on the loose."

"Maggie Burnette nervous? That's a first."

"Are you coming back to take over the case?" I asked hopefully.

"No," she said with a loud sigh.

"Why not?" Staying away had to be driving her crazy.

"Because I want to make Lloyd Monroe eat his words, that's why. When we heard about the murder, I was going to hightail it back to Byerly, but he said he was sure *his* deputy could handle it on her own." She snorted. "Mark Pope may not be the brightest bulb on the chandelier, but at least he knows enough to follow proper procedures. Not like Belva Tucker, who stopped a speeder last month, but was too lazy to run his plates for priors. Turns out he was a known drug dealer driving a stolen car, and he got away with nothing but a speeding ticket. Which he didn't pay, needless to say. Lloyd claims that Belva has learned her lesson, and that she has an 'instinct for the criminal mind,' but that's a bunch of bull hockey. The only criminal minds Belva understands are her brothers'. I told Lloyd that there was no way that Belva was going to solve this case ahead of Mark."

"I smell a bet," I said.

"A big one," she confirmed. "Whoever's deputy arrests a reasonable suspect first, wins. We agreed that neither one of us will go home before the conference is over, no matter what, and we can't interfere, or give advice, or anything else."

"So you want me to stay out of it?"

"Is there something wrong with this connection? I said it's a *big* bet, Laurie Anne. I want you to give every bit of information you get to Mark."

"Don't you think Mark can do it on his own?"

"Laurie Anne, Mark's been my deputy ever since I became police chief, and he was my daddy's deputy for years before that, but everybody knows that he wouldn't be able to put a jigsaw puzzle together to save his life. He'd be able to get all the pieces, but he'd never figure out how they go together."

"I'd noticed that he's not got much imagination."

"But you've got enough imagination for two or three people."

"Hey!"

"That's a compliment."

It didn't sound like one to me, but I let it slide because she was probably right.

She went on. "I have to admit that I'd had a beer or two when I made the bet, and the next morning I was wondering if it was the smartest thing I'd ever done, but then I heard that you and Richard were in town, and I figured y'all would be nosing around. I don't see why I can't take advantage of it."

"Does that mean that you don't want me to talk to Belva?"

"I'm sure she has her own resources, so you don't need to bother her."

That was fine with me. After the way she'd spoken to Aunt Maggie, Belva could go jump in a lake for all I cared. "If you win, do I get a cut?"

There was a pause, then she carefully said, "How big a cut did you have in mind?"

"I'm kidding, Junior. I'd be happy to help you win that bet, but I have a problem. When I tried to talk to Mark today, he wasn't exactly receptive." That was putting it mildly, but I felt funny about bad-mouthing Mark to his boss. Besides, I knew Junior could read between the lines.

There was a long, drawn-out sigh. "I guess I shouldn't be surprised. Can you work around him?"

"Probably. I've worked around you before, haven't I?"

There was another sigh. "Don't remind me."

"Anyway, if I find out anything, I'll tell Mark. I can't guarantee that he'll listen, but I'll do my best."

"I'd appreciate that, Laurie Anne. Now, I can't help you any, because Lloyd made me promise not to even let Mark send me his files."

"Rats! He'll never show them to me and Richard." There were details about Carney's death I wanted to know more about. Then I remembered that Byerly has two deputies. "What about your brother?"

"Trey? The one who adores your cousin Ilene, and who worships you because you got her out of jail last year?"

"In other words, he'll help?"

"He'll do anything short of confessing to the murder himself."

"Great." A source at the police station would definitely come in handy.

Aunt Maggie came up behind me and rattled her keys loudly. "Junior, I've got to go. You have a good time in Florida."

Richard, who'd also heard the keys rattling, came running down the stairs, and we left for the auction.

Chapter 21

As soon as I walked into Red Clark's Auction Barn, I smelled it. "There is a God," I said. "That's Aunt Nora's fried chicken." A sign that said "Chicken Dinners" was taped over a long table covered with big pans of chicken, biscuits, cole slaw, potato salad, and half a dozen other things I wanted to dive into.

But first things first. "Where do we unload your stuff?" I asked Aunt Maggie.

"It can wait until I check in," she said. "Why don't y'all go ahead and get something to eat?"

She didn't have to tell me twice. I was halfway to the table before she finished her sentence.

I'm not nearly so obsessed by food in Boston as I am in Byerly. It's just that there's so many things I can't get up North, either because they aren't available or because I'm not a good enough cook to fix them myself. So I eat like a pig when I'm home, trying to get my yearly allowance of barbeque, pork skins, pecan pie, sausage biscuits, and anything Aunt Nora cooks.

Mrs. Lockard, one of Aunt Maggie's neighbors, took Richard's and my money and said, "It's all you can eat, so help yourself."

I grabbed a paper plate and picked up a pair of tongs to serve myself some fried chicken, but before I could get a piece, somebody said, "Don't you dare take any of that!"

I looked up, startled, and saw Aunt Nora. "Why not? We paid Mrs. Lockard."

"I just don't want you taking the old stuff," she explained. "I've got some fresh out of the frying pan." She took the tongs from me and got each of us two big pieces from the tray she was holding. Then she added a smaller piece to each of our plates. "That ought to hold you awhile."

"It's a start, anyway," I said. Of course I was only kidding. There was no way I could eat more than three pieces. Then I took a good whiff of the chicken, and I wasn't so sure.

"Get whatever else you want, and come on outside. We thought it would be better to set up tables out back rather than have people eating in their chairs."

Richard and I filled up the empty space left on our plates, picked cans of Coke out of the ice chest next to the table, and went out the back door. Aunt Nora was standing by a redwood picnic table with her purse and sweater marking both benches as taken.

"Are you saving those seats?" I asked.

"I sure am." She pushed her things out of the way. "Have a seat. I've got to check on things in the kitchen."

"Thanks, Aunt Nora." It was a good thing she'd saved us a table. Most of the others were already filled with people digging into their food. Richard and I got ourselves settled and did the same.

After a few bites, I said, "This is wonderful."

"Mmmm," Richard agreed.

That was it for conversation for a while. One has to have priorities.

I was long past the point of being starved, but not yet to the uncomfortably full stage, when Aunt Nora came back. I squeezed over on my bench so she could sit next to me.

"I think they can get by without me for a while," she said. "Besides, it's getting hot in that kitchen."

"Would you like a drink?" Richard asked.

"I'll get myself something in a minute. You go ahead and eat."

"I was getting up anyway," he said. "We need more napkins."

Though we could certainly use more napkins, I knew he hadn't planned on moving until he absolutely had to, so that was something else I was going to enjoy making up to him.

"How was the flea market?" Aunt Nora asked.

"Interesting," I said. "Did you hear about the break-in?"

She nodded, which didn't surprise me. Byerly has an excellent grapevine, and Aunt Nora is usually right in the thick of it. "They say it was a bunch of kids, maybe devil worshippers or witches, and all of them high as kites on crack cocaine."

As usual, the rumor mill had added a few details to the story. "I don't know about devil worshippers, but Belva Tucker thinks it was kids looking for a place to get high."

"Does it have anything to do with Carney Alexander's murder?"

"Belva thinks it was the same crew, that Carney surprised them last week and they panicked and killed him."

"Laurie Anne, if I wanted to know what Belva thinks, I could have found that out anywhere. We all heard Aunt Maggie say she wanted you to solve a murder, and since

Carney Alexander's is the only murder we've had around here lately, I know y'all are investigating it. So what do *you* think?"

So much for keeping it a secret. "I think the break-in and the murder are connected, but I don't think it was any kids. I think it was somebody who works out there." I explained Richard's and my reasoning. Then I told her how Mark and Belva had acted when we told them.

"Maybe Belva doesn't know y'all very well, but I'm surprised that Mark didn't want your help."

"Don't get me started on those two! As far as I'm concerned, neither of them have the brains God gave a milk cow."

"What did Aunt Maggie tell you about the case?"

I feel silly using professional terminology when talking about Richard's and my so-called cases, but my family has no such problem, and TV cop shows have taught them all kinds of official-sounding words and phrases. "You probably know as much about the murder as she does, but she does have some ideas about why certain people might have wanted Carney dead."

"I'm not talking about their motives, I'm talking about Aunt Maggie's. Why does she want you to find Carney's killer?"

"She said it's because she's afraid to work at the flea market."

"Aunt Maggie? It would take more than one body to scare her off."

"She also said she didn't want thrill seekers coming out there."

"Shoot, if she thought a murder would improve business, she'd stage a fake one every week."

"I know, but that's what she said."

Aunt Nora looked frustrated, which was how I felt, too.

Richard came back then and handed her a Coke. "Sorry to take so long. There's quite a crowd in there, and I ran into Aunt Maggie, who wants to know when we're going to come give her a hand."

"Right now," I said, finishing my last bite of peach cobbler.

Aunt Nora said, "I better get back to the kitchen and make sure everything is going all right."

"You guys have done a wonderful job," Richard said around a mouthful of potato salad.

"You sure have," I agreed. In fact, it seemed a lot more relaxed than events in Byerly usually are. "That reminds me, where's Vasti?"

"She said she'd be late," Aunt Nora said.

"Is anything wrong?" Vasti usually likes to be present from beginning to end to make sure she gets a chance to order everybody around.

"Don't you remember what she said about the calendar yesterday? She's not sure last night took, so she's got *business* to take care of with Arthur." Aunt Nora giggled all the way back to the kitchen.

As Richard and I were getting up, Aunt Daphine came out with a plate that was nearly as well-loaded as mine had been. "Hey there. Y'all aren't leaving, are you?"

Before Richard could say anything, I said, "I've got to go help Aunt Maggie, but Richard will keep you company." I figured that would pay him back for getting Aunt Nora's drink. He gave me a quick smooch as a thank-you, and sat back down with a sigh of relief.

I found Aunt Maggie at a table talking to a woman with a notebook and a stack of numbered cards.

"Laurie Anne, did you get a number?" Aunt Maggie said.

I looked blank.

"You have to have a number to bid," she explained. "If you want something, you hold up your number so they know who you are. You could use mine, but it'll be easier if you and Richard have your own."

I obediently gave the woman my name and address, and she handed me the card on the top of the stack. I wasn't planning on buying anything, but I didn't want to limit myself.

Once that was taken care of, I said, "Richard said you need some help."

"We ought to go ahead and unload the car. We drew straws in the back, and I've got the third slot."

"Meaning that you're going to be the third dealer to sell?"

She nodded and led the way out.

"Is that good or bad?" I asked.

"Good. You don't want the first slot because sometimes folks get here late or they're not settled down to buy right at the beginning. And you don't want the last slot in case they've spent all their money or have to leave early. Second, third, and fourth are all good slots to have." She unlocked the back of her car. "It's going to be a while before I sell, but there's some tables in the back room where we spread out our stuff so folks can take a look before it goes on sale. With some of these box lots, that's the only way you know what you're bidding on."

We spent the next few minutes ferrying boxes from the car to the barn, and then unwrapped pieces to display them.

Aunt Maggie was mostly selling glassware, though she also had a couple of quilts. "Those old quilts go for good money," she said. "I'd just as soon have an electric blanket, but these are pretty."

Once everything was set out, she said, "Let's go get a seat before all the good ones are gone."

"Is it all right to leave your stuff?"

"Should be." She nodded at a big blond man in a straw cowboy hat. "Red's son Scooter will keep an eye on things. He's not like Bender Cawthorne—I've never had a piece go missing here."

"Scooter?" He didn't much look like a Scooter.

"His real name is Shirley, just like Red's."

No wonder he went by Scooter.

Out front, Aunt Daphine and Richard were already reserving a row of metal folding chairs, and we joined them.

"Did y'all have a nice talk?" I asked.

"Very nice," Aunt Daphine said, "but I'm afraid I don't know anything about those people Richard asked about."

Trust Richard not to miss an opportunity, and trust Aunt Daphine to be discreet in a crowd. "That's all right," I said. I hadn't spoken to Aunt Nora about them yet, and she was the one I relied on most.

The place was filling up quickly. Aunt Maggie had called it a barn, and I guess some time in the past it had been a home for horses, but there wasn't much evidence of it left. At the end farthest away from the front door, there was a high platform with a microphone and a podium where the auctioneer stood. He was flanked by two people Aunt Maggie called spotters. Their job was to watch the crowd and let the auctioneer know when somebody made a bid.

"Don't we have to be careful not to scratch our noses

or blink?" Richard asked. "I've heard that auctioneers will interpret any movement as a bid."

Aunt Maggie snorted. "Not this crew. Some nights you just about have to jump up and down to get their attention. If you get one of the spotters mad at you, you may as well hang it up because they won't see your bid if they don't want to."

There was a table in front of the podium for the clerk, who wrote down the bids and lot numbers and passed the information on to the cashier, who was the woman who assigned bidder numbers. The cashier totalled up purchases and collected money before sending people out back to pick up what they'd bought.

"Looks like a decent setup," I said, "but I bet they'd do better with a computer."

"They tried that," Aunt Maggie said. "It got things so snarled up we like to never have figured out who bought what. This is much easier, believe me."

Despite being a computer nut, I don't think you need a computer for everything, so I didn't argue with her. I did spend the next few minutes figuring out how I'd set up a system for them. Even though computers have their failings, I find them easier to understand than a lot of people.

Speaking of people I was trying to understand, as the barn filled up, I recognized a few people from the flea market. Tammy and J.B. were there, and I saw China Upton and Mr. and Mrs. Samples, the furniture dealers.

"Aunt Maggie, are the other dealers here to sell or buy?" I asked.

"Both, same as me."

"So y'all are going to bid for the same stuff, and then go out to the same flea market to sell it? I don't get it."

"Don't you remember what I said about how important it is to know your stuff? Well, we all know different things. China isn't going to be bidding on books or Depression glass—she's going to want fabric and maybe teddy bears she can fix up. The Samples are going to be buying furniture, stuff I couldn't sell if my life depended on it."

Just then Vasti arrived with a tired-looking Arthur in tow. He sat down with us while she marched into the kitchen. I'd thought the food line had been moving pretty quickly, especially for a charity event, but Vasti soon had it moving as fast as a fast-food restaurant in a TV commercial. Vasti is nothing if not efficient. I looked at Arthur sympathetically. Efficiency isn't always a good thing.

Once she had the kitchen up to speed, Vasti headed for the back room, where the man Aunt Maggie said was auctioneer Red Clark was smoking a cigarette and joking with people. I don't know what Vasti said to him, but he and the other auction workers were in place and ready to start within five minutes.

"Vasti ought to come every month," Aunt Maggie said loud enough for Red to hear. "Red hasn't started on time all year."

Red just grinned at her, and said, "If everybody will take their seats, we'll get this show on the road." He introduced himself as Colonel Red Clark, briefly explained the procedure, and announced that we were there to raise money for Habitat for Humanity.

"He doesn't look like a soldier to me," Aunt Daphine said. "What branch of the service was he in, Aunt Maggie?"

"I don't know that he was in the service," she said.

"He called himself Colonel Clark."

"All auctioneers call themselves Colonel. Even the women."

Whether he was a real colonel or not, Red deployed his staff like a veteran. They ran through an amazing amount of merchandise in an awfully short time, with Red telling folks, "Pay attention, people. You don't see merchandise like this every day," and "Looky here—this would be cheap at twice the price." When an item wasn't quite so impressive, he just said, "Remember, this is for charity," or "This is a nice one. Whatever it is." The more he talked, the more people laughed, and the more they laughed, the more they bought. As I told Richard, Red was the fastest-talking Southerner I'd ever seen.

Aunt Nora came out to sit with us about halfway through the second dealer's turn. "We ran out of chicken," she said.

"Shhh," Aunt Maggie said. "I want to bid on this next lot."

She got it, too, but I didn't know why she wanted a box of beat-up Christmas ornaments. "I thought you didn't put up a tree anymore," I said, because I couldn't imagine that there was anything in the box worth selling.

She grinned, clearly pleased with herself. "Did you see those three boxes of glass balls they held up?"

I nodded.

"You couldn't see it from here, but the boxes were marked 'Made in Occupied Japan.' "

Even I knew that Occupied Japan collectibles were valuable. "Good catch!"

She just grinned, and bid on another lot.

When her turn to sell came, Aunt Maggie went up front to help out, telling Red what each piece was and cheerfully arguing with him over where to start the bidding. Everything she'd brought sold except for one of the quilts. I don't know how much money she'd expected to make, but she was smiling when Red moved on to the next dealer.

About then, my eyes started burning from the smoke. North Carolina isn't known for sympathy toward non-smokers. At least Byerly isn't. Too many families had grown tobacco before they went to work in the mill. There were an awful lot of people smoking, and even though it was a big room, a gray cloud had formed over our heads.

"I think I could use some fresh air," I said.

Aunt Nora said, "I think I could, too. Besides, if I stay here much longer, Vasti is going to hunt me down to get me to help clean up the kitchen."

"Richard?"

"You go on," he said. "Aunt Maggie said the next guy has books to sell."

I handed him our number, just in case. We didn't really need any more books, but if he bought some, that would even us up a little.

Chapter 22

With the auction going strong, everybody had gone inside except two women talking quietly at the picnic table farthest from the barn. We'd gotten paper cups of iced tea on our way out, so we picked a table and got comfortable.

It was a beautiful night, just enough cooler than it had been during the day to cover the benches and tables with dew. There were crickets chirping and lightning bugs blinking past us. Right then, I didn't mind missing Cape Cod at all. But unlike my planned trip to Cape Cod, in Byerly I had a job to do.

"All right, Aunt Nora," I said. "Now that I've got you alone, what can you tell me about the folks at the flea market?"

"Not much."

"You're kidding. You know everybody in Byerly."

"The folks at the flea market aren't from Byerly. They're from Rocky Shoals and Hickory and Granite Falls and Conover and who knows where."

"I never thought of that," I said. How in the Sam Hill was I going to find Carney's killer without Aunt Nora's help?

"Can't you ask Aunt Maggie about them?" she asked.

"You know Aunt Maggie. She's not interested in— In people the way you are." I'd almost said *gossip*, but I was afraid that would sound rude. "She doesn't know much about their personal lives. I was hoping you'd be able to fill in the gaps."

"I'm sorry, Laurie Anne, you know I'd do anything I could to help."

"I know you would." It wasn't her fault that I'd come to rely on her for information. "Are you sure you don't know any of them? Wasn't Carney Alexander from Byerly?"

"Nope, his people are from Wilmington, and he lived in Rocky Shoals. All I know about him is what I read in the *Byerly Gazette*. He was single and had an apartment over his sister's garage. The sister was out of town when he was killed, so she's not a suspect."

"Is she married? Are there other brothers or sisters?" I asked, hoping for a family squabble.

"Just the two of them, according to the paper. She's been divorced for years, and their parents are long gone."

At least that eliminated some possibilities. "You know the Cawthorne brothers, don't you? You were talking about them the other night."

"I used to know them because they grew up in Byerly, but Evan lives in Rocky Shoals now."

"Bender may still live here, depending on where the town line is."

"What do you want to know about them?"

"Anything you know. Aunt Maggie hasn't mentioned either of them having a reason for wanting Carney dead, but maybe you know something she doesn't."

She took a sip of her iced tea. "I always felt sorry for the Cawthornes, particularly Evan. You see, they never had any money. We Burnettes never had any money either, but we always had a place to sleep, and clothes to wear, and enough food to eat. There were many times that the Cawthornes didn't. Evan and Bender's mama died when Bender was six or seven and Evan was two, and their daddy Russ never was the same afterward. He kept saying that if he'd had enough money to live in town instead of out in the woods in an old shack that wasn't fit to cure tobacco in, she wouldn't have died. Russ always had been a hard-drinking man, but after that, he crawled into a bottle to hide and never came out. There was nobody to take care of those two boys. The church took them food and clothes every few months, but otherwise they were on their own."

She looked embarrassed. "Once when I'd been fussing because I couldn't have a new dress, Paw sent me out there with the ladies from the church so I could see what it really meant to be poor. Those two boys shared a cot with sheets so dirty they looked gray, with only one blanket even though there wasn't a bit of heat in the house." She shook her head. "These days they take children away to take care of them, but they didn't step in back then like they should have."

She took another sip of tea. "Anyway, I'll give Russ credit for one thing—those boys were always in school. Of course, with them dressed in rags or hand-me-downs, they got teased all the time. It never seemed to bother Bender, like it did Evan. Evan tried to fight anybody who said anything, but the principal threatened to kick him out of school if he didn't stop. So all he could do was try and keep whatever clothes he had clean and neat."

"He still dresses neatly," I said, remembering those knife-blade creases in his khakis and how even his golf shirt had looked starched.

"Despite all those boys had going against them, they both made it through school, and went to work at the mill."

No surprise there. Most of the young men and women in Byerly start out working at Walters Mill, and a lot of them stay there, including many of the Burnettes.

Aunt Nora went on. "By then Bender had already started drinking, just like his daddy."

"Is Bender his real name?"

"You know, I'm not sure. It seems like I remember Paw and Maw talking about Russ calling him that because he was out on a bender when he was born, but I don't know if that's what they put on his birth certificate or if it's just a nickname. I never heard him called anything else, not even in school."

No wonder Bender drank. With a name like that, it must have seemed inevitable.

Aunt Nora said, "Anyway, it wasn't too long before he drank himself right out of his job. After that, he'd do odd jobs, seasonal work, whatever he could to keep himself in Rebel Yell."

I nodded. Rebel Yell Whiskey is the cheapest way I know of to get drunk, but it tastes terrible, so the only ones who drink it are kids who don't know any better and drunks who can't afford any better. "What about Evan?"

"I don't think Evan's ever taken a drink in his life. That's what having a drunk in the family does. You either drink like a fish or you won't have anything to do with it. The Cawthornes ended up with one of each. Evan did real well at the mill, and got to the point where he was making enough money to get himself a little room away from his father. It was the first time he'd ever had a decent place to live. Of course, this being Byerly, nobody ever let him forget what kind of life he'd had growing up until somebody tried to steal his truck."

"What truck?"

"One of Big Bill Walters's trucks. Evan was driving a load from the mill to Raleigh, and he stopped to eat at some place by the side of the road. While he was inside, a couple of yahoos tried to hot-wire the truck, but Evan saw them and went after them like a bat out of hell. He jumped into the cab and pulled out a big old monkey wrench and knocked the fool out of those boys."

"Really?" I said, trying to picture that pompous man in a fight. "You'd never know it to look at him."

"Big Bill was so impressed by his loyalty that he declared him a hero and got his picture in the paper. He gave him a big bonus, too."

"Big Bill gave somebody a bonus?"

"He figured that it would be a good example to the other workers at the mill. If that truck had been stolen, he'd have been out a lot more money than what he gave Evan."

"True." I was willing to believe that Big Bill could be generous if he directly benefitted.

"Anyway, Evan invested that money, and he was either smart or lucky, because it wasn't too long before he had enough money to start his own trucking business. He just had the one truck at first, but he put every dime he made back into the business until he had a whole fleet. Somewhere along the way, he started buying up land."

"He told me he got the flea market lot in payment for a debt."

"That's what I heard. It was the Rawson family's pig farm, but the pigs up and died one day. The Rawsons never did find out why, so even when they got new stock, people were afraid to buy from them. Evan was the one trucking the pigs to market, and when they went belly up, they gave him the land. I don't know how much the Rawsons owed him, but if they ever get the town line mess straightened out, I bet he'll get his money back and then some."

"Aunt Maggie says he's pretty fond of money." After hearing how he'd grown up, I didn't blame him.

"I think he's afraid of ending up poor again."

"Is he married?"

"No, but I hear he's been dating some woman out at the country club in Rocky Shoals. He wants to get himself established and then marry somebody fancy."

It sounded to me like he was well established already, but some people don't satisfy easily. "I know Bender lives out there at the flea market, so I assume he's not married. Does he have any friends?" Serious drinkers don't always pick their friends wisely, and before Aunt Nora could answer, I'd imagined Bender running with a group of thugs who had taken advantage of his knowledge to get into the flea market. I didn't think a random group of kids would have killed Carney, but I could picture an older gang doing the job. Unfortunately, it was a waste of imagination.

"Not really. He's got some drinking buddies, but the only one he spends a lot of time with is that dog of his."

So much for the Cawthornes. "Do you know Obed Hanford? He sells donuts."

"I've had some of his donuts, but that's all."

"Tattoo Bob Tyndall?"

She shook her head.

"Ronald Lane? He makes jewelry. And there's a Mr. and Mrs. Samples that sell furniture."

"Never heard of any of them."

"J.B. Doughty or Tammy Pruitt? Or Dulcy Lamar?" Okay, I didn't really consider the little girl a suspect, but I was getting desperate.

"Now that name rings a bell."

"Dulcy?"

"No, Lamar. Who do I know named Lamar?"

"Her grandmother is Annabelle Lamar." Had I imagined it, or had one of the women at the other table looked up when I said that? Just in case, I lowered my voice. "Tammy used to be married to Annabelle's son Roy."

"I met Annabelle over at Vasti's house. They're trying to put together a debutante ball."

"You're kidding." I couldn't imagine anything Byerly needed less. "I know Annabelle wants her granddaughter to make her debut, but isn't Vasti a little old for that kind of thing?"

"She's planning ahead. Vasti figures that if she has a girl, it'll be running good by the time she's ready to come out."

For a minute, I imagined Vasti's reaction if a child of hers ever decided to "come out" the way most people talked about it these days. Then I shook my head and took a big swallow of tea. I had to be tired—my mind was really wandering. "What do you know about Annabelle?"

"I know that she's mighty full of herself. She's not from Rocky Shoals originally. She and her boys moved there after her husband passed away. They'd been big shots in some town in Tennessee, but there were too many memories there, and she wanted to make a fresh start. The minute she got to Rocky Shoals, she started running things because she's got enough money to get away with it. She's needed that money, too—her boys have been in trouble more times than I can count. Junior could tell you more about that. I know she's arrested a couple of them."

Actually, I wasn't going to be able to ask Junior, but I could ask Trey if I found enough of a connection with Carney to make it worth the trouble. "Thanks, Aunt Nora. You've been a big help." Not as big as I'd hoped she'd be, but that wasn't her fault.

"You're welcome, Laurie Anne. I want to tell you again how much I appreciate your staying in town long enough for Augustus's party. It means a lot to him, and it means a lot to me, too." Needless to say, her eyes teared up. "Come over here and let me hug your neck."

I was happy to do so, and I don't want to make it sound like I wasn't, but as I hugged her, I saw the two women who'd been talking get up. One went toward the barn, and I recognized Mrs. Samples. The other had her back to me and was wearing a hat, but as she picked her way across the field that served as a parking lot, she lost her footing and the hat slipped just enough for me to see her face, and I recognized her, too. No wonder she'd looked up when I said, "Annabelle Lamar." It *was* Annabelle Lamar.

Chapter 23

Aunt Nora said she was going to claim some of her pots and pans from the kitchen, and I went looking for Aunt Maggie. The auctioneer announced that he was taking a five-minute break right then, so I thought I could get away with talking to her. Luckily, she was sitting by herself, rummaging through a box.

"Where is everybody?"

"Daphine is in the little girl's room, Richard is carrying a box of books out to the car, and Vasti came and dragged Arthur away."

"Did you get anything good?"

"I'm not sure. I thought I saw a piece of Autumn Leaf in here, but now I can't find it. Oh, well. I usually get something worthwhile."

"Aunt Maggie, have you ever seen Annabelle Lamar at any of the auctions?"

"After the way she acted out at the flea market today, I can't see her wanting to spend any time with us lowlifes. Why?"

"I thought I saw her outside just now."

"Really? You think this has anything to do with what I've asked you and Richard to look into?"

Suddenly Vasti was right there next to us. "Laurie Anne, what are you up to now?" she asked loudly. "I swear, I don't know how you and Richard can stand sticking your noses into other people's business."

That was the pot calling the kettle black, especially under the circumstances.

Aunt Maggie said, "Why don't you say it a little louder, Vasti. Some of the people in Boston might not have heard you."

"Goodness, Aunt Maggie, everybody knows about Laurie Anne and Richard's investigations. They might as well hire themselves out as private investigators."

"How on earth could we keep any investigation private with you around, Vasti?" I asked. It seemed to me that an awful lot of heads were turned in our direction. "Would you please keep your voice down?"

"What are y'all investigating this time?" she asked at a slightly lower volume. "It's something at the flea market, isn't it? Somebody told me that you said that you and Richard were going to start working at a flea market, but I told them that there was no way you'd do anything like that."

"Vasti, did it ever occur to you that we might have told people that for a reason?"

"Oh."

"Who were you talking to?" Maybe I could undo some of the damage.

"I don't know his name. One of the dealers. He's got a ball cap on."

I counted at least seven men with ball caps on. "Wonderful. Vasti, please don't discuss Richard's and my business with people. It could really cause problems for us."

"I certainly didn't mean to cause problems," she said

indignantly. "It's just that my mind is on this auction. You have no idea how hard it is to make things run smoothly."

"I realize that it's a lot of work," I said.

"It would help if you'd bothered to tell me what it is I'm not supposed to tell people."

"You're right.'" Of course, we hadn't had a chance to tell her, and even if we had, I don't know that we would have, but I could see her point.

"If you two will excuse me, I have business to take care of, if doing that won't cause you any *problems*."

"Vasti," Aunt Maggie said with a tone of warning, " that was uncalled for."

Vasti backed down. "I'm sorry, but I am in a delicate condition right now."

"Really?" I said. "Then you're—"

"I'm not one hundred percent positive, but I feel like *something* happened this afternoon."

"I sure hope so," Aunt Maggie said with a chuckle.

Vasti ignored her with as much dignity as she could muster. "I'm sorry if I messed things up for you, Laurie Anne."

"Don't worry about it, Vasti. Enough people know about Richard and me that it would have come out sooner or later." I remembered something Aunt Nora had said. "There might be something you can do to help, if you've got a minute."

"What's that?" she said, torn between wanting to get involved and wanting to claim terminal lack of time.

"I need some information about Annabelle Lamar. You know her, don't you?"

"Of course I know Annabelle. She and I are chairing a committee together. You don't think she's involved in—" She stopped herself, bless her heart. Of course, Aunt Maggie clearing her throat just then might have helped. "I can't imagine that she's involved in anything wrong."

"Has she ever mentioned Carney Alexander to you?"

"Never. In fact, I was there when she read the article about him in the paper. At first she thought he was one of the Alexanders from Raleigh, so she read the rest of the article, but when she found out he wasn't related to anybody, she didn't care anymore. Except she said she wondered what kind of people would spend their time at a flea market. No offense, Aunt Maggie."

Aunt Maggie looked like she did take offense, but she controlled herself admirably.

"Anyway, I'm sure she'd never heard of him before that," Vasti said.

Annabelle could have been lying, but Vasti is usually pretty good at spotting lies. "Thanks, Vasti."

"You're welcome." She looked at her watch. "Red said he was going to take a ten-minute break, not an eleven-minute break." She walked purposefully toward the back room.

"Do you think Annabelle is involved?" Aunt Maggie said.

"Probably not," I said. "I'm just doing like you do."

"How's that?"

"I thought I saw something interesting, so I bid for the box to find out for sure. Even if I don't get what I want, I usually get something worthwhile."

A few minutes later, Red Clark stepped back up to the podium, and the scattered Burnettes sat down again. Keeping my voice down so as not to distract Aunt Maggie, I told Richard what I'd found out from Aunt Nora, how I'd seen Annabelle sneaking around, and that Vasti had been talking again. Then he told me about the box of books he'd bought, which included some classic science fiction novels I'd wanted to read for years and a couple of books about the playwright he wasn't quoting.

There didn't seem to be anything else we could do right then, so I was content to relax and enjoy the auction.

Aunt Maggie bought several more boxes of assorted stuff, each time producing nice pieces from what looked like junk. Aunt Daphine and Aunt Nora went in together for a box of China Upton's sachets, saying that they'd be perfect Christmas gifts. Richard and I bid on a couple of boxes of books, and got one. And later on, we somehow found ourselves in a bidding war for an oil lamp that had been converted to electric. We didn't even have a place to put it, but we still bid like our lives depended on it. If Aunt Daphine hadn't taken our number away from me, we'd probably still be bidding.

Afterward, I thanked her. "I've heard about people losing control at auctions, but I never thought it would happen to me."

"It happens to all of us. You know that ugly chair I've got in my front hall?"

"It's not ugly," I protested, then tried to think of something nice to say about it. "It has character." It was upholstered in a sickly yellow fabric, and its stuffing poked through the fabric and the clothes of anyone sitting in it. Even if she had it re-covered, there was nothing she could do about the slant of the back that made it impossible to sit back.

"It's plug ugly," she said, "and I'd be embarrassed to tell you how much I paid for it. I was at a charity auction, and I got carried away. I keep it around to remind me."

"You should have let them buy the lamp so they could learn their lesson," Aunt Maggie said.

"Oh, we've learned our lesson. Haven't we, Richard?"

He didn't answer. He was starting to lift his hand, and when I saw what was up for sale, I grabbed that hand and held on for dear life. "Richard, we don't have room for a church pew!"

After that, I decided that Richard and I needed to get out of there. Aunt Maggie didn't want to leave yet, but Aunt Daphine was ready to go and offered to drop us off. After taking one last load out to Aunt Maggie's car, we gratefully allowed Aunt Daphine to take us to the house, and just barely got ourselves into bed before falling asleep.

Chapter 24

Sunday morning came earlier than it should have, but Aunt Maggie was bright-eyed and bushy-tailed, even though she'd been out later than we had. She rushed us even worse than she had the day before.

"How does she do this week in and week out?" I grumbled to Richard. "I think there's two of her: one to rest while the other one herds us around."

"Surely not," he said. "There couldn't be two Aunt Maggies."

Once again, stopping for sausage biscuits and coffee along the way provided some consolation, so I was nearly awake by the time we got to the flea market.

"No police cars," Aunt Maggie said cheerfully, parking in Carney's old spot again. Obviously she doesn't believe in ghosts.

Everything inside looked all right. Either Bender and Rusty had been more attentive, or the killer hadn't come back. Did that mean that he'd found what he was looking for, or did it mean he was looking elsewhere? Or did it mean that I was crazy to think that he was looking for anything in the first place? I was working from an awful lot of assumptions.

Aunt Maggie put Richard and me to work getting the booth ready for business while she went outside to cherry-pick. She came back with a bunch of odds and ends that she promptly priced and put out on the table.

"Don't people ever come inside and see their stuff on sale?" I asked her.

"Not usually, but even if they do, what are they going to do? The only ones who have ever made a fuss were Mary Maude and Mavis."

Her saying that must have started Mary Maude and Mavis's ears burning, because they showed up a few minutes later, looking even less friendly than usual.

Mary Maude planted herself in front of Aunt Maggie. "I hear there was an auction at Red Clark's barn last night."

"I believe you're right," Aunt Maggie said, and picked up a figurine to dust it.

"You were there, weren't you?"

"Right again."

Mary Maude waved her finger at Aunt Maggie. "You listen to me—"

"Sister," Mavis said, putting a placating hand on Mary Maude's arm. "Miz Burnette, why is it that when Mary Maude asked you about an auction yesterday, you said you were going to be visiting family?"

"First off, it's no business of yours how I spend my evenings." She gave them the look. "But it just so happens my great-niece Vasti arranged a charity auction last night, and asked me to come. My niece Nora was in charge of refreshments, and my niece Daphine was there, too. So we were visiting family. But like I said, it's none of your business." Aunt Maggie looked Mavis straight in the eye until she looked away, then did the same to Mary Maude. "Is there anything else I can help you with?"

Mary Maude muttered something under her breath, but didn't quite dare to say it out loud. Mavis said, "You could tell us if there are any sales this week."

Aunt Maggie pulled her date book out of her pocketbook and made a big show of looking through the pages. Then she pulled out a piece of blue paper. "There's a mini warehouse auction scheduled for tomorrow morning."

Mavis snatched at the paper and read it.

"You can keep that flier if you want," Aunt Maggie said. "Of course, if the renters pay up before tomorrow, they'll cancel the sale. You better call tonight and make sure it's still on."

"Maybe we'll go anyway," Mavis said sweetly. "Somebody might tell us that it's been cancelled when it hasn't been."

"Suit yourself," Aunt Maggie said with a shrug.

They left without even thanking her.

"That was ruder than usual," I said. "If it were me, I wouldn't have told them about that auction."

"No skin off my nose if they go," Aunt Maggie said. "Red told me last night that the renters have paid up, so there's not going to be any auction."

Richard and I laughed.

"I warned them to check first."

That made us laugh even harder, and while Aunt Maggie didn't join in, she did grin.

People must have been waiting outside, because they poured in as soon as Bender opened the main door. Most of the early birds were regular customers, so Aunt Maggie waited on them and put Richard and me to work making change and wrapping purchases. That gave us a little time to talk in between customers.

"I never had a chance to tell you what Aunt Daphine said last night," Richard said.

"I thought she didn't know anything about the people out here."

"She didn't, but she did have something to say about Augustus."

I wasn't sure if I wanted to hear it or not, but I said, "So what's the story?"

"A lot of it we'd heard before. He's been acting distant ever since he got back from Germany, spending a lot of time alone. He doesn't help around the house, he hasn't tried to get a job, and he hasn't tried to get together with his old friends. According to Aunt Daphine, a steady stream of former girlfriends called him his first week home, but he didn't even call them back. She says that Aunt Nora is upset, Uncle Buddy is angry, and Thaddeous is confused."

"What about Willis?"

"Willis hasn't had much to say."

Aunt Nora's youngest son never had much to say, but it stood to reason that he was as worried about his brother as the rest of the family. "Augustus must be smoking a lot to have affected his behavior this way," I said sadly.

"Maybe."

"Maybe?"

"His smoking could be a symptom of some other problem."

"Like what?" I had a horrible thought. "Augustus didn't know Carney, did he?"

"What? No, not that. I was thinking more along the lines

of something that happened in Germany. Maybe he left a lovely fraulein behind."

"He would have said so if he had, unless she were somebody he didn't dare bring home to Byerly." I thought about it, then shook my head. "No, the old Augustus wouldn't have let what anybody else thought stop him."

"Could he have discovered an organization of latter-day Nazis ready to form a Fourth Reich, but been unable to convince his superiors of the coming danger?"

"Richard, have you been reading Aunt Maggie's thrillers?"

"Just the back covers."

I sighed. "Well, whatever his problem is, we've got Carney to worry about right now. Besides, I'm not sure we should be sticking our noses into Augustus's business anyway."

Richard looked like he didn't quite believe me, and I wasn't sure I believed myself. After all, if Augustus was in trouble, was it prying to try to help him, or was I just being a good cousin? We Burnettes tend to err on the side of prying.

Business slowed down around mid-morning, and Aunt Maggie, in her own subtle way, said, "Are you two going to do any detective work today or not?"

Richard suggested that he go talk to people this time, and I was more than willing to give him a shot. I'd had my chance, and I didn't have much to show for it.

"How should I play it?" he asked us. "The nosy Yankee who doesn't know any better or the polite good ole boy?"

Aunt Maggie snickered. "You better stick with the nosy Yankee, because with that accent, you're not going to fool anybody into thinking you're a good ole boy."

He assumed an air of injury. "I can say *y'all* with the best of them."

"Is that right? Do you say 'grits is' or 'grits are'?"

"Grits are?"

Aunt Maggie and I looked at each other, and in unison said, "Yankee."

Richard bowed his head in surrender, and headed on his way.

Chapter 25

Not long after Richard went sleuthing, Thatcher Broods wheeled a padded dolly over to Carney's booth and started loading boxes.

"You moving your stuff outside, Thatcher?" Aunt Maggie asked.

"No, ma'am, I'm taking it home. I wanted to sell today, but I got a late start because I had to go over the inventory with Miz Alexander before I did anything else. I was here late last night getting it done."

"Is that Carney's sister you're talking about?"

"Yes, ma'am, Sadie Alexander. Carney didn't have any records, so she didn't have any idea of what it was she was selling to me. I didn't want her to think that I'd gypped her, so I took her the inventory in case she wanted to check it against the stock, but she said she trusts me. The way she figures it, if I make a little on the deal, it would only be fair. From the way Carney talked, she was pretty sure he'd been cheating me ever since I started working as a point man."

Aunt Maggie said, "Being a man's sister doesn't make her blind to his faults. Sometimes it makes you see them that much more clearly."

"I don't think those two liked each other much, anyway.

He complained about her a lot, said she wouldn't leave him alone and went through his things when he wasn't home. She said he was a lazy slob. She even complained about him when I was over there this morning. I guess when she took the police over to his place, it was a real pigsty, even though she cleaned it before she went out of town Friday. It's like she was mad at him for getting killed and leaving her with the mess."

"I've known a lot of people to lose husbands and wives, and parents, and brothers and sisters, but I've never seen two people show their feelings the same way. Maybe fussing is her way of grieving."

Thatcher said, "Maybe you're right," but I could tell he just couldn't imagine why a grieving sister would complain about her late brother. Aunt Maggie looked at me and shook her head ruefully, and I could tell she was thinking that Thatcher was awfully young, and that someday he'd know better.

As for me, I was wondering how Carney had made such a big mess so quickly. If his sister cleaned Friday and he died Sunday morning, when had he had the time? Even assuming that he'd gone straight home Saturday night, there wouldn't have been but a few hours to make a mess.

Of course, the killer had Carney's keys, including his house key. Since Carney's body had stayed hidden most of the day, that meant that the killer would have had plenty of time to search the apartment, and he wouldn't have cared how much of a mess he made. Presumably he hadn't found what he was looking for, because if he had, he wouldn't have had to break into the flea market later in the week.

I sighed. I was still working on assumptions. Reasonable assumptions, maybe, but still assumptions. My problem was that I'd only talked to Carney's enemies, and I really needed to talk to one of his friends.

"Aunt Maggie," I said, "did Thatcher know Carney well?"

"I couldn't say, but he'd been a point man for a good while."

That was something, anyway. "If you don't need me, I think I'll go see if I can give him a hand."

"Laurie Anne—"

"I know, you've been running this booth by yourself for umpteen years. Why on earth would you need me now?"

"I'm sorry," she said, which was rare for her. "I don't mean to sound like I haven't appreciated you and Richard helping out."

"That's all right. I know you prefer working alone."

"Usually, but there's times when it'd be nice to have somebody else around. Your granddaddy used to come out once in a while, and he went to some of the auctions with me. Since he's been gone, I've been on my own."

I'm an only child, so I can't really understand what it means to lose a brother or sister, but I could tell that Aunt Maggie missed Paw as much as I did. I was thinking about giving her a hug when she stepped away, like she'd known what I was going to do.

She said, "But you aren't here to mess with the flea market—you're here to find out what happened to Carney. So you go ahead and talk to Thatcher."

I walked to where Thatcher was working and said, "Can I give you a hand with those boxes?"

He smiled, and I could tell that he was going to be nice-looking if he ever filled out. "That would be a big help. Mr. Cawthorne said he was going to have to charge me for today if I don't get cleared out of here by noon."

Thatcher was taking the boxes home so he could spend the week sorting and pricing, and he was so excited about it that I couldn't get a word in edgewise until we'd carted a couple of loads out to his mother's station wagon.

Finally, as I held the dolly for him to load boxes, I said, "It sure is terrible, what happened to Carney. Had you known him long?"

"A couple, three years. I bought my first knives from Carney."

"Is that right?"

"Do you know much about knives?"

"No, but my husband does have a sword."

"Is it a real one, or just for show?"

"I'm not sure." Richard had used it in a production of *Hamlet*, so I'd always assumed it was just a prop, but I didn't want to tell him that. "I know it's seen at least one battle." Okay, I was the one who'd taken it into battle, but I had swung at somebody with it and I'd even connected.

"I'd like to get into swords someday, but the good ones are expensive. If you send me a picture of it, I'll try to track down how much it's worth."

"Thanks, that would be nice to know." To edge us back on subject, I said, "I take it Carney didn't deal in swords."

"No, he preferred knives. Knew a lot about them, too. Of course, he had to, or he wouldn't have been able to—" He stopped short.

"To do what?" I prompted.

"To sell them," he finished, but it wasn't very convincing.

I thought I knew what he'd been about to say, and why he hadn't. Paw taught me it wasn't nice to speak ill of the dead, but I thought he'd understand, given the circumstances. "I'd heard something about Carney restoring a lot of his knives."

"I guess that's what you'd call it. I knew he did some of that, but it wasn't until I was doing the inventory that I realized how many of his knives are restored."

To give him a chance to get over his embarrassment, I waited until we'd taken another load out before asking the next question. "You're not nervous about taking over his business, are you? I mean, considering what happened to him."

"I never thought about it," he said. "Deputy Tucker said it was just a coincidence that Carney was here when the place was broke into, that it didn't have anything to do with him."

"Do you believe her?"

"I guess," he said. "I've been so busy getting the money together to buy the business and then doing the inventory that I haven't thought much about what happened to Carney. Makes me sound kind of cold, doesn't it? But I really didn't know him that well, just enough to talk about knives."

"Y'all never went out together or anything like that? Not even to a knife show?"

"Nope. Carney never went to the shows. Sometimes he'd pay my way to get things for him, but he never came along."

"Really? It seems like he'd have enjoyed it." Aunt Maggie was always talking to other dealers, comparing notes. Richard liked talking Shakespeare and departmental politics just like I liked talking computers. What better time could a knife aficionado have than to mingle with others?

"He wasn't one to make friends easily."

"So I've heard." I waited a minute to see if he'd say

anything else, then added, "In fact, I hear he went out of his way to make enemies."

"You might say that," Thatcher said, clearly uncomfortable again. "I never had any problems with him."

Obviously he knew somebody who had. "What about the other point men? That's what he called you guys, isn't it?"

"I thought that was right smart—Carney was good with puns."

I think Thatcher was glad for an opportunity to say something nice about Carney. "Did Carney not get along with the other point men?" I persisted.

"Some of them said he didn't pay them what he ought to, and they might have had a point." He stopped and grinned. "Hey, I just made a pun."

"So you did. Seems like working with knives would be a natural for jokes. Cut to the chase, cutting edge, pointed remarks."

"I'll have to remember those," Thatcher said admiringly. "You're fast with words, just like Carney was. He could make a play off somebody's name as soon as he heard it, or out of what they did, or anything. Some of them were funny, too. Like calling Bender Cawthorne a border guard, because he was a boarder and a guard. And there's what he called your aunt."

"I didn't know he had a nickname for Aunt Maggie."

"He never said it to her face," he said, looking nervously in her direction.

I probably shouldn't have asked, but I couldn't resist. "What did he call her?"

"Old Maid-in-Japan, because of what she sells and because of her not being married."

It's a good thing he hadn't used it to her face, or he might have died sooner. "I'd heard some of his puns were nasty."

"Some of them were," Thatcher admitted. "You know how Evan Cawthorne was poor when he was growing up? Every time Carney saw him, he'd ask him if he knew a good place to get a poor boy sandwich. Just last week, he asked Evan if he was feeling poorly, because he'd heard his business was taxing."

"Making fun of Evan having been poor and that tax audit at the same time."

"I guess. Now, Evan Cawthorne can take care of himself, but Carney shouldn't have picked on Wyatt," Thatcher said. "Wyatt's a point man, too. He's my age, but he started losing his hair early. Carney started making jokes about Wyatt having his receipts all balled up. All *bald* up. And he'd ask if Wyatt knew a good place to get a haircut, or if he had a comb Carney could borrow. One day Wyatt showed up in a toupee, and we all waited for Carney to say something, but he didn't say a word until Wyatt was about to leave. Wyatt said he was going out dancing, and Carney told him to have a good time cutting a rug. Then he looked right at the top of Wyatt's head."

"Ouch! I can understand why nobody's sorry that Carney's gone."

"I wouldn't go that far," Thatcher objected. "Some of us point men were sorry. We went in together to get flowers for his funeral."

"Even Wyatt?"

"He didn't put in much, but he was short on cash. Wyatt and the other point men spent last weekend at a knife and gun show in Raleigh, and he spent purt near everything he had. They said it was a heck of a show. I wanted to go, but Saturday was my mother's birthday."

Great! All of the other point men had just been eliminated from the running in one fell swoop. For a second I thought about a bunch of them working together, saying that they'd gone to Raleigh while staying in town to kill Carney, but that didn't seem likely. I consoled myself with the thought that at least I hadn't wasted any time tracking them down.

There was still Thatcher, of course, but darn it, he seemed too nice. Of course, his fascination with knives probably said something Freudian about his personality, but it sure didn't show. So I gave up on questions while we finished taking boxes out to his car. To thank me for my help, he gave me a nifty Swiss Army knife with two blades, a nail file, a bottle opener, a screwdriver, a toothpick, and a pair of tweezers. I was sure Freud would have something to say about Thatcher giving a woman a knife, but all I said was, "Thank you."

Chapter 26

Thatcher said he was going to tell Bender that Carney's space was ready, and a little while after he left, Bender and Rusty showed up. Bender was carrying a broom and a plastic milk crate filled with cleaning supplies.

Rusty wagged his tail, and Bender said, "Howdy, Miz Burnette, Miz Fleming. How are y'all doing?"

"Pretty good, Bender," Aunt Maggie said. "How about yourself?"

"I woke up with a little headache this morning, but I'm feeling better."

Aunt Maggie looked at me and shook her head, and I knew she was thinking that Bender's headache had been nothing more than a hangover. "What's Evan got you doing now?"

"I'm just making sure that Carney's booth is ready for J.B. and Tammy to move in."

"Need any help?" I asked, thinking I might talk to him like I had Thatcher.

Bender shook his head. "It won't take me but a few minutes to clean up." I was surprised to see that once he got moving, he was an efficient worker. I had to wonder what he could do if he stayed sober.

"That's that," he said when he'd finished sweeping and wiping the tables down. "I just have to throw these boxes away. I don't guess Thatcher needed any more wrapping paper."

"Did you say those boxes have paper in them?" Aunt Maggie asked.

"Yes, ma'am."

"Then let me have them. I'm running short on newspaper."

Just then Evan came in the back door. "Is the booth cleared out yet?" he asked.

"Just finishing up," Bender said, handing the boxes to Aunt Maggie.

"What's that? Did Thatcher leave something behind?"

"Just scrap paper," Aunt Maggie said.

Evan nodded, and then inspected the empty booth as Bender watched him anxiously. I wouldn't have thought it warranted such a thorough inspection. Evan checked for dust, rubbed the tops of the tables to make sure the laminate was secure, even bent down to look under the tables.

"Gum chewers," he explained when he saw me and Aunt Maggie watching him.

Aunt Maggie snorted and went back to what she'd been doing.

"It looks fine, Bender," he said. Rusty wagged his tail, and I think Bender would have, too, if he'd had one. "Go tell J.B. and Tammy they can move in any time."

"All right, Evan," Bender said, and he and Rusty left.

I said, "Mr. Cawthorne, have the police come up with any leads about the murder or the break-in?"

"Not that I've heard. I was hoping that they'd solve the

case quickly to avoid negative publicity, but I guess there's no chance of that now."

I didn't say anything, but as usual, my face gave my feelings away.

"I don't mean to be uncaring," Evan said, "but this is a difficult time for me. I've just bought into a very big project. A group of businessmen is putting together a package for building luxury vacation condominiums."

"In Byerly?" I said.

"No, in Boone. We're hoping to cater to successful professionals from Charlotte and the Research Triangle who want to enjoy the natural beauty of the mountains without leaving modern convenience behind."

He sounded like he was quoting from a brochure. I said, "That could be a winner."

"Oh, it will be. The market research has been incredibly encouraging, and I was lucky to be asked to join in. If Carney's death were to be linked with the project, I could be pushed out."

"You should be safe," I told him. "Boone is far enough from Byerly that I bet nobody there even knows about it."

"So far, you're right, but I am concerned. This project is very important to me." He looked around the booth one more time, then said, "I hope you two ladies have a profitable day," and went out the door he'd come in.

"What do you think, Aunt Maggie?" I said. "Are you going to buy yourself a luxury condo in Boone?"

"Why on earth would I want to go to Boone?" she asked.

I knew it wasn't because there was anything wrong with Boone. Aunt Maggie just isn't much of a traveler.

She said, "I heard Evan was in hock up to his eyeballs

because of some deal, but I didn't know it was condos. He better be careful—he could lose his shirt."

"Really? Aunt Nora said he was well off."

"He does all right, especially compared to me, but a lot of his money is tied up in his business and in property like this place. Evan being Evan, he doesn't want to let any of it go. So he got mortgages and loans to raise the money."

"Did he tell you that?" Businessmen aren't usually forthcoming when it comes to their finances.

"No, but he talked to Arthur, and Arthur told Vasti. Which means that the whole county knows by now."

Vasti is a darned effective means of communication. She has more information than most web sites, and is a lot easier to log onto than the Internet.

"The only piece of property he was wiling to sell was this lot out here," Aunt Maggie said, "and he was fit to be tied when he found out he couldn't."

"He said it was something about zoning," I said, remembering yesterday's conversation.

"The Byerly part is zoned residential and the Rocky Shoals part is zoned business. Then there's property taxes to deal with. Both Byerly and Rocky Shoals want their cut, and want to make sure they get the right amount. Evan can keep this place running forever, because it predates the zoning regulations, but since nobody can do anything else with the land, nobody will buy it until they get the town line settled."

"That must be frustrating," I said. Evan Cawthorne was clearly a man with plans.

"You know why he wants to do that deal in Boone, don't you? It's because nobody up there knows how poor his family was."

I remembered what Aunt Nora had said about the other kids teasing Evan. He probably saw those kids every day, all grown up now, but still knowing what he used to be. No wonder he wanted to get away. Hadn't I wanted to move up North to make a fresh start?

If Carney had been standing in the way of that fresh start, I could see where Evan might have wanted him dead, but it sounded like Carney's death was a hinderance, not a help.

I sighed. I was learning an awful lot about these people, especially Carney, but none of it explained why he'd been killed. I looked over at his booth, now swept clean. As nasty as Carney had been, it seemed odd that he'd left no more mark than he had.

Chapter 27

Richard came back a few minutes later, but we had customers milling around, so it was a while before I had a chance to ask him what he'd found out.

"You were right not to let me investigate on my own," Richard said. "I didn't get a thing out of those people."

"We always end up with a lot of useless information," I said consolingly.

"You don't understand. I didn't get any information, useless or otherwise. Nobody would talk to me."

"Didn't you introduce yourself as Aunt Maggie's nephew?"

"Of course. And I told them how interested I was in learning about their businesses. Maybe I'm no Kenneth Branagh, but after all my years in academia, I can convincingly pretend to be interested in almost anything. These people weren't convinced. Tattoo Bob said he was too busy to talk, even though there was nobody around him, and Obed was short with me." He winced. "Sorry. Obed told me he didn't think I was cut out for his kind of work. China wasn't exactly rude, but she was definitely nervous, and I couldn't even catch Ronald's eye. Admittedly he was making a ring, but he had time to talk to everybody else who came by.

The furniture people said they don't have time to give free advice."

"What in the world?" I wondered. "Everybody was perfectly friendly to me."

"I thought I'd have better luck outside, but J.B. glared at me and Tammy looked hurt. Even the little girl acted like she was mad. I was so desperate that I went over to Mavis and Mary Maude's booth and gave them any number of openings to complain, but they wouldn't say a word." He shook his head. "I know Yankees aren't the most popular people in Byerly, but I've never had a reception like that."

"I can't imagine it has anything to do with your being from Massachusetts," I said. "Heck, Obed traveled all over the country. He couldn't have done that if he was rude to Northerners."

"Then what? I didn't flash my Harvard ring or quote Shakespeare. I didn't make rude comments about their merchandise. I know I brushed my teeth and used deodorant this morning."

"Maybe it wasn't you at all," I said. "Maybe it's me. I talked to them all yesterday—maybe they figured out what we're doing. I tried to be careful, but I'm not used to being undercover. Or maybe somebody heard Vasti talking last night. She was pretty loud."

"I can understand the murderer not wanting to talk to me, but why would everybody else avoid me unless they're involved, too?"

"Like in *Murder on the Orient Express*? I don't think so. Besides which, wouldn't a smart murderer try to be extra friendly to throw us off the track?"

"The murderer may not be all that smart."

"He must have been pretty smart to plan the murder,

not to mention the break-in and getting into Carney's apartment."

"What about Carney's apartment?"

I quickly caught him up on my conversations with Thatcher, Bender, and Evan.

"Great," he said. "I go off to find facts, and get nothing. You sit here and they come to you. Maybe I should let you do this alone—it might go faster."

"Not on your life!" I said, and gave him a big hug.

"I'm glad somebody still likes me," he said with a smile. "Which reminds me, when I was at China's booth, I ran into a friend of mine."

"In Byerly? Who?"

"Do you remember my mentioning Vivian?"

"That's not that redheaded freshman who had such a big crush on you last semester, is it?"

"Hardly," he said dryly. "Vivian is the army nurse I met at the V.F.W. post."

"That's right, the Jane Austen fan. How is she doing?"

"She looked as hale and hearty as ever, which is remarkably hale and hearty."

"You're forgetting that I never met her."

"Picture a woman six feet tall, solidly built, and dressed in fatigues."

"I can't imagine a woman like that being a fan of Jane Austen. Would she be comfortable in a silk dress with an empire waist and lace at the throat?"

"Maybe not, but there's definitely a side to Vivian I hadn't seen before. She bought an entire box of China's sachets."

"The ones with lace and ribbon, or the ones with hearts and silk flowers?"

"Neither, actually. The ones she picked out weren't that elaborate, just plain gingham and calico. Even so, she looked a little embarrassed by my catching her. I wanted to ask her opinion of some of the Austen movies and TV shows that have shown up recently, but she was in a hurry."

"It's a shame China doesn't have any sachets made of camouflage material," I said with a giggle.

"With army insignia sewn on," Richard added.

"What's so funny?" Aunt Maggie asked as she came up behind us.

"Just wondering if China would be interested in adding some new styles of sachets," I said.

"I swear, I wonder if I shouldn't make some of them things," she said. "They sell like hotcakes."

"Really?" I wouldn't have thought the average flea market shopper was interested in sweet-smelling lingerie. Customers at Victoria's Secret, yes, but not at Tight as a Tick.

Aunt Maggie said, "She sells them by the crate, and not just to women either."

"Men buying gifts, I guess. Unless you think they're—" I stopped, not sure how to put it politely.

"You mean do I think they've got lace on their underdrawers?" Aunt Maggie said, which was her euphemism for gay men. "Not hardly. I've seen big, strong men over there."

I could have pointed out that big, strong men are quite popular in Boston's gay community, but instead I said, "That's kind of odd. Sachets aren't what I'd consider a high traffic item. What are people doing? Putting one in every drawer in their house?"

"Do you think it means anything?" she asked.

"Problably not," I admitted.

It was getting past lunchtime, so Richard went to the

snack bar to pick up food for the three of us. I'd hoped that eating would increase blood flow to my brain so I'd come up with something else to look into, but instead I got sleepy. Richard and Aunt Maggie looked snoozy, too. It was considerably hotter than it had been the day before, and there wasn't much business.

Between the heat and business being slow, I guess I shouldn't have been surprised when Aunt Maggie got testy. It was about an hour and a half before closing time when I heard a woman say, "Would you take a dime for this?" She was holding a white bud vase with pink flowers along the edge.

Aunt Maggie took it from her and checked the price tag. "It's marked a dollar."

"Would you take a dime for it?" the woman asked again.

Aunt Maggie looked disgusted. "Lady," she said, "it's not worth anything if it's not worth more than that." She threw it into the metal trash barrel hard enough that we could hear it break.

The woman stared at her for a couple of minutes, then walked away without saying a word.

Once the woman had turned a corner, Aunt Maggie snickered and said, "I swear, it was worth a dollar just to see the look on her face."

Chapter 28

Right after Bender gave the fifteen-minute warning, a thin man with just enough hair to comb over his bald spot rushed up to the booth. "Miz Burnette, are you buying?"

"What have you got, Luther?"

"I moved two old ladies this week, and they sold me boxes and boxes of glassware. Are you interested?"

"I suppose it wouldn't hurt to look at it," Aunt Maggie said casually, but I saw a gleam in her eye. "Pull your truck around back, and I'll come out and see."

"Okay, but we've got to hurry. I'm due for Sunday dinner in less than an hour."

"I'll meet you out there," Aunt Maggie called after him as he nearly ran back the way he'd come.

"Do you think he's got anything good?" I asked.

"I never know with Luther. He and his wife run a moving company, and they've got a deal with the Byerly Nursing Home to help people clean out their houses before moving into the home. There's no way they can take all their stuff with them, so Luther buys anything they can't keep."

"Sounds kind of mercenary," I said.

"If Luther didn't buy it, they'd just throw it out. He only gets called in when there's no family willing to help. Luther may not pay them much, but it's more than they'd get without him. He turns around and sells it to me, which gives him a way to make a little money on the side without telling his wife."

Aunt Maggie pulled out her lock box to get a fistful of cash. "Richard, why don't you come with me? If he's got anything worth buying, we'll load it into the car and take it home so I can price it before next week."

After making sure I didn't mind, he said he would, and off they went. I was expecting them to be back shortly, but they were still gone when Bender locked the front door. I didn't think Aunt Maggie would want me to leave the cash box unattended, so I straightened up like I'd seen her doing the day before.

When Tammy, J.B., and Dulcy came by to stock their new booth, I thought I was going to have company, but I'd have been better off alone. J.B. looked mad, and Tammy looked like her feelings were hurt, just like Richard had said. They didn't say a word to me when I said, "Hey there."

When Aunt Maggie and Richard finally came back, I could tell from the look on Aunt Maggie's face and the tired way Richard was moving that Luther really had had something worth buying. "Well?"

"Laurie Anne, I can't remember the last time I got so much stuff. There's an ironstone pitcher and at least six Jubilee tumblers and Carnival glass and Occupied Japan figurines and . . . I don't know what all is in there. Do you have any idea of how much I can get for that stuff?"

I didn't, but it didn't matter, because she didn't give me a chance to answer.

"Just the pieces I recognize are worth more than I paid for the whole lot."

"That's great." I was getting excited, too. Richard was right—working at a flea market was like going on a treasure hunt.

"I'm going to have to carry some of my books home to look things up." She started filling an empty box with the books she needed. "By the way, Laurie Anne, we've got a problem. I bought so much that there's not enough room in the car for all of us. Somebody is going to have to wait here while the other two go to the house and unload."

Great. All I wanted was to get into an air-conditioned room and put my feet up. Not to mention the fact that I was hungry, and the snack bar was long since closed.

"I'll wait out here," Richard said. "You go on with Aunt Maggie."

I was going to turn him down anyway, but I didn't get a chance before Aunt Maggie said, "I'd rather have Richard to help unload the car." She looked over at Tammy and J.B. "Maybe they'd give you a ride."

"I doubt it," I said, and explained.

She was as mystified by the way they were acting as we were, but said, "We'll work it out later. Right now, I want to get at those boxes."

I could tell Richard was trying to decide if it would be more chivalrous to leave me alone or to have me unload boxes, so I said, "Why don't I ask Thaddeous to come get me? That way I won't have to wait so long, and we can all help unload."

"Good idea," Aunt Maggie said.

I used the pay phone at the snack bar to call Thaddeous, but ended up talking to Aunt Nora, who told me that he wasn't there and that Augustus had her car. Since Augustus was due home any minute, she said she'd send him after me as soon as he got back, and since she was Aunt Nora, she invited the three of us over for supper. I was tempted, but I was also tired. Besides, I knew Aunt Maggie would never be able to sit through supper with those boxes waiting. So I told her we'd come for supper Monday night instead. Maybe I'd be rested by then.

When I went back to the booth, I passed all of this on to Richard and Aunt Maggie. Richard gave me a quick kiss before they left, and I got one of Aunt Maggie's paperbacks to read while I waited for Augustus outside.

I could have waited inside, but I didn't want to hang around Tammy and J.B. Besides, they were getting ready to go just as Aunt Maggie and Richard were, and I think it would have been creepy even if Carney hadn't been killed there the week before.

It was creepy outside, too. The dealers were long gone, leaving nothing behind but filled trash barrels and odd scraps of paper and metal. Every footstep echoed, and with no trees, I couldn't blame the random noises I heard on squirrels or birds. At least it was still light, but that meant that there were long shadows everywhere, making it look like somebody was following me. I hoped Augustus was on his way.

I felt the rumbling before I heard it, and at first I thought it was thunder. Then I recognized it as a motorcycle revving. More than one, I corrected myself. In fact, it sounded like a dozen.

I walked on toward the road as I tried to forget every movie about motorcycle gangs I'd ever seen. Then a motorcycle came out of nowhere and crossed in front of me. The rider was wearing a helmet with the visor down.

I turned back the other way—Augustus would just have

to come find me—but I hadn't gone a dozen steps when a second motorcycle cut me off. Where was Bender? More importantly, where was Rusty?

I turned around again, but didn't have a chance to move before yet another motorcycle appeared. I started walking in that direction anyway. If I didn't move, those motorcycle riders were going to be able to see my legs shaking.

Two more cycles zoomed past me, but I walked on, hoping that they weren't going to run me down. I'd seen movies where a man on foot tripped up a motorcycle by sticking a rod in the spokes, but even if I'd had a rod handy, it didn't look possible from where I stood. I could have tried to knock one of the riders off with my pocketbook, but what would I do about the other four?

Now they were circling me, coming closer and closer until I had to stop. Five motorcycles don't sound like a lot until you're surrounded by them, and I'd never realized how much noise five motors could make.

They circled for what seemed like forever, but was probably no more than a couple of minutes. Then one of them raised his hand, and they all slowed to a stop. The one who'd signaled climbed off of his motorcycle, and came over to look down at me. He wasn't that tall, but he was right much taller than I am. His visor was mirrored, so instead of his face, all I could see was my own pale reflection.

I was so scared I could hardly breathe, but I wouldn't let myself look away from him. Didn't people like this respect strength, or was that another myth from the movies? I didn't care—I wouldn't be able to face myself the next day if I didn't hold my ground. Assuming that I saw another day.

Finally he reached up and pulled off his helmet. It was J.B. Doughty.

I'd thought that seeing a face would make me feel less threatened, but the fierce look he was giving me was worse than the visor. Was he Carney's killer? Why else would he be so angry? Had Belva been right about Carney having been killed by a gang? She'd thought it was kids, but couldn't it have been bikers? I couldn't very well ask J.B., so I just waited him out.

I think he was trying to wait me out, too, but finally he said, "I want to talk to you."

"Go ahead," I said as calmly as if I spent every other day surrounded by biker gangs.

"You've been asking questions about things that are none of your concern. I want you to stop."

I've been accused of sticking my nose into other people's business more times than I can count, and even if it's true, it still makes me mad. "J.B., if you knew me, you'd know better than to try to tell me what to do. I'm going to keep on asking questions until I find out what I need to know."

His eyes shifted to the other bikers. I don't think that was the way he'd scripted this encounter. "I don't want to hurt you, but if you do anything to Tammy, I'll . . . You don't want to know what I'll do."

I hadn't considered Tammy that strong a suspect, but maybe we'd missed something. "Are you saying that Tammy—"

"Tammy is a good mother, and Dulcy belongs with her."

Finally I realized what he was worried about. "You think I'm trying to take Dulcy away from Tammy?"

"I'm not stupid!" he snapped. "Maybe we didn't go to college like you and that husband of yours, and maybe we don't have the money Annabelle Lamar has, but we can take care of Dulcy just fine. I'm not about to let you take her away from us."

"Nobody is trying to take Dulcy away from you and Tammy."

"The hell you say!"

I amended that to, "I mean, Richard and I don't have anything to do with Mrs. Lamar trying to get custody of Dulcy."

He didn't look convinced.

"J.B., would Aunt Maggie let me do something like that?"

He looked like he was thinking about it, and I could tell he wanted to believe me, but he said, "Then why have y'all been asking so many questions? Nobody believes that y'all want to become dealers. And why were you with Annabelle Lamar at the auction last night? I saw her leave right after you came inside, and then I heard that other woman talking about you and your husband investigating something. It doesn't take a genius to figure out that you're trying to dig up something on Tammy and me so Annabelle can take Dulcy away, but there's nothing to dig up."

No wonder he was mad. "J.B., I was not with Mrs. Lamar." He started to speak, but I talked right over him. "I saw her, but it was Mrs. Samples she was talking to, not me. Ask Mrs. Samples if you want to."

"Yeah, right," he said, sounding skeptical. I didn't blame him. My being outside at the same time as Annabelle was just a coincidence, but coincidences look bad sometimes. "Then why have you been asking questions?"

I knew that if J.B. had killed Carney, I might be getting myself into worse trouble, but I didn't think I could avoid telling him the truth. "We're trying to find out who killed

Carney Alexander. Aunt Maggie asked us to because she doesn't think the police are doing a good job."

"She's right about that. They're more worried about one-upping each other than they are about catching a killer. But why bring you two into it?"

"Because we've done this kind of thing before." He looked skeptical again, so I added, "I've worked with Junior Norton on several cases."

He nodded, so I guess that was official enough for him.

I said, "You don't have to worry about me unless you killed Carney."

"Of course I didn't kill Carney. What kind of man do you think I am?"

I just looked at him.

"I'm not like this, usually. Yeah, I got into trouble with the law a long time ago, but it ain't ever going to happen again. Me and Tammy, we've got plans. Besides, I had no reason to go after Carney. He was a low-down snake, but if I killed every low-down snake in the world, there'd be a lot fewer people walking around."

He had a point, but he also had a reason to want that particular snake gone. "I heard Carney was the one who told Mrs. Lamar about your police record."

"I don't know that for sure, but I think you're right. I wanted to have a talk with him, but the cat was already out of the bag, and it wouldn't do us any good to have me in jail for beating up Carney. There's no way I'd have risked killing him, not when I knew that we'd lose Dulcy forever if I got caught."

That explained everything but the possibility of his killing Carney in the heat of anger, and what he said next put the kibosh on that idea.

"Besides, if I'd killed Carney, I wouldn't have settled for trying to scare you."

That was logical, if not comforting. Maybe it wasn't evidence, but I was willing to take J.B. off our list of suspects. "Then like I said, you don't have to worry about me."

"I'm glad to hear that," he said, sounding relieved that I believed him. I wondered if he'd been as scared of what I could do to him as I'd been of what he could do to me.

J.B. remembered that we were still surrounded by bikers, and told them, "Y'all can go on home. I made a mistake—this lady isn't trying to make any trouble."

The riders lifted their visors, and I felt right foolish. They weren't exactly Hell's Angels material. In fact, I recognized two of them from the church in Byerly. They looked like they felt foolish, too, and before they rode off, one of them muttered, "Sorry to alarm you, ma'am. We didn't mean no harm."

Once the sound of their engines faded, I said, "No offense, but motorcycles sure are noisy. I'm surprised Bender and Rusty didn't come running to see what all the commotion was about."

"I told him that me and some of my friends were going to be racing out here so he might want to keep Rusty out of the way," J.B. said.

No wonder they hadn't come to my rescue. "While we've got some privacy, I'd like to ask you a couple of questions about Carney."

"I owe you that much for trying to scare you."

"Do you have any idea of who would have wanted to kill him? Or why?"

He hesitated, then said, "I don't want to get anybody into trouble, but when I first heard about Carney being dead, I wondered about Tattoo Bob. Carney could have put Bob out of business by setting the public health people on him."

"But Bob passed the inspection."

"I know he did, but I also know that Carney hadn't given up. The week before he died, I heard him telling a man that Bob had given one of his customers AIDS. I know Bob keeps his needles clean, and Stan got that tattoo years ago. He got AIDS by being queer as a three-dollar bill."

That name sounded familiar. "Stan Upton? China Upton's husband?"

"No, her son. China kept the AIDS quiet, but I went to school with Stan and I knew he was that way. When I saw how he looked right before he died, it wasn't hard to put two and two together. Anyway, spreading that rumor could have put Bob out of business. Since he uses needles all the time, blood doesn't scare him, and everybody knows that artists can be nervy."

I think Bob would have appreciated his reputation as a temperamental artist, even if he didn't care for why J.B. was saying it. "Did Bob find out what Carney was telling people?"

"Not that I know of. I was going to tell him, but Carney was killed before I got a chance."

"If Bob didn't know, then he didn't have a reason to kill Carney."

"I guess not," J.B. said. "Then I hope you find whoever it was soon. We can't have a murderer running around. I've got a family to take care of."

"Tammy and Dulcy are lucky to have you," I said. "One other thing. Would you let the other dealers know that we're not working for Mrs. Lamar? We really got the silent treatment today."

"Sorry about that. I'll spread the word." He looked at his watch. "I heard you tell your aunt that somebody was going to pick you up. Do you want me to keep you company until he shows up? This is a lonely place to be by yourself."

He was the most dangerous thing I'd seen, but I thought it would be rude to say so. Instead I said, "No, thanks. My cousin should be here any time now."

"Then I better be getting home. If there's anything else I can help you with, you just ask." He got back on his Harley. "You know, I thought you'd be more scared than you were."

"Are you kidding? I was petrified."

"It sure didn't show. You acted like you were ready to take on every one of us."

"I think you're trying to pull my leg, but I appreciate it anyway."

He kept the visor up as he drove away, and for some reason, the motorcycle's engine didn't sound nearly as loud as it had before.

Chapter 29

I'm sure the encounter with J.B. and his friends didn't last nearly as long as it seemed to, but I was surprised that Augustus hadn't shown up by the time it was all over. Thirty minutes later, I was beyond surprised and all the way into mad. Aunt Nora had said he was due any minute. Was this another case of his forgetting what he was supposed to do? I couldn't help but picture him off toking somewhere while I fumed.

A full forty-five minutes after I'd told J.B. my ride would be there any time, Richard pulled up in Aunt Maggie's car.

"Sorry to leave you waiting so long," he said as I climbed in. "Aunt Nora called right after we got the car unloaded and said that Augustus hadn't shown up yet so we might want to make other arrangements."

"I should have known not to count on Augustus," I said as he drove out of the parking lot.

"Aunt Nora said the same thing."

"Really?" It takes a lot to get Aunt Nora mad.

"I hope you weren't too bored."

"Actually, the first few minutes were quite exciting," I said, and told him what happened.

"Jesus, Laura. You must have been scared to death!"

"I kept thinking of *Mad Max*, and wishing Mel Gibson would show up."

"I should never have left you alone! What kind of idiot am I? There 's a murderer on the loose, for God's sake!"

"It's okay," I said, reaching over to pat his leg. "I'm none the worse for the wear."

"You could have been. What if J.B. hadn't believed you?"

"He wouldn't have hurt me. He just wanted to scare me."

"Still, from now on, we're going to be more careful."

I was willing to go along with him there, but I was starting to wonder where it was we were going. "Richard, you do know the way back to Aunt Maggie's, don't you?"

"Of course I do. Aunt Maggie said that as long as we were out, we should pick up something to eat. What would you say to some barbeque from Pigwick's?"

"I'd say, 'Hello, handsome. Where have you been all my life?' "

"I think I'm jealous."

"Don't be. My relationships with barbeque platters never last long." Then I had a thought. "Do you think Aunt Maggie would mind if we took a detour?"

"The way she was diving into those boxes, I don't think she'd even notice. There are boxes all over the basement, and she's as happy as . . . "

I could tell he was trying to come up with something to say without the Bard's help. "As happy as a pig in slop?"

"Exactly. What did you have in mind?"

"I thought we could go visit Trey Norton and see how the investigation is going."

"Good idea, but we should call first and make sure Mark Pope isn't there."

We found a pay phone, and I called and found out that Trey was on duty at the station and that he'd be glad for us to come visit.

When I got back into the car, Richard said, "I think I detect a theme in our activities. Aunt Maggie is acting like a pig in slop while we're on our way to get pork barbeque. And we're stopping off to see a policeman. I trust you remember what some people call police officers."

"That's awful!" I said, but I added, "You forgot about my encounter with a Harley hog."

We kept on for a while longer, but fortunately had pigs out of our systems before we got to the police station.

Byerly's police station is neither large nor fancy. There's a front room with a couple of metal desks, some filing cabinets, a radio transmitter, and a photocopier. I knew from past visits that there were cells and storage space in the back. That's all, but it's usually enough to do the job.

Trey was waiting for us inside with three cold Cokes. "I'm glad y'all stopped by. Have you found out anything about Carney Alexander's murder?"

"That's what we were going to ask you," I said as I sat down and gratefully took a swallow of my Coke. "Has Mark had any luck?"

"Nope. Belva says she hasn't either, but I don't know that she'd tell Mark if she did find anything."

"What's that about, anyway?" Richard asked.

"Two of her brothers started acting up at the Mustang Club once and Mark arrested them. If it'd been me or Junior, we'd have just called their folks and got them to come get them, but you know Mark. Belva heard they were in jail, so she came down here to try to get Mark to drop the charges. She tried to sweet-talk him first, but he didn't catch on. Then she got mad, and by the time Junior showed up, they were in the middle of a shouting match. Junior got it all cleared up and sent the boys home with Belva, but Belva still has a grudge against Mark. As for Mark, he thinks she shouldn't be in law enforcement if she can't keep her own family out of trouble. Their feuding has made this case real uncomfortable."

"I imagine it has. Trey, I know this is against the rules, but do you suppose Richard and I could take a look at your file?"

I expected him to fuss a little, but he said, "I've got it right here." That either meant that he and Ilene were getting along real well, or that Junior had told him how much money she had riding on the case.

Richard read the file while I filled Trey in on what we'd found out. I left out the parts I'd promised not to tell, and downplayed the bits with J.B. and his biker friends, but I was careful to tell him all the information and guesses we'd come up with. I finished just as Richard closed the file.

"What do you think?" I asked Trey.

"It sounds like you're on the right track, but Mark wouldn't see it that way. As a matter of fact, he said he doesn't want me talking to y'all any more than absolutely necessary."

I'd been afraid of that. "Do you think you could convince him to check out the people at the flea market without mentioning me and Richard?"

"I'll try, but this is the first time Mark's handled a big case without Junior around, and he's bound and determined to do it his own way. He doesn't always like the way she handles things."

"Junior is a terrific police chief," I said.

"You won't get any argument from me, but Mark thinks he should be police chief instead of her because he's worked here longer. So he's not likely to listen to anybody, especially not y'all."

"Rats," I said. I liked the idea of solving the case and rubbing Mark's nose in it, but I liked the idea of catching the killer quickly even more. "Do what you can, and we'll let you know if we get anything else."

As Richard and I got up to leave, Trey said, "Have you heard anything from Ilene?"

"Not directly, but I hear that the tour is going well."

"She's still supposed to be home this week, isn't she?"

"I'm sure you'd find out about any changes in plans before I would."

He grinned. "I guess I would. Y'all be careful now."

I drove the next leg of the trip so Richard could tell me what he'd found out from the police files. Unfortunately, there wasn't much to tell.

"The medical examiner's report verified what Aunt Maggie told us," Richard said. "They know Carney was killed Sunday because of the contents of his stomach. He had multiple wounds, but was killed by a stab in the back." He grimaced. "The photos were quite explicit."

"Poor Richard."

"Dr. Connelly thinks there was only one attacker, despite Belva's gang theory."

"That's not necessarily a flaw in the theory," I had to admit. "One member of the gang could have actually done the stabbing. If there'd been a gang, that is."

"There were no useful fingerprints on the knife, in Carney's booth, or in his van. Nobody saw the attack, and nobody saw the murderer abandon the van. Though Carney was not well-liked, Mark hasn't discovered any likely motives for murder."

"He's got none, and we've got more than we can handle."

"That's about it."

"Really? I expected more."

"There were notes from his interviews of people at the flea market, including Aunt Maggie, but nothing we didn't already know. And I got Carney's address and his sister's name."

"Maybe we should go see her. I can't think of anything better to do. Aunt Maggie's got to be wondering why she asked us to help."

"Cut that out! We've only been on the job since the night before last, and we've learned quite a bit, especially considering how little sleep we've had."

"I guess," I said, not convinced.

"This is our vacation, after all. I think that tonight we should remember that—and forget about Carney Alexander."

So that's what we did. We got our barbeque and, despite how wonderful it smelled, got it back to Aunt Maggie's before digging in. Then Richard and I watched TV and read while Aunt Maggie looked at her new acquisitions. We did offer to help, but she said she could work faster alone.

At ten or so, I went to tell her we were going to bed.

"See you in the morning," she said, paying more attention to the bowl in her hand than to me.

"*Late* in the morning," I amended.

"Not too late," she said. "The thrift store opens at ten."

"What thrift store?"

"Didn't I tell you? I like to get to the thrift store first

thing Monday morning. They stock the shelves Sunday night."

"Do you need us to go?" I asked plaintively.

"I see other dealers there sometimes."

I sighed. "Okay, count us in."

"Good." She turned back to the bowl. "It'll be nice to have company."

I stared at her. Had I heard that right? Or was I more tired than I thought? I trudged upstairs and broke the news to Richard.

"Ten o'clock isn't so bad," he said philosophically. "If we go to bed right now, we should get nine hours of sleep."

"Of course, that assumes that we'll be going right to sleep," I pointed out.

"Eight hours of sleep will be more than enough," he said with a big smile.

Chapter 30

Aunt Maggie is usually a slow, careful driver, but not that Monday morning. After staying up into the wee hours going through boxes, she'd slept late, and then Richard and I hadn't moved fast enough to suit her, so she was trying to make up for lost time. She went way over the speed limit, pushed through two yellow lights, and went through a four-way stop two cars ahead of her turn. I was still half-asleep when I got into the car, but I was wide awake when we made it to the thrift store.

Aunt Maggie swerved into a parking place by the front door, and even though hers was the only car in the parking lot, she hopped out and said, "Come on! They're already open."

Richard and I had to run to keep from being left behind, then bumped into her when she stopped just inside the door. "Good morning, Davy," she said to the man at the register. "What have you got for me today?"

"Morning, Miz Burnette." Davy scratched his chin, which looked like it had three or four days' worth of beard on it, and turned to look at the shelves. I wondered how he could pick out the new merchandise from the old. It all looked old to me.

The front of the store was filled with furniture: sagging couches, wooden end tables, partial bedroom sets, and a couple of fifties-style dinette sets. Behind that were mismatched racks of mismatched clothing and bins filled with shoes and battered pocketbooks. Then came stuffed animals and board games, and a motley assortment of dolls ranging from clowns with porcelain heads to naked Barbies with their hair teased in all directions. Next were appliances: toaster ovens and can openers colored harvest gold and turquoise and other colors nobody uses in kitchens anymore.

Near the center were racks and shelves of dishes, glasses, vases, and other breakables. Along the right wall were books in boxes, on shelves, and in stacks on the floor.

The last third of the store held everything else: two lawn mowers, framed pictures of sad clowns and dogs playing poker, an exercise bike, a stack of needlepoint kits still sealed in plastic, a case of eight-inch floppy disks, a pink manual typewriter, and boxes of chartreuse mini-blinds.

Davy said, "There's some big bowls like those you got before, and we got a good load of paperbacks. Some of them look like they've never even been read."

"Thanks, Davy." She paused, and I guessed that she was trying to decide where to start. "Richard, you sold a lot of books this weekend, so you know what kind I need. See if you can find any good ones. Laurie Anne, you get a cart and come with me." She went on, not waiting to see if we obeyed.

The shopping cart was rusted and marked with the name of a grocery store that had closed at least four years before. By the time I wrestled it free of the line by the door and caught up with Aunt Maggie, she already had two mixing bowls in one hand and was inspecting a third. She put all three into the cart.

"Those two with the brown stripes are McCoy," she said. "I bet I can get fifteen dollars apiece for them."

I looked at the price tags. They were marked two dollars each. "That's twenty-six dollars profit," I said in awe.

"Any idea how much that one with the apple on it is worth?"

I didn't have a clue, but I turned it over to look at the bottom like I knew what I was doing. Unfortunately, there wasn't anything on the bottom. "Twenty-five dollars?" I finally guessed.

"Multiply that by four. I think it's a piece from Watt Pottery."

"A hundred dollars?" I looked at it more closely, but it still just looked like an old bowl. "How come it's worth so much?"

"Because there's people who'll pay that much. That's the only reason I know." She turned back to the shelves and slowly worked her way down them. Occasionally she'd pick up a glass or a dish and look at it, and about a third of the time she'd add it to the growing pile in the cart.

I pushed the cart behind her, trying to guess which pieces she'd take. I didn't do too well. In fact, it seemed like anything I thought was worthwhile was junk, and vice versa. I told myself I wasn't asking questions because I didn't want to disturb her, but in fact, I didn't want to demonstrate how ignorant I was. When she picked up a cheap-looking ceramic bird with its head pointed up and its beak wide open, I had to say something. "Why on earth would somebody want that?"

"Don't you know what it is?"

I shook my head.

"It's a pie bird."

"Looks more like a canary."

"It may be a canary, but it's also a pie bird." She stuck her finger down the bird's mouth, and it came out the bottom. "You see the hole? You put this in the middle of a pie to release pressure on the crust so the filling won't overflow while it's baking. It'd come in handy, if I ever baked."

"I'm hopeless, Aunt Maggie," I said. "If I ever tried to make a living at this, I'd starve to death."

"Don't worry about it," she said with a grin. "You've got to remember that I've been doing this for a long time, and I'm old enough to remember when you could buy Watt bowls in the store and when people used pie birds." She kept looking as she talked. "I've made plenty of mistakes. Most of the time I don't know what it was I should have bought, or what I sold for less than it was worth, but there was that one time." She stopped, and I wasn't sure if it was so she could look more carefully at a dish or because she was stalling. "Once I bought a box at an auction, and inside was this vase, I guess you'd call it. It was a pitiful-looking thing. Red-brown clay with splotches of paint, and I don't think it would have held water, but I stuck a quarter price tag on it and put it on the table. There it sat for six months."

She picked up a stack of saucers, shuffled through them to check the markings on the bottom, and put half of them in the cart and the other half back on the shelf. "One day a man came by, and I could tell he was just looking around while his wife shopped, but when he saw that vase, his eyes got as big around as this plate here." She held up a plate, put it back on the shelf, then reconsidered and put it in the cart. "He picked it up to look at it, and put it down real careful. Then he asked me if the price marked was right. I said it was, and he got out a twenty-dollar bill and a five-dollar bill. 'That's twenty-five *cents,*' I told him, which may be the stupidest thing I've ever said. He looked at me like I was crazy, but he gave me a quarter and picked up the vase. Then he asked if I knew what I'd just sold. He said that thing was American Indian pottery, good enough for the Smithsonian. I asked him how much it was worth, and he said it was priceless. Here I'd just sold it for a quarter."

As we started down the last row of glassware, Aunt Maggie said, "It's impossible to know about everything you find, because you never know what you're going to run into."

The front door opened, and in walked Mavis and Mary Maude.

Aunt Maggie frowned. "See what I mean? You never know what kind of junk you're going to run into."

I hid a grin as the two of them made a beeline for us.

Aunt Maggie said, "Don't take your eyes off that cart for a second. They're going to look to see what's in it, and if you're not careful, they'll 'accidentally' pick up something and put it in their own cart."

I got a firm grip on the handle. Meanwhile, Aunt Maggie nearly ran down the last aisle, picking up pieces without even looking at them. She reached for a pair of blue candlesticks, but Mary Maude grabbed them first.

"Don't often find pieces like this, do you, Miz Burnette?" Mary Maude said with a triumphant grin. "How much do you suppose these are worth?"

"I wouldn't know," Aunt Maggie said, and turned around to make another pass through the shelves.

Mary Maude turned the candlesticks over to look at the bottom, but from her expression, I knew she didn't have any idea of what it was she was holding. I didn't either, but I hadn't practically stolen them from Aunt Maggie.

I stopped watching Mary Maude just in time to see Mavis peering into our shopping cart with one hand out. "Excuse me," I said, and pushed the cart out of her reach, just barely missing her toes.

"By the way, Miz Burnette," Mavis said, sounding miffed, "we went to that mini warehouse auction you told us about, but it turned out it was cancelled."

"I told you to call ahead," Aunt Maggie said.

"Do you know about any other auctions this week?" Mary Maude demanded.

"Not off hand," Aunt Maggie said.

"Why don't you check that date book of yours?" Mary Maude said, poking at Aunt Maggie's pocketbook.

"I can't," she said, sounding pleased. "I left it out at the flea market. One of my suppliers brought me a big load of stuff yesterday, and I was so busy packing the boxes into my car that I forgot to pick it up."

That's why she'd sounded so pleased. She'd been hoping for an excuse to mention the new merchandise Luther had brought her. From the look on Mary Maude's face, the gloat hit home.

It may have backfired, because Aunt Maggie spent the next few minutes sandwiched between Mary Maude and Mavis. Mary Maude was in front so she could get to everything ahead of her, and Mavis was behind her, watching everything she picked up. I don't know how Aunt Maggie stood it. I was expecting her to either explode or give up when she grabbed a glass bud vase.

"Is this what I think it is?" she said. She held it up to the light, checked the bottom, then showed it to Mavis. "You know what this is, don't you, Miz Dermott?"

Mavis said, "Lord, I don't remember the last time I saw one of those. It's in good condition, too."

"I've got a collector who comes by every week, and I know she'll pay a hundred dollars for it."

"Really?" I said, looking at it in amazement.

Aunt Maggie said, "You know how collectors are. This lady isn't satisfied with just one of anything—she wants as many as she can get. If I could find a dozen like this one, she'd buy them all. She used to try to fool me into thinking she was broke, but I know better now. She's got plenty of money, even if she does dress like country come to town—always wearing that bright pink coat and carrying the tackiest black-and-white checked pocketbook." Aunt Maggie admired the vase a minute more, then gently placed it in the cart. "You be careful, Laurie Anne. I don't want that getting chipped."

"Yes, ma'am," I said, but I was getting suspicious.

"I think I've found everything I'm going to. Let's go see what Richard's got," she said.

As soon as we were out of earshot, I said, "What are you up to?"

She tried to look innocent, but spoiled it with a devilish grin. "Just getting those two out of my hair for a while."

"That vase isn't really worth a hundred dollars, is it?"

"I'd be lucky to get a quarter for it."

Right about then, I heard Mary Maude and Mavis chattering about something. Mary Maude was holding a cardboard box, and Mavis was so excited she was nearly jumping up and down. They just about ran for the cash register.

"What do you suppose they found?" I asked.

"Problably the box that vase came out of," Aunt Maggie said. "I saw it when we went by the first time. The box originally held a dozen, but there were only eleven in the box."

"So they think they've got eleven hundred dollars worth of bud vases. Aunt Maggie, like they say in Boston, you are wicked smart."

"Thank you, Laurie Anne."

"What about the lady in the pink coat? Did you make her up?"

"Nope, she comes by every couple of weeks. I don't know if she's got any money or not, but I know she'll bargain for an hour just to get a nickel off the price."

"Wicked smart," I said again.

"Maybe that'll teach them not to grab things out of my hand."

When we got to Richard, I saw that he'd found an empty box and had nearly filled it with books.

"What did you find?" Aunt Maggie asked.

"Some amazing stuff." He held up a large paperback. "This one is a classic."

"*The Norton Anthology of Poetry*?" Aunt Maggie read out.

"And a complete set of Shakespeare's tragedies in paperback."

"Richard—"

"You were right to get us up early—I'm surprised this stuff is still here."

"Richard, did you see any books like this out at Tight as a Tick?"

"No—you should corner the market. The flea market that is."

"The reason you didn't see any books like this," she said patiently, "is because books like this don't sell at the flea market. My customers want Stephen King, not Shakespeare."

"But these are good books."

"It doesn't matter. They won't sell." She picked up a fat historical romance. "Now, I'll sell this the first day I put it out." She grabbed a couple more romances and a John Grisham book. "These, too. But what you've got—"

"What I've got won't sell," he said sadly.

"We'll buy them for ourselves if you want them," I said, though I didn't know where we'd put them.

That cheered him up, and after Aunt Maggie went through the rest of the books, we headed for the register. Aunt Maggie stopped to put the glass bud vase back on the shelf and came away with a big grin. In their rush, Mary Maude and Mavis had left the blue candlesticks.

"These are Fenton," she said. "I can get thirty-five, forty dollars for them."

Once we got the car loaded, I said, "What next?"

"There's still the Goodwill store, and I thought we might go by a place in Hickory if you two don't mind."

"Lead on, MacDuff," I said cheerfully, and Richard groaned from the back seat. He couldn't even correct me while the bet was going on.

We didn't have much luck at the next two stores. Mary Maude and Mavis beat us to both of them, and bought anything worth buying before we got there. After that, we were ready for lunch, so we stopped at Hardee's.

"Now what?" Richard asked when we finished eating.

"Nothing else today," Aunt Maggie said, "but I think there's a sale tomorrow." She fumbled in her pocketbook. "Shoot, I forgot I left my book at the flea market."

I said, "I thought you just said that to bug Mary Maude and Mavis."

"No, I really did leave it. Do you two mind if we ride out there and get it? I can't remember who's having the sale."

Since Richard and I didn't have any other plans, other than a persistent longing for sleep, we said we didn't mind a bit.

Chapter 31

The flea market lot was as empty as it had been on Sunday afternoon, but not nearly as creepy with company.

"We better go by Bender's trailer to let him know we're here," Aunt Maggie said.

"Why don't you drop me off and let me tell him?" I said. "I haven't really had a chance to talk to him, and according to Tattoo Bob, Bender ought to be our prime suspect."

"Bob is talking through his hat," Aunt Maggie said with a snort. "Bender doesn't stay sober long enough to plan out something like Carney's murder."

"Still, he might know something useful."

"Shall I come with you?" Richard asked.

I knew he wasn't crazy about leaving me alone after what had happened with J.B., but I didn't think Aunt Maggie should be by herself, either. "No, you go on with Aunt Maggie. I'll get Bender to walk me to the building." That should keep us all reasonably secure.

Aunt Maggie had told us that Bender lived on the flea market grounds rent-free, but from the way the outside of that trailer looked, he wasn't getting much of a bargain. I'd have been ashamed to use that rusty, dented thing for storage, let alone as a place to sleep.

Before I could knock, I heard a muted woof from inside, and Bender opened the door, dressed in the same clothes he'd been wearing over the weekend.

"Hey, Miz Fleming."

"How are you today, Mr. Cawthorne?"

"I'm doing all right, but I want you to call me Bender. Everybody calls me Bender. Isn't that right, Rusty?" He patted the dog. "What can I do you for?"

"Just wanted to let you know that Aunt Maggie, my husband, and I are out here. After all the troubles you've had, I didn't want y'all getting worried."

"I appreciate that, but you could have saved yourself the trouble. Rusty had already let me know that somebody was here, but since it was somebody he knows, he didn't put up a fuss. If a stranger comes around, he gets all riled up."

"Since I've already got you away from what you were doing, can I talk to you for a minute?"

"Sure thing. Come on inside."

I peered through the door he was holding open. It was dark and smelly inside, and I swear I saw a pile of old clothes move. "Why don't we talk out here? It's an awfully nice day."

"That's fine, too." He and Rusty came outside, and I noticed Bender didn't bother to lock the door behind him. Maybe that pile would keep watch. "Let's us go sit out back."

There were a couple of mismatched lawn chairs on the other side of the trailer. They were ancient, and though I didn't think they'd collapse under us, I sat down carefully, just in case.

"This is nice," Bender said. "I ought to get outside more, but I get busy and lose track of time." Since he smelled like a brewery, I thought I knew what he'd been busy doing. "What did you want to talk to me about?"

"I was just wondering if you'd heard anything else about the murder." I didn't think he had, since I'd been at the police station the night before, but I had to start the conversation somewhere.

"Not a word. I still feel bad about that happening on my watch. Poor old Carney."

That was as much sympathy as I'd heard anyone express for Carney. "Did you know him well?"

"I can't say as I did. He wasn't much of a mixer, and I never saw him out anywhere."

"Aunt Maggie and I were talking," I said, trying to sound casual, "and she says she doesn't believe there's a gang running around here. She thinks that whoever killed Carney must have had something against him personally. Did you ever know him to have problems with anybody?" Considering the number of people I knew of who'd had run-ins with him, I expected Bender to start listing them off.

Instead, he said, "Nope, he seemed to get along with everybody out here."

Even Rusty gave him a disbelieving look. Maybe when you're focused so much on a bottle, you're oblivious to everything else.

We sat a little longer while I tried to think of something to ask. Bender seemed perfectly happy to sit in the sun. Finally I said, "This is nice, but I better go catch up with Aunt Maggie and Richard. Do you mind walking me over there?"

"Now, why would I mind escorting a pretty lady?" he said gallantly. He was a nice man, but it was a shame he didn't keep himself cleaner. False teeth would have helped, too.

Rusty ran in front of us as we walked, sniffing at everything and marking his territory. "Did you know Rusty used to be a hunting dog, back when I used to hunt?" Bender said with pride.

"Is that right?" I said, trying to suppress a shudder at the idea of Bender with a gun.

Could Bob have been right about Bender? Could he have gotten drunk and killed Carney, and then forgotten about it? The more I thought about it, the less likely it seemed. I'd seen Bender drunk—in fact, I wasn't sure I'd ever seen him completely sober. Bender was a gregarious drunk, not a mean one.

When we got to Building One, I started to circle around to the door where Aunt Maggie usually parked.

"You don't have to go all the way back there," Bender said. "I'll let you in the front." He pulled out a ring of keys and unlocked the small door to the side of the main entrance, then opened it and reached in to flip on a light switch.

I started in, but we heard a car driving away quickly, wheels squealing.

Rusty ran toward the noise, and Bender said, "I better go check that out. You go on inside." He trotted after his dog.

I thought about going with them, but I wanted to make sure Richard and Aunt Maggie were okay. I called out their names, but there was no answer. Figuring that they must have already found the date book and gone outside to wait for me, I started for the door near Aunt Maggie's booth. As I reached for the doorknob, I saw her lying behind the table facedown on the concrete floor.

I must have screamed for Richard, because he told me later that he heard me from outside, but I didn't know I'd done it. I knelt down beside her, not wanting to touch her because I was afraid of finding out that she wasn't breathing. There was blood seeping from that ridiculous jet black hair, and a thin trail of it ran onto the concrete. I made myself put my hand on her back, and thought I'd cry when I felt her breathing.

Then Richard was there. "What happened?" he asked.

"I don't know. I just found her."

"How badly is she hurt?"

"She's breathing, but I can't tell anything else. We've got to get an ambulance out here."

"I'll use the phone at the snack bar," he said, and was gone again.

"Who is it?" a voice asked.

"It's Aunt—" I stopped, and turned around. Aunt Maggie was standing behind me. "I thought it was you!"

"In that shirt? I wouldn't be caught dead in that shirt. She's not dead, is she?"

I shook my head, and looked at the woman on the floor again. Now that I had proof standing beside me, it was obvious that it wasn't my great-aunt. Like Aunt Maggie said, she'd never have worn a black and white mock turtleneck, but I thought I'd seen somebody in a shirt like that earlier. "I think it's Mavis."

Aunt Maggie leaned over, trying to see her face. "Looks like Mary Maude to me. Let's roll her over so we can get a better look."

"Is it all right to move her?"

"I think so," she said. "It's only folks with back and neck

injuries you're not supposed to move. I'd say somebody knocked her upside the head."

Gingerly we rolled her over so that she was lying on her back, with her head in my lap. It was Mary Maude, all right. Her face looked pasty white, but it was hard to tell if that was from her injury or just her usual heavy hand with powder.

I said, "Aren't you supposed to keep people warm to prevent shock? This floor is awfully cold."

"I'll get something to put on her."

I have to give Aunt Maggie credit. She could have made do with one of the sheets she uses to cover her tables, but she found the handmade quilt that she'd tried to auction off and wrapped it around the injured woman.

"Maybe you should go look for Mavis," I said. "She might be hurt, too."

"She's all right. At least she was. Their car was out back, and as soon as we drove up, she came over and started talking a mile a minute. I don't know why she didn't come in with us, but I'm not leaving you here by your lonesome when there's some nut on the loose. There's no way this could have happened by accident."

Her saying that started me thinking. "I thought she was you when I first found her."

"So you said, but I can't see why."

"Y'all are about the same height," I said defensively. "Your hair and hers are about the same length, and the same color."

"Don't remind me," she said, ruffling her hair. "I hope this mess grows out quick."

"And she was hit from behind."

"That's what it looks like."

"Maybe whoever it was thought it was you, just like I

did. From behind, it would have been an easy mistake to make."

"Why would anybody come after me?"

"I told J.B. what Richard and I are up to, and he might have told somebody else. Or the killer might have figured it out for himself. He could have been trying to scare us off." As soon as I said that, I knew it didn't make sense. "No, this was the worst possible thing he could have done. If he'd laid low, there was a chance that Richard and I would give up and go home. Hurting you would guarantee that we'd never give up."

"Laurie Anne, I think that's the nicest thing you ever said to me," Aunt Maggie said.

I looked down at Mary Maude, a little embarrassed. It was true that I wasn't overly demonstrative with Aunt Maggie, but that's the way I thought she wanted it. Didn't she know how much I cared about her? I'd have to make sure that she knew, but this wasn't the time or the place.

"Come to think of it," Aunt Maggie said, "how would anybody know I'd be here? We didn't decide to come until we were on the way."

"Good point," I said, relieved that she hadn't been the target. "Maybe he was searching for whatever it was that Carney had." Of course, I was still assuming that Carney had had something worth killing for.

"So Mary Maude showed up while he was looking, and he hit her with that?" She nodded at a cast-iron bookend that was under one of the tables. In all the excitement, I hadn't seen it. "That wasn't there last night, and I don't think those stains are rust."

"I think you're right." Our killer's ability to find weapons everywhere made me nervous.

"I'd like to know what Mary Maude was doing in my booth."

"We'll ask when she wakes up." I didn't bring up the possibility that she might not wake up. Mary Maude wasn't a young woman, and it looked like her attacker had meant to kill her. I was surprised he hadn't hit her again to be sure she was dead. Maybe he'd heard Richard and Aunt Maggie outside, or me and Bender at the front, and ducked out one of the building's other doors. It had probably been him that Bender and I had heard leave. I kept telling myself that so I wouldn't imagine him lurking nearby.

Richard came back, and said that the ambulance was on its way and that he'd called both police departments. He also brought Bender and Rusty, who hadn't been able to catch the car we'd heard.

After we quickly explained the situation to Bender, he and Rusty went to find Mavis. A few minutes later, in she ran, calling for her sister.

Aunt Maggie said, "Miz Dermott, I'm afraid your sister's been hurt."

Mavis screamed and threw herself at her sister so hard I was afraid she'd hurt herself and Mary Maude. I didn't get all of what she was saying, but it was clear that she thought we'd attacked Mary Maude.

I was trying to keep Mary Maude from being too badly jostled while Richard tried to gently untangle Mavis. Then Aunt Maggie got a hold of one arm and pulled her up. Mavis was still screaming at us when Aunt Maggie slapped her right in the face.

I'd heard about slapping hysterical people for years, but that was the first time I'd seen it done. It worked. For the first time since I'd known her, Mavis was speechless.

"Miz Dermott," Aunt Maggie said, "you don't know what you're saying. We did not hit your sister. Laurie Anne found her this way, and we're doing what we can for her. Making all this fuss isn't going to help her one bit!"

Mavis looked down at me, and I did my best to look like somebody who'd never dream of hitting an old woman.

"Who else would care about your date book?" Mavis demanded.

"What's my date book got to do with this?"

Mavis didn't say anything, and after a second, Aunt Maggie answered her own question. "That's what you two were doing here. I told y'all I'd left my book out here, and y'all wanted to find out when the auctions are. Mary Maude came in to find it while you played lookout and kept us talking outside so we wouldn't catch her in the act."

Mavis looked embarrassed for maybe ten seconds, but then said, "It doesn't matter now. Mary Maude's hurt!"

It must have been a strain for her, but Aunt Maggie said, "You're right, Miz Dermott. Taking care of Miz Foy is the important thing."

Mark arrived then, followed a few seconds later by Belva, and they tried to make sense of our stories. It would have been easier if they'd quit interrupting each other, and if Mavis had quit interrupting Aunt Maggie and me. I don't know how much they'd figured out when Trey Norton brought in the EMTs a minute later.

They examined Mary Maude and got her out of my lap and onto a stretcher to carry her to the ambulance. Mavis trailed along behind them, looking nearly as sick as her sister.

Belva said, "This puts a whole new light on the Alexander

case. I think it's pretty obvious that we're dealing with a serial killer preying on flea market dealers."

Richard and I looked at each other. That possibility hadn't occurred to us, but it sure didn't sound right. In fact, it sounded downright silly.

I guess it sounded silly to Mark, too, because he said, "You're making something out of nothing, Tucker. It was another robbery attempt. Drug-related, probably. Nine times out of ten, it comes down to drugs."

That didn't make sense either, because nothing had been taken. In fact, Aunt Maggie didn't have anything that would be attractive to a thief wanting to convert goods to cash in a hurry.

I wanted to add my opinion, and I could see that Richard was dying to join in, too, but we both resisted. Mark and Belva were too busy arguing with each other, and they'd made it plain that they wouldn't listen to us, so we just asked if it was all right for us to leave. When they said it was, Aunt Maggie got her date book, and we headed to Aunt Nora's for supper.

I realized I was shaking once I got in the car, and at first I thought it was delayed reaction. Then I figured out what it really was. I was angry. I hadn't known Carney Alexander and maybe I hadn't taken his death all that seriously, but I was taking it seriously now. Somebody had nearly killed Mary Maude, and I was furious because it could have been Aunt Maggie in that ambulance.

Chapter 32

Out of deference to Uncle Buddy's queasy stomach, we waited until we'd had our fill of pork chops, mashed potatoes with gravy, and string beans to tell Aunt Nora, Uncle Buddy, Augustus, Thaddeous, and Willis what had happened to Mary Maude.

After warning us to be careful, Uncle Buddy settled in front of the TV, Willis left to work the night shift at the mill, Thaddeous grabbed the phone to call Michelle, and Augustus said he was going to take a walk. I knew they all knew about Richard's and my investigation and were probably curious, but I also knew that Aunt Maggie had told Aunt Nora to keep anything she knew under her hat. Besides, everybody knew that all the Burnettes were going to find out sooner or later.

That left Aunt Maggie, Aunt Nora, Richard, and me sitting around the kitchen table to hash over what we knew and what the police thought they knew.

"A serial killer?" Aunt Nora said.

"Belva figures that Carney's death was just the first," I said.

"Don't serial killers usually kill the same kind of person?

Like all tall blondes, or all women who look like their mothers?"

Richard raised one eyebrow.

"I watch *Unsolved Mysteries*," she explained.

"I think you're right," I said. "Serials also tend to use the same M.O." I watch *Unsolved Mysteries*, too. "Switching from a knife to a blunt instrument doesn't fit, but Belva thinks the pattern is using the dealer's own merchandise: Carney's knife and Aunt Maggie's bookend." I imagined Bob killed with needles and Tammy run over by a Harley, and what I came up with for Obed was enough to turn my stomach.

Aunt Maggie said, "The only serials around here are the Saturday morning ones Belva watched too many of when she was a little girl. Carney's killer was looking for something, but Mary Maude showed up, and he wanted to shut her up."

"What could he have been looking for?" Aunt Nora asked.

"We don't know," I said. "Aunt Maggie, did Carney ever give you anything?"

"He never gave me the time of day, but now that you ask, I've got an idea. He usually got out there before I did, so he could have hidden something in my booth."

"Don't you think you'd have found it by now?" Richard objected. "You had to sort through most of it to clean up after the break-in."

"That's true," Aunt Maggie said.

We kicked around other ideas, ranging from the unlikely to the outlandish, but none of it was very useful. Finally Aunt Maggie said she was going to watch TV with Uncle Buddy, and Aunt Nora said she wanted to get the supper dishes cleaned up.

"Can I help?" I asked, expecting to be turned down.

Instead Aunt Nora said, "I hope so, Laurie Anne." I reached for a dirty plate, but she put one hand over mine. "Not with the dishes. What I'd really like is for you to talk to Augustus. You know he was two hours late yesterday afternoon? That's why I didn't send him to get you. I am at my wit's end with that boy, and Buddy is out of patience. If something doesn't change soon, I'm afraid there are going to be hard words."

"Don't you think it would be better if Thaddeous or Willis talked to him?"

"They've tried, Laurie Anne. I've tried, Buddy's tried. Maybe he'll listen to you. He's always respected you for being the first to leave Byerly. He says you inspired him."

"Really?" I hadn't known that. We'd talked about our plans to get away, but I'd never thought of him as following in my footsteps. "I'll try, Aunt Nora."

"I sure would appreciate it."

"Do you want me to come with you?" Richard asked.

"No, I ought to talk to him alone." I didn't want Augustus to think we were ganging up on him.

"Then I'll help Aunt Nora with the dishes," he said.

"No, you won't," Aunt Nora said. "You go watch TV."

"But I don't want to watch TV."

They were still arguing when I went outside.

Augustus wasn't hard to find. I just followed my nose. He'd climbed up into the tree house he and his brothers had built years ago. It didn't take a psychologist to figure out that there was something meaningful in his retreating to a boyhood hiding place.

"Hello up there!" I called out. "Does your club allow girls?"

There was some hurried scuffling, and then he called back, "I guess I have to—I wouldn't want you to sue."

I climbed the rungs that were nailed into the trunk to make a ladder, thinking that it had been an awful long time since I'd done that, and hoping the tree house was strong enough to hold us both.

The tree house was just a wooden platform with a ceiling that slanted down away from the trunk, but it was roomy. The boys used to keep crates of comic books and baseballs and such in there, but the only thing still up there was an ashtray that Augustus dumped overboard as soon as I got up.

I sat down next to him, both of us leaning up against the thick tree trunk.

"I thought you and Mama were gossiping," Augustus said.

"It's not gossip. It's networking."

"My mistake," he said, and there was still enough light for me to see him grin.

I didn't say anything for a while, partially because it was a nice evening and I didn't want to spoil it, but mostly because I was stalling. Finally I said, "Is this where you do your toking?"

He didn't answer for a long while, but then sarcastically said, "You really have become a detective."

"It didn't take much detecting. Aunt Nora's bound to catch on soon, if she hasn't already."

"Well, it can't do anything but confirm her opinion of me."

"Augustus! She always thought the world of you, and you know it."

"Did you use the past tense? Does that mean she no

longer thinks the world of me? Why is that? Because I'm a pot-head?"

"I'm not being judgmental," I said, hoping it was true. "A lot of our friends in Boston smoke pot, but you just don't seem the type."

"Why? Because I'm a good ole boy, and us good ole boys are supposed to get high on Budweiser instead of on weed?"

"You're not a good ole boy, Augustus. You've seen as much of the world as I have, maybe more."

"But here I am again," he said bitterly.

"Don't you want to be here?" Aunt Nora had told me he'd decided not to reenlist.

"Wanting doesn't have anything to do with it. I *have* to be here."

"Augustus, you can go anywhere. If you'd like to give Boston a try, you're welcome to stay with us. Our place is small, but—"

"You don't get it, Laurie Anne. I have to be *here.*" He shoved his hair back from his forehead. "You remember how I was when I left? I couldn't wait to leave. I knew that if I stayed, I'd end up working at the mill for the rest of my life, and I couldn't stand the thought of that. Don't get me wrong. Daddy makes a good living there, and Thaddeous and Willis have done well, too, but the place would have been like a prison for me."

"I know how you feel. I used to love visiting Paw at the mill, but the older I got, the less I wanted to go there. I kept picturing myself in one of those smocks the women used to wear, working my way through the ranks until I became one of those cranky old women who fuss when somebody else puts his lunch in her spot in the refrigerator. Going to college was my way of making sure that never happened."

"My problem was that I wasn't smart enough for college."

"You were plenty smart enough," I protested. "Your grades were always good."

"All right, maybe I could have," he admitted, "but I didn't want books; I wanted the real world. The army seemed perfect. They said they'd train me and give me a chance to travel. I was so happy to get that uniform that I thought I'd bust. I was sad to be leaving Mama and Daddy and everybody else, but I didn't look back."

"So what happened?"

"At first I loved it. Germany was even better than I'd dreamed it would be. The buildings, the people, the food—it even smelled different over there. The other countries I went to were just as wonderful. I made friends all over, and I dated women with accents that made my name sound like something special. For the first year or so, I thought I had the world by its tail."

"Then what?"

"Then I started to realize that I wasn't having fun anymore. The buildings were incredible, but after a while they didn't look right to me. And the people's faces were funny, and the food didn't taste good. I got tired of being with women I could barely understand. At first I thought it was something physical, but the doctor said I was fine. He thought I needed a change of scenery, so I transferred to another post. That helped for a while, but after a few months, I was as bad off as before."

"What was it?"

He wouldn't meet my eyes. "One of my bunk mates figured it out first, but I didn't want to believe him. It sounded right foolish to think that a grown man would have that happen."

I waited for him to go on.

"I was homesick, Laurie Anne, pure and simple. Just like a little kid."

"Augustus, that's nothing to be ashamed of."

"That's easy for you to say. You've never been homesick."

I had to laugh. "If you had any idea of how miserable I was my first semester in Cambridge, you wouldn't say that."

"But you got over it, didn't you? Not me. I'd talked so big, and here I was pining for home. I'd never felt so ashamed in my whole life, so I decided I was going to fight it, that I wouldn't come back."

"Is that when you stopped coming home on leave?" Aunt Nora had fretted about it, but had convinced herself that Augustus was just using his time off to see more of Europe.

"That's right. I was afraid that if I came to Byerly for even a little bit, I'd never leave again. So I went anywhere but here: Paris, London, Amsterdam. It didn't help."

"Is that why you started smoking pot?"

"It wasn't pot—it was hashish. Hash is stronger; but I can't get it in Byerly, so I switched to pot. Anyway, I was in the red light district in Amsterdam and one of the guys had some. It's legal over there, so I figured it couldn't be that bad. I tried it, and I found out that when I was high, I wasn't homesick anymore. Drinking didn't help me a bit, but hash sure did the trick."

"How long have you been smoking it?"

"A couple of years. I guess my commanding officer could tell after a while. He didn't say anything, but there were surprise inspections, and they posted the rules about drugs on our bulletin board. I thought I'd be safe as long as I didn't smoke on base, but one day the CO found me in a park smoking. That was it for my army career."

"He didn't court-martial you, did he?" I asked.

"No, he just took my stash away and made sure I didn't get off base much after that. And he suggested that I not reenlist. He didn't actually say that I'd be in trouble if I did, but I got the idea. So here I am, back in Byerly, and I guess I'll end up working at that damned mill after all."

"There's other things you can do."

"Like what? Byerly isn't exactly a hotbed of industry. The army did teach me some things, but I can't make a living around here repairing radio equipment."

"What about someplace else in North Carolina?"

"I thought about that. After I was discharged, I spent a couple of days in Charlotte and a week in Raleigh, seeing if it was just the States I was missing. I was still miserable. It's got to be Byerly. So tomorrow I'm going to go see Bill Walters."

"Don't do it, not yet, anyway. You'll come up with something else."

"Like what? All I'm good for is being homesick and smoking this shit." He pulled a joint out of his pocket, looked at it in disgust, then flipped it out into the darkness. "The mill is as good a place for me as any."

"Augustus Crawford, you listen to me!" I said, shaking my finger at him. "If you want to work at Walters Mill, that's fine, but don't you dare go down there unless you're going to give it your best shot, because it wouldn't be fair to the mill and it wouldn't be fair to you. There's lots of other work you can do." He started to object, but I wouldn't stop talking. "I don't know what, but I do know that we're going to figure it out."

"Do you really think so, Laurie Anne?"

"I really do."

He leaned back against the tree. "I hope you're right, because, despite everything, part of me is just so damned glad to be back home that I want to cry." His voice broke.

I hugged him as hard as I could. "You know, you are so much like Paw. He was just as attached to Byerly as you are. He once told me that he thought he'd up and die if he ever had to leave. Sometimes I was jealous, because I'd never been that way about a place, not Byerly and not even Boston. I never really understood how he felt, but talking to you, I almost do. He'd be awfully glad you came back."

Augustus started sobbing, and we stayed like that for a long time.

Chapter 33

After Augustus quieted down, we decided go back inside before anybody came looking for us. Besides, the mosquitoes were starting to bite.

Everybody was in the living room, and both Aunt Nora and Richard looked up when we came in. I nodded to let them know that it had gone all right, and both relaxed. Augustus's problems weren't over, but he was better off than he had been before.

We all settled down to watch TV for a while, but I wasn't paying much attention to the show. I wasn't thinking about Carney Alexander, either. Instead I was trying to come up with something Augustus could do with himself. I had one idea, but I wasn't sure if he'd be interested.

Aunt Maggie eventually announced that she was ready to head home. That meant that we had half an hour of Uncle Buddy asking Aunt Maggie about the leak in her attic, and Thaddeous remembering that Michelle had given him Richard's and my new plane reservations. I'd been cowardly enough to leave her a voice-mail message rather than call directly, but she must have forgiven me because the new plane tickets weren't costing us any extra.

Aunt Nora pulled me aside and said, "Laurie Anne, I

was thinking. I know you're pretty sure that the killer wasn't after Aunt Maggie, but what if you're wrong? Is it possible that she's in danger?"

What she was saying was that none of us would forgive ourselves if anything happened to Aunt Maggie because of our guessing wrong. "You think we should keep an eye on her, don't you?"

She nodded.

"Then Richard and I will be all over her like white on rice." Considering the way she'd talked Richard and me into accompanying her so far, I didn't think it would be a problem.

"If it gets too much for y'all, you be sure to ask for help. Thaddeous can help at night, and Willis can help during the day. I don't know about Augustus."

"I'm sure Augustus will help, too," I said.

"I won't ask you what y'all said, but do you think he's okay?"

"He's got some things to work out," I warned, "but I think he's going to be fine."

"Thank you, Laurie Anne."

"Don't cry!" I said quickly. I'd already had one person crying on my shoulder—I didn't need another.

Aunt Nora sniffed a couple of times, but managed to stem the flow by changing the subject. "We'll have to be careful that Aunt Maggie doesn't figure out that we're watching her. You know how she is. She'd be right put out at us for thinking that she can't take care of herself."

After that, Aunt Maggie, Richard, and I headed back to the house, and we all went straight up to bed. As soon as I was alone with Richard, I told him what Aunt Nora had suggested, and he agreed that we shouldn't leave Aunt Maggie alone. Then I described my conversation with Augustus. "Now all we have to do is find him a job."

"Wouldn't he rather do that himself?"

"I don't think he'd mind a little help."

"Laura, your idea of a little help is to write his resumé, get him a job interview, and hide behind him during the interview to feed him answers."

I stuck my tongue out at him. "I'm just trying to do what Aunt Nora asked."

"I thought she asked you to talk to him."

"If she knew what we'd talked about, she'd ask me to help him find a job, too."

"My wife reads minds."

I stuck my tongue out at him again.

"So, what career have you chosen?"

"I'm not going to tell you," I said with as much dignity as I could scrape up. Which wasn't much, since I couldn't resist sticking out my tongue one more time. When he tickled me in response, we lost track of what we'd been talking about anyway. We only quit when Aunt Maggie banged on the wall and told us to hush up and go to sleep.

I could tell something was wrong when I woke up the next morning, but it took me a while to figure out what it was. Then it hit me. I actually felt rested for the first time in days. When I looked at the clock, I saw that we'd slept for ten hours.

Without waking Richard, I went downstairs to make sure everything was okay. Not that I really thought that somebody had come in and attacked Aunt Maggie in her sleep, but Aunt Nora's worrying was contagious.

I could have stayed in bed. Aunt Maggie was in the basement sticking price tags on plates.

"Good morning," I said.

"Just barely," she said. "I thought you two were going to sleep all day."

"We had some catching up to do. You've been keeping us pretty busy." I'd had no idea how much work Aunt Maggie's business entailed. She worked much longer hours than I did.

"I was just kidding, Laurie Anne. If I hadn't wanted y'all to sleep, I'd have made enough noise to wake y'all up."

"What's the plan for today? Didn't you have a sale in your date book?"

"Nope, it's next week."

"Are we going to hit the thrift stores?"

"No reason to. They won't restock until Wednesday night. You and Richard have the day off, unless there's something dealing with Carney you want to take care of."

"Nothing that I can think of," I admitted. "That reminds me, have you heard anything about Mary Maude?"

"I called the hospital, and they said she's going to have to stay there a day or two; but they don't think she suffered any permanent damage. I guess it would take more than cast iron to bust through her thick skull."

"Did she identify her attacker?"

"I didn't ask. I was talking to a nurse, and I didn't think she'd know anything about it."

"Then I'll give Trey Norton a call." A few minutes later, I reported back. "She doesn't remember a thing."

"Is he sure she's not faking so she won't have to explain what she was doing in my booth?"

"Knowing Mary Maude, I wouldn't put it past her, but Trey says it's normal for her not to remember. Apparently people who are hit hard enough to lose consciousness usually forget the events just beforehand. The last thing Mary Maude remembers is driving to the flea market."

"What about Mavis? Did she not see anything?"

"Just you and Richard. Trey didn't say so outright, but I think she wanted to pin it on us. Fortunately, since you were with her, and I was with Bender, we all have alibis."

"If I wanted to try to knock some sense into Mary Maude Foy's head, I'd have done it long before now." Then she said, "Looky here!"

"What?" I said. Since we'd been talking about the attack on Mary Maude, I thought she'd found something to do with that, but she was holding a ratty red felt pennant with the words "Byerly Bobbins" in white letters.

"Who are the Byerly Bobbins?" The Byerly high school team is the Bobcats, not the Bobbins.

"The Bobbins were the Walters Mill baseball team, back when there was a textile league," she said.

"Don't they still play ball?"

"They've got a softball team, but it's not the same. Back then, we had real baseball players playing for the mill. Some of them were players hoping to get good enough for the major leagues, and some knew they'd never make it to the majors, but they all played a sight better than the boys around here. Big Bill would give them cushy jobs at the mill, but they were really only hired to play ball. There was a catcher named Pudd'nhead Wilson . . . " Her voice faded away, and and she stared into the distance.

"Pudd'nhead Wilson?" I said. "Like in the Mark Twain book?"

"His name wasn't really Pudd'nhead," Aunt Maggie said, still with that faraway look. "It was a nickname. Ballplayers had to have nicknames. I can see him now, prancing out onto the field at the beginning of the game like he was something special. He told me he always felt that way when he stepped onto a ball field. I always wanted to see him play in one of the big ball parks up North, but I never got the chance."

"Aunt Maggie, were you sweet on Pudd'nhead?"

"Maybe I was and maybe I wasn't," she said with a grin.

She clearly had stories I'd never heard. I was tempted to ask her for more, but I remembered another story she hadn't told me, one that was more important right then. Like why she was so set on our finding Carney's murderer. I'd been waiting for her to volunteer the information, but it didn't look like she ever would. So I started, "Aunt Maggie—"

Then she said the one thing that was guaranteed to distract me. "By the way, Vasti called a while ago. She's working on Augustus's party and wanted to know what you and Richard are up to."

"What did you tell her?" I wanted Augustus to have a nice party, but not if I had to spend the day running errands for Vasti.

"That you two were still asleep and I didn't know what y'all had planned. She said she was going to be out anyway and she might stop by."

"How long ago did she call?"

"About half an hour ago."

"Good." Vasti lived about ten minutes away, and it normally took her nearly an hour to get ready to go anywhere, which meant that Richard and I had just enough time to get away. "Aunt Maggie, can we borrow your car?"

"I was going to go to the grocery store, but I guess it can wait."

"Thank you!" I said as I ran up the stairs.

Forty minutes later, Richard and I got the car keys from Aunt Maggie on our way out the door.

"Do you want me to tell Vasti where you're going to be?" she asked.

"You are kidding, aren't you?" I said.

She just grinned.

It turned out to be as busy a day as it would have been if Vasti had caught us, but a lot more pleasant. Our first stop was Aunt Nora's house. I knew she'd be happy to feed us the breakfast we'd been in too much of a hurry to eat at Aunt Maggie's. Next we went to see Aunt Nellie and Uncle Ruben and heard about the failed video store. Then came Aunt Edna, who raved about her trip to Charlotte and about how wonderful Caleb was. We met Aunt Daphine for lunch, and she told us what she knew of Vasti's schedule to make sure we didn't run into her accidentally.

After lunch, we went to Linwood and Sue's house. Linwood was at work, but we spent some time with Sue and the kids: Tiffany, Jason, Crystal, and Amber. It was hot by then, so we adults took turns sticking our feet into the kids' swimming pool while the kids splashed around.

Sue told us that Aunt Ruby Lee and Uncle Roger were back, so our next stop was their place. Clifford, Earl, and Ilene were in the middle of rehearsing, and I couldn't believe how good they sounded. I told Uncle Roger that those three were going to be giving his Ramblers a run for their money.

We hightailed it out of there when we found out that Vasti was on her way to tell the kids what she wanted them to play at Augustus's party. By then it was nearly five, and we figured we'd be safe at Aunt Maggie's house. As far as I could tell, Aunt Maggie hadn't left the basement, though

I supposed she must have gone to the bathroom. She said she didn't have any plans that night, so we could keep the car if we wanted to.

Richard and I got bottles of Coke and went to the living room to relax. At least I wanted to relax, but my mind kept wandering back to Carney's murder. As usual, Richard could tell.

"Are you brooding?" Richard asked.

I nodded. "What happened to Mary Maude yesterday has got me rattled. How many more people are going to get hurt while we putter around?"

"You call this puttering? We've hardly had a minute to ourselves since we've been in town. Even the police are entitled to time off." He leaned over to nuzzle my neck. "I know some wonderful ways to spend time off."

I tried to nuzzle back, but my heart wasn't in it. "I'm sorry," I finally said. "I'm too distracted."

"Okay," he said with a heavy sigh. "What do you want to do?"

Unfortunately, I was fresh out of ideas. "Let's look at our suspects again. We've got Tattoo Bob, Obed, China, J.B., Tammy, Mary Maude, Mavis, Bender, and Evan. At least, those are the ones we know about."

"Let's not add to the list if we don't have to."

"We can eliminate Mary Maude because there's no way she could have faked that attack. Mavis was outside with you and Aunt Maggie, so she's in the clear, too."

"Bender was with you, so that eliminates him."

"Right. After what J.B. said Sunday night, I don't think it was him or Tammy."

"If our suspects knew that threatening you was a way to establish their innocence, we'd be in serious trouble."

I ignored him. "That leaves Tattoo Bob, Obed, China, and Evan."

"Did Evan have a motive?"

"Not that we know of," I said, "but he had access to the flea market, and he'd have known that Rusty was going to be at the vet's the morning Carney was killed."

"What about Rusty? He had access, and Bender will vouch for him being smart enough."

"Richard!"

"First he snuck out of the vet's. Opening a door would be hard without opposable thumbs, but I'm sure he could have managed it. Then he held the knife in his mouth to stab Carney. It would have been easier to bite him, but he was trying to throw off our suspicions."

"How did he move the car?"

"He drove it, of course. He's got a license—I've seen it on his collar."

"That's a dog license."

"You're right. Add unlawful use of a vehicle to his list of crimes."

"You're overlooking something. Actually, you're overlooking lots of things, but you knew that."

"Mere details to a mastermind like Rusty."

"Except that he was with me and Bender when Mary Maude was attacked."

"You're right! You know what that means?"

"I'm afraid to ask."

"Somebody is trying to frame Rusty!"

The only logical answer to that was a tickle fight, with no holds barred. This time, Aunt Maggie didn't interrupt, so it went on until we were both exhausted and claiming victory.

I know Richard had intended to get my mind off of Carney, but it didn't work for long. After I got my breath back, I said, "What did Sherlock Holmes say about a dog not barking?" I knew he'd remember the quote.

Richard said, " ' "Is there any point to which you would wish to draw my attention?" "To the curious incident of the dog in the nighttime." "The dog did nothing in the nighttime." "That was the curious incident," remarked Sherlock Holmes.' "

"Change that to the curious incident of the dog in the daytime. Carney told me that I didn't have to let him know we were at the flea market because Rusty doesn't fuss if it's somebody he knows. So the person who hit Mary Maude must have been somebody Rusty knows."

"Of course Rusty knows him. We already knew it was somebody at the flea market."

"No, we didn't. We were just making assumptions, most of which are based on things Aunt Maggie told us. This is our first outside confirmation that Carney was killed by an insider."

Richard nodded, but I could tell he didn't think it was that big a deal.

"Okay, maybe it doesn't make a lot of difference. It's just that so much of what we've got is based on Aunt Maggie's insisting that it was an insider, but she won't tell us why she's so sure. Besides which, she admits that she doesn't know that much about these people. Aunt Nora would have known a lot more."

"Probably more than we needed to know," Richard said.

"I still wish we had more information. None of my family other than Aunt Maggie hangs around Tight as a Tick, and I don't think any of my old friends go out there either." That reminded me of something. "Didn't you say you saw your friend Vivian at China's booth Sunday? Do you think she spends a lot of time out there?"

"I heard her call China by her first name, and she said something about seeing her in a couple of weeks."

"Perfect! If she knows China, she might know some of the other dealers. You don't know her phone number, do you?"

"I don't even know her last name."

"Rats!" But then I remembered where he'd met her. "What about the V.F.W.? Doesn't she hang out there? Do you suppose it's open tonight?"

"Probably," Richard said, with a certain lack of enthusiasm.

"Great! Since Aunt Maggie doesn't have anything for us to do tonight, you can go over there after dinner and see what you can find out from her."

"I can?"

That sounded odd, so I said, "Would you rather I come with you? I thought that since you know Vivian, it would be better for you to talk to her alone."

"I'm so glad you've thought it all out."

This time I couldn't miss the sarcasm. "What's wrong?"

"Not a thing. Just because I've spent every minute either working at the flea market or visiting your family, there's no reason to think that I might want to relax for one evening. I love spending my vacation rounding up suspects."

"You said you wanted to help Aunt Maggie."

"Why not? We may as well do something while we're stuck in Byerly."

"That's not fair!" I said, stung. "You said you wanted to stay until Augustus's party."

"What was I supposed to say, Laura? With you looking at me like that, and Aunt Nora crying. Schopenhauer was right. 'To marry is to halve your rights and double your duties.' "

"Richard!"

"Don't I get a little time off? Maybe I'd like to decide for myself what I want to do."

"Fine!" I snapped. "Go ahead and do whatever you want."

"Thank you so much. If you don't need the car to chase suspects, I'd like to use it."

"What about supper?"

"I think I can manage alone."

"Fine!" I said, too mad to care that I was repeating myself. He stormed out and I stomped up the stairs.

I stayed furious for about ten minutes. After all, I decided, he had no business complaining when he'd agreed to what we were doing every step of the way.

Then I spent ten minutes feeling like there might be some justification for him being angry, but that he shouldn't have been so nasty about it. Okay, our vacation hadn't been what we planned, but I was missing out as much as he was. If it seemed like I was ordering him around, it was only because I wanted to find Carney's killer quickly.

Somewhere during the next ten minutes, I realized that the real reason I was so mad was that I felt guilty. Maybe Richard had agreed to spend the week in Byerly and help Aunt Maggie, but like he'd said, it would have been hard for him to refuse.

By the time Richard had been gone an hour, I was wishing I knew where he'd gone so I could find him and apologize for everything, especially being so pushy. Maybe I'd been spending too much time with Aunt Maggie. She can be awfully determined when her mind is set on something, and her mind was definitely set on finding Carney Alexander's killer. Why on earth did she care so much?

That's when I decided that I was going to get a straight answer out of her. Richard deserved to know why it was he was spending his vacation following her around, and so did I.

Chapter 34

Of course, I couldn't just ask her. I had to work my way up to it, and what better time to get Aunt Maggie talking than over something to eat. So I went downstairs and said, "Are you about ready to get some supper?"

"I suppose so," she said, standing and stretching. "What do you and Richard have in mind?"

"Richard went out," I said. "He had some errands to run."

"Oh," was all she said, but I wondered how much of our fight she'd heard. "Since I didn't make it to the store, there's not much here to eat. Do you want to order a pizza?"

"That sounds good."

We went back upstairs to find the menu for Domino's, and called for a pepperoni pizza. I stalled while we were waiting by telling Aunt Maggie the family news I'd gathered while hiding from Vasti. Aunt Maggie hadn't always been interested in all our carryings on. She'd never been married, and didn't seem to mind that most of her family was distant relatives. Then Paw died, and she'd taken his place as head of the family as best she could. I think it was for her sake as much as for ours.

Then the pizza arrived. I didn't want to bring up an

unpleasant subject while we were eating, so I told her stories about Boston. But the pizza didn't last forever, and by the time we'd had three pieces each, Aunt Maggie was starting to look like she wanted to get back to her treasures downstairs.

I took a deep breath and said, "Aunt Maggie, there's something I've been wanting to talk to you about. You know Richard and I are committed to finding out who killed Carney. You asked us to, and there's no way we'd quit after what happened to Mary Maude, but it seems to me that you haven't been completely honest with us."

"I've told you everything I know about the other dealers."

"Everything except why it is you wanted us to start snooping around in the first place." I rushed on before she could argue. "I know you said you're nervous about having a killer on the loose, but there's more to it than that. I don't think it's asking too much for me to want to know what it is."

She didn't say anything for a long time, and I was sure that she was mad at me. The only question in my mind was how mad—mad enough to fuss or mad enough to kick me and Richard out of the house? But when she spoke, she didn't sound mad at all.

"You're right, Laurie Anne. I do have another reason for wanting you to catch Carney's killer. The fact is, I owe it to Carney. I helped that killer stab him in the back just the same as if I'd handed him the knife."

I didn't know what she meant, so I just waited for her to go on.

She said, "A couple of months ago, Carney was running late and I was running early, so I got to the flea market first and parked in that spot he always took. I didn't mean anything by it—it was just the closest spot, and I had some boxes to bring in. About fifteen minutes after I got there, Carney came inside, white as a sheet and sweating like a pig. I thought he was going to pass out right there on the floor, so I went to see what the matter was.

"He looked at me, and in this tiny voice said, 'Miz Burnette, would you mind changing parking places with me?' Of course I asked him why, and he told me he had agoraphobia."

"Fear of heights?"

"That's acrophobia. Agoraphobia is the fear of open spaces. For Carney to get inside after having to park those extra few feet away from the door nigh about killed him."

"How did he live that way?" I asked.

"I guess you can work around most anything if you have to. Carney said he was okay in his van, because it felt like he was inside. When he got home, he parked in a garage that had stairs to his apartment. He got a lot of his stock through the mail and had his point men to scrounge for him, so he could run his business, and he lived with his sister, who ran errands for him. If he absolutely had to go somewhere other than home or the flea market, she'd drive him there and let him off right at the door, and he could generally manage to get inside. But for him to stay outside more than just a second or two would bring on panic attacks. That's what happened that morning. He said it wasn't even a bad one."

"That's awful." Though I hadn't heard much good about Carney, he hadn't deserved that. "Couldn't he get therapy or something?"

"I didn't ask him, Laurie Anne. It was plain that it wasn't something he liked to talk about. I'd known him for years and never knew before that. I just got his keys and moved my car so I could park his van in his regular spot. He thanked me, but I knew he was ashamed that I'd seen him like that. He never mentioned it again."

"Did anybody else at the flea market know?"

"Not until I opened my big mouth," she said. "About a month after that, Carney pulled another one of his stunts. This lady who sold costume jewelry brought a bunch of kittens to the flea market to give away. She said she already had the legal limit for having cats in Rocky Shoals, so she had to find homes for this litter before anybody noticed.

"It was a big litter, and you know it's hard to find people to take kittens. She brought them out there two or three weekends, but she still had three kittens left the day Carney tried to get her to trade a ring with a skull on it for one of his knives. She didn't want the knife, so she offered him a discount, but Carney got mad and wouldn't take it.

"By the end of the day, she was in tears because the dogcatcher had come by. He'd heard about her having more cats than she was supposed to, and said she better find homes for them that day because he was going to inspect her house that night. If there were any extra cats, he was going to take them to the pound, and she was afraid they'd be put to sleep."

"Don't tell me. Carney called the dog catcher."

"Of course he did. You should have seen him grinning when he saw how upset she was. Fortunately, it worked out all right. One of the dealers took one for her daughter, and I got Dr. Josie to take the other two. Her being a veterinarian means that she can have more animals than other people, and the laws in Byerly are different anyway."

"Do you think the cat lady had something to do with Carney's death?" I asked.

"No, she's not selling at Tight as a Tick anymore. She went on the cat show circuit. I only told you about her to explain what comes next. After closing time that day, some of us were talking about how mean Carney was, and how we ought to teach him a lesson. One fellow wanted to let the air out of his tires, and one woman wanted to see if we could put together a petition to get him thrown out of the flea market. I said that all we had to do was take him out to the middle of the parking lot and leave him there. Of course, then I had to explain why.

"Everybody jumped on the idea, not meaning to really do it, of course. We just liked knowing his weak spot." She paused. "The same way Carney liked knowing ours. Maybe he wasn't that much worse than the rest of us after all."

"None of y'all used the information to hurt him," I pointed out.

"Maybe somebody did," she said softly. "You asked why Carney didn't run away when he was attacked, why he tried to get into his van instead. It's because the killer was between him and the door to the building. He couldn't get inside, and the door to his van was locked, but Carney was so afraid of being in the open that he *couldn't* run away. Here he was being stabbed, and all he could do was try and try to get into that van."

"Oh, Lord," I said. I'd known that Carney had had a hard death, but it was even worse than I'd realized.

Aunt Maggie said, "Anybody else would have run, so for the plan to work, the killer had to have known about Carney's agoraphobia. That means that I'm the one who told him how to kill Carney."

"You don't know that for sure. Maybe the killer found out some other way."

"How? I knew Carney as well as anybody out there, but I didn't know it until recently. There wasn't anybody else out there he'd have told."

I hated to admit it, but it sounded like she was right. "Who did you tell? That should limit the possibilities."

"I don't remember who was there, but it doesn't matter anyway. That was on a Saturday, and by noon on Sunday, there wasn't a dealer out there who hadn't heard. A couple of people made cracks where Carney could hear, and he knew I'd told them about his agoraphobia. If looks could kill, I wouldn't be here now."

"He didn't ask you to keep it a secret, did he?"

"That's not the point, Laurie Anne. I knew he didn't want it spread around. I felt so guilty about it that I didn't blame him for being mad, but that's nothing to what I feel now. It's my fault that he's dead."

"Aunt Maggie, if somebody wanted Carney dead, he'd have found a way."

"He didn't need to find a way—I gave him the way. It wouldn't have been easy to kill Carney anywhere else. With the agoraphobia, he almost never went anyplace but the flea market and home. He might have been safe if I hadn't opened my big mouth. That's why I want you to find out who killed him, Laurie Anne. It won't make things right, because it's too late for that, but it's the best I can do for Carney now."

"Don't you worry," I said. "We'll find out who killed him." I didn't know how, but I wasn't going to let Aunt Maggie down if I could help it.

Chapter 35

Aunt Maggie decided to watch TV after that, but fell asleep during the movie. When it was over, I woke her up, told her how it had ended, and sent her to bed. Then I read while waiting for Richard. It was nearly midnight before he finally came in.

"Hi," I said.

"Hi." He sat down on the couch next to me. "What are you reading?"

"One of Aunt Maggie's historical romances," I said, showing him the cover with its flame-haired heroine and her heaving bosom.

"Any good?"

"Not really. The heroine expects her beloved to drop everything to defend her family's honor, and can't understand it when he wants a little time alone with her. Totally unrealistic! Who'd be dumb enough to treat a handsome, brilliant, sexy man that way?"

"Sounds like quite a hero," he said with a smile.

"He's amazing," I said. "I don't know why he puts up with her."

"She must be beautiful, brilliant, and sexy herself."

I borrowed a page from the book and threw my arms

around him to give him the steamiest kiss I could manage. From the length of time it took, I'd say it was a success.

After that kiss, and several more, I said, "I'm sorry, Richard. I've been a royal pain."

"I'm the one who should apologize. If I don't like the way we're spending our vacation, I've got no one to blame but myself."

"No, it's my fault. You only agreed to help because it's my family."

"*Our* family," he corrected me. "Shakespeare said it better, but the fact is, they treat me like one of their own. I owe them nothing less in return."

"You're the best, Richard."

"You deserve the best."

"I still think I owe you an apology."

"I'll accept it, but only if you accept mine."

"Fair enough."

We kissed some more and, after we went upstairs, did quite a few other things. After all, we couldn't let ourselves be outdone by the hero and heroine of Aunt Maggie's book.

As we snuggled afterward, I told Richard what I'd found out from Aunt Maggie. Like me, now that he knew why we were after Carney's killer, he was more determined than ever to finish the job.

Then he said, "Aren't you going to ask where I went? I thought curiosity would be driving you crazy by now."

"You're the only thing driving me crazy."

"You must be a little curious."

"Maybe a little," I admitted.

"I went to the V.F.W."

"I thought you didn't want to."

"After I'd eaten and gone to all three bookstores in Hickory, I was at loose ends anyway. Besides, don't you remember what Trollope said?"

"No, but I have a hunch that you're going to tell me."

" 'Oh husbands, oh, my married friends, what comfort there is to be derived from a wife well obeyed!' "

"What about Emerson? 'I hate quotations, tell me what you know.' "

"Touché. I left that dictionary of quotations here, didn't I?"

"You did," I said smugly. "Was Vivian there?"

"She was," he said. "The bartender told me that Tuesday night is the night she runs a veterans' support group. They were still meeting when I arrived, so I pulled out a copy of Jane Austen's *Persuasion.*"

"An apt title," I said.

"I thought so. After the meeting broke up, Vivian and several men came into the bar. It didn't take long for Vivian to hear the siren call of Miss Austen and come my way."

"You're so seductive when you're reading," I said.

"We talked about literature, Jane Austen movies, unusual editions of Austen books, and then flea markets where I've picked up interesting books."

"I was hoping you got to the flea market eventually."

"These things must be done delicately."

"Is that a quote?"

"The Wicked Witch of the West."

"I hope there was nothing Freudian about that choice," I said, thinking about the way I'd badgered him into going to the V.F.W.

"When I referred to seeing her at Tight as a Tick and asked about China's sachets, Vivian started to get a bit itchy."

"Do I dare make jokes about ticks and fleas?"

"Maybe later. By now I was getting suspicious that she knew something that connected China to Carney's death, particularly when she made excuses about having to leave. I persevered, which considering her combat training, could have been dangerous. But I knew the job was dangerous when I took it."

"Poor Richard," I said. "Reduced to quoting Super Chicken."

He looked forlorn, then manfully strong. "I laid my cards on the table and told her we're trying to find out who killed Carney and that China is a suspect. Of course, I was talking about the way he harassed her and mentioned the possibility that he'd done more than talk, but I could tell from the way Vivian looked at me that I was on the wrong track. When I asked her why she was so worried, she hemmed and hawed, but then swore me to secrecy and told me."

"Well?"

"China Upton, respectable widow, grieving mother, and friend to gingham everywhere, distributes marijuana."

"You're kidding."

He shook his head. "Nope. She sells sachets filled with pot. Home-grown, too."

I started to laugh. "I can't believe China is a pusher."

"She's not exactly a pusher," Richard said, his voice serious. "Do you remember how her son died?"

"J.B. said it was AIDS."

"That's why she started growing pot. It's one of the few things that can help AIDS patients."

I stopped laughing.

Richard said, "Vivian told me that AIDS is one of the

reasons California made it legal for medical practitioners to dispense pot."

"There's no law like that in North Carolina."

"That's right. Stan Junior used to grow his own, but after he got too sick, China took over. As time went on and they met other AIDS patients, she started supplying pot to them, too. When word got around certain circles, others came to her."

"She must make more money from that than from stuffed geese."

"Vivian said she barely meets expenses. She does it in remembrance of her son."

"How did Vivian get involved?"

"There are several vets in her support group who rely on pot when their dreams get bad, so she keeps some around for them. You can see why she swore me to secrecy. If Junior were to find out—"

"Junior would understand," I said, but then I wasn't sure. Though Junior turns a blind eye on some things, there's a line she won't cross. I didn't know which side of that line China's and Vivian's activities would fall on. "Did Carney find out?"

"Vivian doesn't know. She knew him, but only as someone not to buy knives from."

Then I remembered something Aunt Maggie had said. "Potpourri," I said, mispronouncing the first syllable to rhyme with spot. "That's what Carney called China's sachets. He knew all right!"

"That means she had a motive to kill him."

I nodded. As soon as possible we were going to have to have a talk with China Upton to find out if she could handle a knife as well as she did sewing scissors.

Chapter 36

Aunt Maggie wanted to go to an auction the next day, which meant that Richard and I needed a car and somebody to watch Aunt Maggie. A call to Aunt Nora took care of both problems. She sent Augustus over with her car, and Augustus casually mentioned that he didn't have plans. When Aunt Maggie said he could come with her as long as he helped out, he winked at me behind her back.

China Upton was listed in the Rocky Shoals section of the phone book under Stanley Upton, which reminded me that she was a widow and did wonders for my morale. Then I thought of the man who killed his parents and asked for leniency because he was an orphan. If China had stabbed Carney, widow or not, she deserved to be caught.

China's house was a cute little place, with brightly painted shutters and petunias growing in the yard. I felt like we were about to interrogate the Easter Bunny.

"I'm out here," China called out when we rang the bell, and we followed her voice around to the backyard. The yard was surrounded by a white picket fence, freshly painted, of course, and when we opened the gate, we saw China kneeling by a flower bed. The place looked like something out of a home gardening magazine. There were rows of gorgeous flowers and plants I supposed were herbs, and even I could tell they were healthy and well-tended. In the back corner was a greenhouse, filled with more color. There was even a scarecrow wearing a gingham dress, a straw bonnet, and plenty of ribbons that blew in the breeze.

"What a nice surprise," China said as she stood up. "Did y'all come by to get those seed catalogs?"

I said, "Actually, we wanted to talk to you, if you've got a few minutes."

"Why don't y'all come inside and have a glass of lemonade. That sun's getting awfully hot." She pulled off her gloves and led us through the back door. "Of course, I can't complain about the weather. It's been one of the best growing seasons I've ever had."

The kitchen wasn't as bad as I'd expected. There were plenty of ruffles and ribbon, but the room was cozy without being overpowering. China kept on talking about the weather and her garden as she sat us down in the breakfast nook and poured tall glasses of cold lemonade.

"I made the lemonade this morning," she said. "Is it sweet enough? I was just about out of sugar, and I was afraid it would be too sour to drink."

Richard and I took sips. "It's wonderful," I said, wishing it had been sour. Anything to make me feel less guilty.

"What can I do for y'all?" she asked. "If it's gardening advice you want, I can give you more than you'd ever need."

"Actually, it does kind of have to do with gardening." I looked out the window. I'd seen marijuana growing once or twice, but there was nothing like that in her yard. "That's a nice greenhouse," I said.

"Stan Senior built it for me. I hated waiting for spring to grow things. This way I can plant in the winter, too."

"Is that where you grow marijuana?"

She didn't answer, and when I looked at her, she hadn't lost her smile, but she was very still, like she was afraid moving would bring down disaster. Finally, she said, "That's where I grow it. I don't care if it is illegal. Stan Junior needed it to help him through his bad spells, and him using it didn't hurt a soul. I don't imagine my neighbors would know marijuana if they saw it, but I thought it best to be careful." She hesitated. "Are you going to tell the police?"

I wanted to tell her that we wouldn't, but I couldn't yet. "Did Carney know about your special sachets?"

"Yes, he knew. You see, I put the pot in sachets to make it easier to give to people. Nobody thinks twice if they see me selling sachets, but they might wonder if they saw me slipping people plastic bags under the table. Of course, I don't sew them all that well, not when the boys are going to rip them open as soon as they get home. I just use a basting stitch, which usually holds, but one got caught on a nail one day, and out came the pot. I tried to sweep it all up before anybody could see, but Carney picked that moment to come over, and he knew what it was right away."

"Did he blackmail you?"

She nodded. "He insisted I come over to his apartment that night. I went, and tried to explain about Stan Junior and the other boys, but Carney didn't care. He threatened to call the police if I didn't start . . . start seeing him."

She blushed, and I knew just what "seeing him" meant. "Did you?"

"Of course not! I'd rather have gone to jail."

"But he didn't turn you in."

"When he realized he couldn't get what he wanted, he

came up with another idea. He wanted free sachets, one every weekend. And he wasn't even sick!"

China was so indignant it was almost funny. "Then what?"

She looked surprised that I was asking. "I gave him the sachets. He'd flirted with me before, so nobody was surprised when he came by every weekend. I hated having to do it, especially when he teased me with that silly mispronunciation of potpourri, but so many boys depend on those sachets. Stan Junior would have wanted me to help them, just like I did him. After a while, I knew Carney wouldn't turn me in because he was breaking the law, too. I thought about telling him that to make him leave me alone, but it was easier to keep giving him the sachets. With him gone, it's not a problem anymore." She stopped, then cocked her head. "Y'all don't think I had anything to do with his death, do you?"

Richard and I looked at each other; then we both looked down at our hands. "Not really," I said.

Darned if she didn't start laughing. "You did! You two thought I was a murderess."

"They say that anybody is capable of murder given the right circumstances," I said hurriedly. "Aunt Maggie has told us how Carney pestered you, and we know how he liked his little power trips. It seemed like he could have pushed you too far."

She was still laughing, and I wasn't sure if that was a good sign or not.

"We're sorry if we've upset you," Richard said.

"Upset me?" she said. "I'm flattered. Most people don't take me very seriously, but here you thought I could stab a man to death. I shouldn't laugh, not when Carney is dead, but you've tickled my funny bone. Me, a murder suspect. Neither Mark Pope or Belva Tucker gave me a moment's thought."

"But they don't know you're a drug pusher," Richard pointed out.

"That's right," she said, dissolving into giggles. "We pushers are dangerous. I may have to rub y'all out for knowing too much."

After that, we didn't bother to ask any more questions about Carney. We finished our lemonade, shared China's giggles, and told her how much we admired what she was doing for AIDS sufferers.

China insisted that we take a big bouquet of fresh flowers with us, which made her the first person who'd ever thanked us for suspecting her of murder.

Chapter 37

"Now what?" I asked Richard as I drove away from China's house.

"Lunch?"

"Why not?"

As we lingered over the remains of two large barbeque platters at Pigwick's, I said, "We've eliminated China from the running, so that still leaves us Tattoo Bob, Evan, and Obed. I don't want to hear anything else about Rusty."

"Agreed. No more shaggy dog stories."

I ignored him. "Unfortunately, Bob's motive is weak, we don't have any motive for Evan, and I still have problems picturing Obed killing Carney the way he was killed."

"We could go talk to one of them."

"Maybe," I said, but I wasn't at all sure of the reception we'd get. Either they'd still be mad at us because they thought we were helping Annabelle Lamar, or, if they'd talked to J.B., they'd know we were investigating Carney's murder. "I wish we could find whatever it is that the murderer was looking for, but it could be anywhere." I looked around the restaurant, thinking of how many places there were to hide things in just one room.

"Wait a minute," Richard said. "If Carney was agoraphobic, there aren't that many places he could have hidden something."

"You're right," I said. "Aunt Maggie said he almost never went anywhere but the flea market and his apartment."

"We know the killer searched the flea market, Carney's van, and probably his apartment. Do you think his sister would suggest any other places?"

"She might with official encouragement."

We paid our bill, which took a while because the owner of Pigwick's was still trying to repay us for a favor we'd done him a while back. We compromised by letting him give us a discount, then headed for the police station.

We were lucky. Trey was on duty, not Mark. I told him what we wanted, and he cheerfully called Carney's sister Sadie on our behalf.

I'd been expecting to have to go see her at work, but Trey said, "You can go over to her house right now. She works at the post office, but she's off today."

Sadie Alexander's house and yard were neat, but businesslike, not at all like China's place. I figured that Sadie either took care of the lawn herself or paid somebody to do it. Surely Carney wouldn't have been able to help.

When we rang the bell, a middle-aged woman in slacks opened the front door, but kept the screen door securely fastened as she looked us up and down. "Yes?"

"Miz Alexander? My name's Laura Fleming and this is my husband Richard. Deputy Norton called and asked if it was all right for us to stop by."

"He said somebody was coming, but that's not the name he gave me."

"Trey probably called me Laurie Anne."

She nodded and opened the screen door. "Come on in."

Just from looking around as Sadie lead us into the living room, I knew one reason she and her brother hadn't gotten along. Aunt Maggie had said Carney kept his booth messy, while Sadie's house was pristine, almost shrink-wrapped. There were plastic runners on the carpet, plastic covers on the couch and chairs, and plastic wrappers on the lamp shades. Even the coffee table had a sheet of lucite on top to make sure nobody ever touched the wood.

"Make yourself comfortable," Sadie said, and Richard and I did the best we could. "Deputy Norton said that y'all were helping the police investigate my brother's death."

That wasn't strictly true, but since Trey had said it, I wasn't about to contradict him. "We're sorry to intrude at a time like this."

"I'm getting used to the idea of Carney being gone." She picked up a framed picture from the coffee table and looked at it critically. "I remember Mama telling him not to play with knives when he was a little boy, but he never listened."

"May I?" I asked, and took it from her. It was the first time I'd seen a picture of Carney, and it seemed odd that I knew so much about him without knowing what he looked like. The picture was a snapshot of a man around forty years old with thinning hair and pale skin who was trying to smile at the camera. Maybe it was because of what I knew about him, but Carney didn't look very happy to me. For the first time, I felt real sympathy for him, not just curiosity about who had killed him.

"Nice-looking man," I said politely.

"He looked a lot like Daddy," Sadie said, and put the picture back exactly where it had been. How she could do that without a dust outline to mark the spot, I didn't know. "What can I do for you?"

"We have a theory we're working with. It's a little unusual, but it seems to fit the facts. We think the person who killed your brother was looking for something. The killer had your brother's van long enough to search it, and his booth out at the flea market could have been searched the day he was killed or during the break-in this past week-end. There was also an incident out there yesterday."

"Belva told me about the break-in, but she said it was a gang of kids, and that they probably killed Carney, too. Today I heard something about a serial killer."

"Deputy Tucker is investigating those theories," I said, trying to sound polite, "but we want to investigate all possi-bilities."

Sadie nodded, so what I said must have made some sense. "What do you think the killer was looking for?" she asked.

"To tell you the truth, we don't know, but after what happened yesterday, we're fairly sure he hasn't found it yet. I was told that when the police examined your brother's apartment, it was messy even though you'd just cleaned it. Do you think that it could have been searched on Sunday? The killer took Mr. Alexander's keys."

Sadie put one hand to her mouth. "I just thought Carney had made a mess. It never occurred to me that it could have been anything else; but I was out of town until Sunday afternoon, so anybody could have gone up there while I was gone. The killer could even have come in here!" She looked around in alarm as if expecting to see traces of an intruder. I didn't think anybody could have set foot in that room without her being able to tell immediately, but I understood how the idea of somebody being in her house would upset her.

"Did Carney have a key to the house?" Richard asked.

She nodded.

"Then, if I were you," he said, "I'd get the locks changed."

"I already did. Deputy Norton suggested it."

Good for Trey. I bet Mark never would have thought of it. "Anyway, we still don't know what the killer was looking for or where it is. Other than his van, the flea market, and his apartment, where would Carney have been likely to hide something?"

"I don't know," she said slowly. "Carney didn't go out much."

"We know about the agoraphobia," Richard said.

"Then you understand that there's no place else he could have hidden anything because there's nowhere else he could have gone," she said. "He used to try to go outside or into a store or over to a friend's house, but it was like he couldn't breathe. Of course, he wasn't always like this or he'd never have been able to finish school. It came on after his wife left him, right after he was laid off. Or maybe it was when Mama and Daddy died. It all happened in there together, which may be the problem. I've read that stress can bring on agoraphobia.

"Once he got it, he never could shake it. I imagine it's been three years or more since he even tried to go out. The last place he added was Tight as a Tick, and if his booth hadn't been inside, he'd never have been able to do it. Are you sure it's not somewhere out there?"

"Pretty sure," I said. "The killer searched, and then Thatcher looked at everything when he bought Carney's stock. There's nowhere in the booth itself to hide anything—the floor is concrete, and the walls are made of cinder blocks."

"Then I don't know where else to look. You could check his apartment, but it sounds like the killer looked there. I've cleaned in there many times, and I never saw anything unusual."

"Tell me, how does someone survive with agoraphobia that severe?" Richard said. "Mr. Alexander couldn't get a job, could he?"

"No, but he had money from our parents. They had a big insurance policy because our cousin sold insurance, so we both inherited a good amount. I used mine to buy this house, and Carney put his away and lived on the interest and what he made with his knives."

"How did he eat, buy clothes, get his van serviced?"

"I did what I could, and anything I couldn't do, Carney paid somebody else to do or did it by mail. You'd be surprised at how many catalogs there are. He bought knives and most of his clothes and just about anything you can think of by mail. Since I work at the post office, he didn't even have to go out to buy stamps."

"By mail?" I said slowly, thinking. "Could he have hidden something in the mail? He could have mailed it to himself, or mailed it to somebody else to mail back to him."

"He did ask me to mail a bunch of envelopes the Friday before he was killed," she said.

"Has he gotten any mail since he died?"

"Lots of it. He was always getting packages and catalogs and such. I haven't even had a chance to look at it yet."

"Would you mind taking a look at it now?" I asked.

"Of course not. Come on into the kitchen."

The kitchen wasn't quite so perfect as the living room. I even saw a stain on the counter.

"I've got it all right here," Sadie said, putting a plastic post office bin on the counter. "Let's see what we've got."

Sadie's time at the post office had paid off. She sorted

that mail much faster than I could have, and in just a few minutes got it down to three manila envelopes. "This one is from a knife collector friend of Carney's in Wilmington, this one is from a cousin, and I don't know this return address."

She opened the envelope from the address she didn't recognize, pulled out a magazine, and blushed. "So that's where he got those things," she muttered, and shoved it back into the envelope.

Then she opened the envelope from the cousin, but after a minute, she shook her head. "Just some clippings from the classifieds in Wilmington from people with knives for sale."

She opened the last envelope, slid out a note and a smaller envelope, and read the note aloud. "Carney, here's your envelope back with the stamps cancelled. Hope your sister is enjoying her stamp collection—my mother has collected for years and has a real good time with them." She looked up at us. "I don't collect stamps."

It was hard not to grab the sealed envelope from her, but I managed to wait as she opened it and pulled out an old piece of paper that had been folded several times over. "It's a map," she said, and spread it over the counter.

I recognized the outlines of Byerly and Rocky Shoals even before I saw the title on top.

"A treasure map?" Richard said, only half joking.

We all looked to see if any location was marked, or if there were any directions scribbled on it. We even checked the back. Nothing.

"Carney certainly didn't need a map," Sadie said. "The only place he ever drove to was Tight as a Tick."

"Which is right there," I said, pointing to an area that straddled the town line. That's when I realized what we had. "I'll be darned. I think this is the map they've been looking for, the original one that shows where the town line is." Sure enough, the border between the two towns was plainly marked with surveyor's marks.

How had Carney ended up with it? It had to be what the killer was looking for, but why was it worth killing for?

Chapter 38

"This is very interesting," Mark Pope said, but I could tell he wasn't at all interested. Richard and I had talked Sadie into letting us take the map to the Byerly Police Station, and even though we'd explained how we'd found it, Mark still asked, "But why do you think this map has something to do with Carney Alexander's murder?"

I explained Richard's and my reasoning, and it did sound a little specious, but Junior would have believed me, and I told Mark so. That was a mistake.

"I'd never contradict my superior," Mark said, "but she left me in charge, which means that I have to rely on my own experience. In my experience, hidden maps don't have anything to do with police cases except in Hardy Boys books." He had the gall to smile at us. "I am curious as to why you've been involving yourself in this case after I asked you not to."

I didn't want to tell him that Junior wanted me to, or that Aunt Maggie didn't think he was up to the job, so that didn't leave me much in the way of explanations. "Let's just say I'm a concerned citizen."

"Uh huh," he said in a tone that made it clear just what kind of citizen he thought I was. "Then let's say that I appreciate your concern and I'll be sure to take note of this important information."

"Don't you want to keep the map?"

"That's all right. I'll let you know if I need it."

Trey looked embarrassed, but there was nothing he could do. There was nothing I could do either, except to try to hold on to my temper until I got back out to the car.

"What an idiot!" I said as soon as I slammed the car door shut. "He hasn't got enough brains to direct traffic, let alone run a murder investigation." I gunned the motor and screeched out of the parking place.

"You're absolutely right," Richard said. "Watch out for that telephone pole."

"I should have known better than to try to talk to him, but I told Junior I would," I said, jerking into traffic.

"I'm sure she'll appreciate it. That's a stop sign."

I braked sharply. "She better. I don't take that kind of abuse from anybody."

"Unless they're related. That car is turning—you might want to slow down." Then he asked, "Would you rather I drive?"

"Sorry." I made an effort to slow down to something resembling the speed limit. "The last thing I want is for that nitwit to have an excuse to give us a ticket."

I continued to rant about Mark's lack of intelligence, manners, and physical charms for the rest of the drive to Aunt Maggie's house. Of course, I was as mad at myself as I was at Mark, and Richard knew it. Partially it was because I hadn't found a way to convince Mark we were right, but mostly because the map was a dead end. I'd thought that once we found what the killer wanted, we'd know who he was. As it was, all we had were more questions and no idea of where to go to ask them.

That's what I told Aunt Maggie and Augustus when I found them eating a late lunch at her house. I finished with, "I know the city council wants this map to establish the town line, but why would anybody kill for it?"

"Are you sure there's not something else written on it?" Augustus said.

"We didn't find anything," I said, but I spread it out for us all to take another look. Aunt Maggie pulled out the magnifying glass she uses to check for trademarks, and we went over every inch, back and front. We even held it up to a lightbulb to see if something had been written in invisible ink. Mark Pope would have been sure we'd been reading Hardy Boys mysteries if he'd seen that, but I wouldn't have minded his jokes if we'd found something. We didn't.

Richard said, "If Carney was running true to form, he would either have been using this map for blackmail or for revenge. Our remaining suspects are Evan, Obed, and Tattoo Bob. Aunt Maggie, do you know how any of those three would be harmed by this map being found?"

"Certainly not Evan. He wants it found so he can sell the land," Aunt Maggie said.

"Maybe Carney told him he'd hidden it and wouldn't give it to him unless Evan did something for him," Richard said.

"That dog won't hunt," Aunt Maggie said. "Evan would have called the police and told them. It's public property so Carney would have had to give it up."

That was another mark against Mark, come to think of it. Even if he didn't think the map had anything to do with Carney's death, he should have realized its importance to Byerly. I said, "Whether Evan knew it or not, with his agoraphobia, Carney would never have risked being arrested. Besides, killing Carney meant that the map might never be found, which is the last thing Evan would want."

"How about this?" Richard suggested. "Carney knew that if the map were found, Evan would sell the flea market, ruining Carney's only way of making a living."

"Nope," Aunt Maggie said. "Evan told us a while ago that he has another lot for us to use. He'll never shut down Tight as a Tick as long as he can make money off of it."

"Wouldn't it have been hard for Carney to move?" I asked.

"He could have paid Thatcher and the other point men to move his things," Aunt Maggie said. "As long as his new booth was close to a door, I think he'd have been all right."

"What about Obed?" I asked.

"What about him? It would have been easy for him to move to another lot—his booth is on wheels."

"Does he have property near there?" Richard asked. "Maybe he didn't want Arthur building a car dealership next door."

"I've never heard him mention owning land, but even if he did, I can't see him killing over it."

"Tattoo Bob?" I said. "Maybe the zoning regulations at the new location won't let him do tattoos there."

"Laurie Anne, I think you're grabbing at straws," Aunt Maggie said.

"I know," I said, and Richard reached over to rub my shoulders. "It's just that I'm sure this map is important, but I don't know why."

"Ask Arthur," Augustus said. "He's been hunting for it high and low, so he might know something."

"That's not a bad idea. He should still be at work." I

reached for Aunt Maggie's phone book to get the number of the dealership.

"Why don't you use that pager Vasti's been making him carry?" Augustus said with a snicker.

"A pager?" I asked.

Aunt Maggie rolled her eyes. "So she can get him at any time of the day. I told her that people have been having babies without pagers since Adam and Eve, but she won't listen."

Aunt Maggie said that by dialing the number she gave me, Arthur's pager would beep and flash Aunt Maggie's number. I tried it, and a few minutes later, the phone rang.

"Is Vasti there?" Arthur asked, sounding tired.

"Not this time. I want to talk to you about some city council business, if you've got a minute."

"You bet," he said, sounding considerably less tired. "It's quiet around here, anyway. Why don't I come on over to Aunt Maggie's?"

"That would be great," I said, and hung up. "He's on his way."

"I'll let you handle him," Aunt Maggie said. "I want to ride over to the flea market and drop off the stuff I bought today. The basement is full, and I need the space in the car because there's another auction tomorrow night."

Richard, Augustus, and I exchanged glances.

"You want me to come with you, Aunt Maggie?" Augustus said.

"I thought you said you had to get Nora's car back to her," she said.

"She won't care if I'm late. In fact, I think she'd pass out on the floor if I showed up on time."

Aunt Maggie shrugged, and Augustus winked at me again. Clearly, my cousin was on the mend.

Arthur got there a few minutes after they left, and after the preliminaries of getting something to drink, deciding to sit at the kitchen table instead of in the living room, and talking about how hot it was, he asked, "What can I do for you, Laurie Anne?"

"Actually, I think I can do something for you." I spread the map out in front of him with a flourish. "Is this what you've been looking for?"

He looked at it, and did a double-take. Then he took the magnifying glass Richard had ready and took a closer look. "Damn! It's genuine and it's dated *before* the Rocky Shoals map! Where did you find it? Vasti said you were up to something, but I didn't know you were looking for the map."

"We weren't," I said, and explained how we'd ended up with it. "I know you'll want to get this to City Hall, but before you do, do you know why anybody would want to prevent Evan Cawthorne from selling the Tight as a Tick lot?"

"Not as far as I know."

"What about the neighbors?" Richard said. "Would any of them mind having a car lot next door?"

"They'd rather have that than a flea market. They're expecting the value of their land to go up."

"What about zoning? Could they prevent Tattoo Bob from running his business in another location?" Like Aunt Maggie had said, I was grasping at straws, but straws were all I had left.

"No, zoning isn't a problem," Arthur said. "In fact, I've already started the paperwork to change the Byerly side from residential to business. Once Evan gets the taxes squared away, and we agree on a price, we're all set. I sure do appreciate your finding this map. I just wish it was helping you with your problem as much as it's going to help me with mine."

"I do, too," I said. I was so busy feeling disgusted that I missed something he'd said.

It was Richard who asked, "What about taxes?"

"Evan has to pay back taxes before he can sell the property," Arthur explained. "With the town line in dispute, neither Byerly or Rocky Shoals could collect, so he owes for quite a few years."

"You mean he's never paid taxes on that property?" I said.

"Not a penny. There was no way to figure out how much he owed each town, and our tax rates are different, so he was given a special extension until the town line is settled."

"Didn't he have to pay estimated taxes or put money in escrow?" Richard asked.

"No, and I'm surprised Big Bill let him get away with it. Evan must have done him a big favor. Big Bill even arranged the same deal with Rocky Shoals."

"How long has it been since Evan paid taxes?" I asked.

"He never has," Arthur said. "Byerly and Rocky Shoals didn't start collecting property taxes until 1964, and that was a couple of years after he got the land."

"How much money are we talking about?"

"I'm not sure," Arthur said slowly. Like any good car salesman, he always carries a calculator, so he pulled it out. "From this map, it looks like about sixty percent of Evan's lot is in Byerly and forty percent is in Rocky Shoals, so if I multiply the acreage by . . . " He mumbled about tax rates and such, then said, "Is that right?" He punched more numbers. "Well, I'll be. He owes nigh about as much as the land is worth! By the time you figure in closing costs and lawyer's fees, Evan could actually lose money by selling!"

"Are you serious?" I said, suddenly excited. "He's in the middle of a deal that's got him mortgaged up to his eyeballs. If he has to take a loss on that property, he could go bankrupt."

Aunt Maggie had said that Evan was tight as a tick. What better motive for murder could he have than money? "He could have heard about Carney's agoraphobia from one of the dealers, and must have known that Carney came early," I said. "He'd have known that Bender was going to take Rusty to the vet, and Rusty wouldn't have fussed if he'd smelled Evan at the flea market the day Mary Maude was attacked."

"Do you think Carney knew about the back taxes?" Richard asked.

I remembered something Thatcher had told me. "Of course he did! Not long before he was killed, Carney told Evan that he'd heard that his business was taxing. I thought he was making fun of that tax audit, but I bet he was really teasing him about the map, just like he teased China and J.B. He must have tried to get something out of Evan in return for not giving the map to the city council."

"Free rent?" Richard suggested.

"Maybe. Either Evan wouldn't give it to him, or he thought that Carney was going to give it to the city council anyway. So he killed Carney, and hid the body so he'd have time to search for the map."

"Which he couldn't find, because Carney didn't trust Evan, either, and hid it in the mail," Richard continued. "He broke into the dealers' booths a second time so he could search more thoroughly, making it look like vandalism so the police couldn't be sure it was connected to Carney's death."

"He must have been tickled to death when Belva Tucker came up with that gang theory, but he still didn't have the map."

"Why did he come back to look for it the day he attacked Mary Maude?"

I thought about it for a minute, then said, "There were two boxes of scrap paper in Carney's booth that Bender was going to throw out, and Evan was there when Aunt Maggie asked if she could have them."

"You didn't tell me about that."

"I didn't think it was important." Aunt Maggie had said something about taking notes, and I should have listened to her. "Anyway, Evan came back to check out the paper, and Mary Maude caught him at it. So he clobbered her to keep her quiet."

"Which means that Aunt Maggie wasn't in danger after all," Richard said. "That's a relief."

"Are you sure about this?" Arthur asked.

Richard nodded, so I said, "Pretty sure."

"Can you prove it?"

"I don't know." Before we could try to think of a way, the phone rang. I picked it up. "Burnette residence."

"Laurie Anne? You better get down here right away!"

"Augustus? What's wrong?"

"I think something's happened to Aunt Maggie."

Richard told me later that every drop of color drained out of my face when I heard that. "What happened?"

"Mr. Cawthorne asked if I'd help him with some boxes in his office, and when I turned my back, he hauled off and hit me. It wasn't enough to knock me out, but it was enough to keep me out of commission while he locked me in. Now he's out there with Aunt Maggie, and I think I heard gunshots."

"Which Mr. Cawthorne?" I said, but I already knew what he was going to say.

"Evan. I think—" The line went dead.

Chapter 39

"Augustus? Augustus!" There was no answer, and after a second, a dial tone kicked in. I slammed the phone down, shouted, "Come on!" and was halfway out the door before Richard caught me.

"What is it?"

I explained it as fast as I could.

"We can't go off half-cocked," Richard said. "We need a plan."

"We need to get out there," I said.

"What about the police?" Arthur asked.

"There's no time," I said. "Mark doesn't trust us, and I don't know Belva well enough to trust her."

"But—"

Richard said, "Arthur, go talk to Mark. Throw your weight around, threaten him—do whatever it takes to get him out there. If that doesn't work, call the rest of the Burnettes and get them out there."

I think he said he would, but I was already out the door by that point, with Richard right behind me. This time, he didn't complain about my driving.

When we got to Tight as a Tick, I drove around to the

back door. Aunt Maggie's car was there, but every one of her tires was flat.

"I think they've been shot out," Richard said.

I was out of the car and reaching for the doorknob when he said, "Wait a minute. I want to get into the trunk."

"What for?"

"To see if Aunt Nora has a tire iron."

I threw him the keys, and while he got the tire iron, I told myself that running around like a chicken with its head cut off wasn't going to do Aunt Maggie or Augustus any good. I needed a weapon, too. My Swiss Army knife wasn't going to do it, but there were some rocks about half the size of my fist on the ground. I don't have much of an aim, but I shoved a couple in my blue jeans pockets anyway.

Richard, carrying Aunt Nora's tire iron, said, "Okay, let's go in. But be careful. And quiet."

I nodded, took a deep breath, and turned the doorknob. Thank goodness it was unlocked. Breaking it down wouldn't have been careful or quiet. I opened the door slowly, and we peered inside. There was nobody in sight, and all I could hear was the pounding of my heart.

I nodded in the direction of the flea market office, and we were almost there when a dog barked and I nearly jumped out of my skin. Rusty came bounding up and scratched at the door.

So much for keeping quiet. Maybe Evan wouldn't panic. After all, Rusty was supposed to be there. It wasn't until I was standing at the door next to the dog that I remembered that Evan and Bender were brothers. How did I know that they weren't in cahoots?

I decided it was too late to worry about that. I had to

know if my cousin was all right. I called out, "Augustus, are you okay?"

"Laurie Anne? Get me out of here!"

The door was locked, and Richard was trying to use the tire iron as a pry bar when Bender showed up.

"Hey there. What are you two doing out here?" He saw what Richard was trying to do. "Is there a problem?"

If he was working with Evan, he was hiding it well, so I took a chance. "My cousin is locked in. Have you got a key?"

"You bet." He pulled out his keys. "Evan sent me to get office supplies, but as soon as we got back, Rusty could tell something was wrong." I swear that he was about to stop long enough to pat the dog, but he remembered what he was doing. "Here we go," he said, putting the key in the lock and turning it.

Augustus swung the door open. "Have you found her? Is she all right?"

"We don't know—we came to get you first," I said.

"What did you do that for? She could be hurt."

"Hold on there," Bender said. "Who are you talking about?"

"Aunt Maggie." I didn't know if he'd believe his brother was a murderer or not, so I said, "The man who killed Carney has her, and we think they're out here somewhere. We've got to find her."

I don't know how much Bender had drunk that day, but he sobered up quickly. "Have you called the police?"

"The line's dead," Augustus said, which explained why we'd been cut off.

"Where would he have taken her?" I asked nobody in particular. The flea market suddenly seemed terribly large, with all the buildings and nooks and crannies. Would we hear Aunt Maggie if she called for help?

"Rusty can find her," Bender said. "All we need is something with her scent on it."

"What about the sheets at her booth?" I said. "She handles them every week."

"That should do it."

We hurried to her booth, and I put one of the sheets on the floor in front of Rusty.

Bender said, "Scent, boy."

The dog buried his nose in the folds of the cloth, then trotted purposefully off.

"This way," Bender said, and we ran after Rusty. For some reason, I expected him to bay as he followed the trail, but I should have known he was too intelligent for that.

"Do you know who's got her?" Bender asked.

I looked at Richard, and he shrugged, leaving the answer up to me. "We think it's your brother."

I expected surprise or even denial, but all Bender did was inhale deeply and look away for a minute. Then he said, "I guess it could be Evan, couldn't it?" No matter how much he drank, Bender wasn't a stupid man.

Rusty led us out the back door and toward the building Aunt Maggie called Taiwan Alley, but instead of taking us to the door, he went on past. He stopped when he got to the end of the building.

We stopped, too, and looked around the corner. Evan Cawthorne was standing next to a Dumpster, holding Aunt Maggie's forearm in one hand and a gun in the other. We all froze.

"Miz Burnette, why did you run away from me?" he was

saying in a frighteningly normal tone. "All I want is the map. Take me to it, and I'll let you go."

"Don't you know when you're licked? Too many people have already seen that map, including the police."

"It won't matter once it's destroyed," he said. "They can't officially establish the town line without it."

"The town line is the least of your worries, Evan. You ought to be worrying about getting caught for Carney's murder. Not to mention what you did to Mary Maude Foy and my nephew. If that boy's hurt, so help me—"

"You're not in a position to make threats. I am. Tell me where that map is or I'm going to hurt you."

"Find it yourself."

"Like you said, I've already killed once. I've got nothing to lose by doing it again. This is your last chance." He lifted the gun.

"Go to Hell!"

She sounded defiant, but I knew she was scared. Aunt Maggie never cusses.

Augustus and Richard were nudging one another, and when Richard hefted the tire iron, I knew they were planning to rush Evan. It wasn't a bad idea, but it seemed likely that somebody was going to end up with a bullet hole. I wasn't willing to bet on it being Evan.

Then I remembered the rocks in my pockets. I pulled one out and showed it to Richard and Augustus. They nodded, and Augustus pointed to a spot a few feet away from Evan. He was telling me not to try to hit him—the rock was just to distract him.

I threw the rock as hard as I could, and it hit the Dumpster with a satisfying clang. Evan was startled enough to loosen his grip on Aunt Maggie, but when she tried to get away, he pushed her down onto the ground. Then Augustus and Richard were on top of him. Richard swung the tire iron, but Evan ducked and hit him in the face with the gun. Blood splashed from my husband's nose. Augustus got a choke hold, but Evan fired toward him, and Augustus had to let go.

Evan whirled, waving the gun, but I couldn't tell who he was going to try to shoot. I pulled out the other rock and was running toward him when I heard Bender say, "Stop him, boy," and a red blur streaked past me. Evan screamed as Rusty clamped his jaws around his arm.

There were shots, I'm not sure how many, but they all went wild as Evan tried to fling Rusty away. Aunt Maggie grabbed one of Evan's legs and pulled him off of his feet, and the gun fell to the ground, out of his reach. Evan scrambled to get it, but Rusty still had his arm. A second later, Richard had the other, and Augustus was sitting on top of his chest. Even then, Evan kept struggling. He didn't give up until we heard the siren.

Chapter 40

It took forever to get it all sorted out. Mark didn't want to believe us, especially when Evan calmed down enough to deny everything. I think Mark might have let him go if Trey hadn't said, "If you don't want to arrest him, Mark, I will. Or would you rather Belva Tucker took him in?" That got him, and he finally handcuffed Evan and put him in back of the cruiser.

Other than scrapes, bruises, and Richard's bloody nose, none of us was injured. Rusty hadn't even hurt Evan all that badly, which I thought was a shame. Once we were sure everybody was all right, we let Mark take our statements.

When Augustus and Aunt Maggie got to the flea market, they found Evan hanging around Aunt Maggie's booth. He said that he wanted to make sure all the doors were locked, and since Aunt Maggie had known Bender to forget, she believed him. Then she mentioned that his problems out there should be over because the map had been found and he'd be able to sell the place. He played it cool at first, just said he was glad to hear that. Then he wanted to know where Richard and I had found it.

Right after she explained, Evan asked Augustus to help him with those imaginary boxes in the office. While they were gone, Aunt Maggie started wondering how Evan knew Richard and I had found the map. It's not like we were actively looking for it, so he couldn't have heard any rumors. He could have heard rumors about us looking for Carney's killer, but the only person who would have connected the murder with the map was the murderer.

That's when Aunt Maggie decided to see what Evan was up to. She got to the office just as he was locking the door and saw that Augustus wasn't with him. Then she went for the back door, meaning to get to the car and go for help. Evan caught sight of her, drew a gun, and fired, so she ran out another door, intending to double back to the car. He got there first and shot out the tires, then cut the phone wires.

Not knowing if Bender was in on it or not, Aunt Maggie decided to try to get to the road and flag down help, but Evan kept cutting her off. She hid behind the Dumpster for a while, but he had just found her when Rusty led us to the two of them. It was a good thing we got there in time. I didn't have any idea that Evan would have let her go.

As for Augustus, he was all got away with that he'd left Aunt Maggie alone. He just wasn't suspicious of Evan because we'd been so sure that the map eliminated him as a suspect.

Of course, when Augustus said that, Aunt Maggie figured out that we'd been watching her. I was afraid that she'd be mad, but she seemed more amused than anything else, although she did sound wistful when she said, "I thought he just liked going to auctions."

Mark was still acting peeved about us getting involved until Belva showed up. She'd seen the Byerly police cruiser while driving by, and wanted to know what was going on

Before Mark could explain, she lit into him for arresting Evan, saying that he ought to be sued for false arrest.

Maybe Mark hadn't believed us before, but he wasn't going to admit it then. He told her that he had evidence that Evan Cawthorne was a murderer, and if she didn't like it, she could take it up with the judge. Then she said that she should be the one to take Evan into custody, but Mark wasn't about to let her get away with that. When she fussed, Arthur, who'd arrived right after Trey and Mark, showed her the map. It proved that Carney's murder had taken place in Byerly, giving Mark jurisdiction.

After Belva drove off in a huff, and Mark and Trey left to take Evan to jail, I noticed Bender standing off to one side, alone except for Rusty.

I went to pat the dog. "Good boy, Rusty," I said, and I meant it. I didn't want to think about what could have happened if he hadn't been there. Then I said, "Bender, I'm sorry about your brother."

"I am, too," he said sadly. "Money has always been real important to Evan, but I didn't think it was that important."

"The love of money is the root of all evil," Richard said, coming up behind us.

"I don't think it was just the money," Bender said. "It was him wanting to prove that he's something more than trailer trash." He shook his head sadly, and he and Rusty went back to his trailer.

The rest of the week was busy by most standards, but compared to what we'd been doing, it was quite relaxing. We spent a lot of time visiting folks, but we got to sleep late. We had to tell Junior everything when she got back in town, but she was a very appreciative audience. Winning that bet had made her mighty happy.

We also got to spend time getting reacquainted with Augustus. One evening, Richard took him to the V.F.W. to introduce him to Vivian, and she talked him into joining her veterans' support group.

By the time his birthday party rolled around on Saturday night, Augustus looked like he was ready to start a new year. I hadn't found the right time to tell him my idea for his new job, but as it turned out, I didn't have to.

Aunt Maggie, Augustus, Richard, and I were going through the whole story again for Aunt Nora. She'd heard it all before, but wanted to make sure she hadn't missed any of the details.

When we finished, she said, "All these years I felt so sorry for Evan. Who'd have thought he'd stoop low enough to take advantage of a man's mental illness."

"I still feel bad about that," Aunt Maggie said. "If I'd kept my mouth shut, Carney might still be alive."

But I said, "Probably not, Aunt Maggie. I ran into Bender at the police station, and he told me something. You remember saying how Carney needed a booth right by the door? It wasn't a coincidence that he got that spot. He specifically asked for it. Evan wasn't going to let him have it, because somebody else had asked for it first, so Carney had to tell him why he needed it."

"Then Evan already knew about the agoraphobia?" Aunt Maggie said.

"He's known about it for years."

She looked like she felt better for a minute, but then said, "At least he never told anybody like I did."

"Think about it this way. If you hadn't felt guilty about telling people, you wouldn't have asked me and Richard to find out who killed him. And if we hadn't known about the agoraphobia, we wouldn't have been able to find where Carney hid the map, and we probably wouldn't have figured out who killed him. If you did owe Carney anything, you're even now."

She didn't say anything at first, but then she said, "Thank you, Laurie Anne." If I hadn't known better, I'd have sworn she teared up a little, but if she did, it didn't last long.

"How on earth did Carney end up with that map anyway?" Aunt Nora wanted to know.

"Thatcher Broods sold it to him," Aunt Maggie said. "Thatcher bought some knives from an estate sale at Clara Jean Hemby's house. Do you remember Clara Jean, Nora? She used to be town clerk."

"Didn't Big Bill fire her a long time ago for stealing?" Aunt Nora asked.

"I don't know if she stole anything before she was fired, but if she didn't, she made up for it when she cleaned out her office afterward. She took all kinds of papers that didn't belong to her, just to make trouble. Somewhere along the line, that map ended up wrapped around the knives Thatcher bought. He told Mark he thought it was just trash, but when Carney bought the knives from him, he knew exactly what it was."

I continued the story. "We're not exactly sure what happened next, because Evan's lawyer won't let him say anything. We think Carney tried to sell the map to Evan and Evan said something that made Carney realize that Evan didn't want it found, and somehow Carney figured out Evan's tax problem. We know Evan knew about the taxes, too, because Belva found a spreadsheet where he'd worked out estimates of how much he owed. Anyway, Carney tried to blackmail Evan, but Evan didn't trust Carney to keep quiet, so he decided to kill him."

Aunt Nora shook her head, and I could tell that she didn't understand how Evan could have done it. I didn't really understand it, either. I knew there were circumstances under which I'd kill, but I couldn't imagine killing for money. Then again, I've never been as poor as Evan Cawthorne had.

"What's going to happen to the flea market?" Aunt Nora asked.

"Bender is going to keep running it," Aunt Maggie said. "Even though he's in jail, Evan hasn't given up, and he'll need the flea market money for lawyer's fees. Everything else is still tied up in the condos. The funny thing is, if the condo deal works out, he might still end up rich."

Richard said, "Speaking of the flea market, what did the other dealers think about Evan being the killer?"

Aunt Maggie rolled her eyes. "Most of them had the story wrong, and of course Mary Maude and Mavis made out like they'd suspected Evan all along. Everybody was real sorry you two didn't come out today. They wanted to apologize for the way they acted and congratulate y'all for catching Carney. Ronald even made y'all a pair of rings—I've got them in the car."

"Thank him for us, and give them all our regards." It would have been nice to have gone out there, but Richard and I had spent a very pleasant day alone.

"Laurie Anne, J.B. said he wanted to thank you," Aunt Maggie said.

"For catching Carney's killer?"

"No, for helping him get Annabelle Lamar to drop the custody suit. You told him that you saw Annabelle with Mrs.

Samples at the auction, and he asked Mrs. Samples about it. It turns out that Annabelle was trying to bribe her to keep quiet."

"What does Mrs. Samples know about Mrs. Lamar?"

"Despite Annabelle being so snooty about Tight as a Tick," Aunt Maggie said, "she spends a lot of time at the Metrolina Flea Market in Charlotte. It turns out that most of those antiques she's been claiming are family heirlooms were bought from the Samples. When Annabelle saw them at Tight as a Tick the day we met her, she was worried that her secret would come out. J.B. figured that if she was lying about that, she just might be lying about other things. So he went to see her and told her he was going to ask some questions about her in her hometown. She turned white as a sheet, and begged him not to. She offered him money, too, but all he wanted was for her to leave him and Tammy alone."

"That's wonderful," I said.

"Well, Aunt Maggie, after all these carryings on, I know you'll be glad for things to get back to normal," Aunt Nora said.

"I guess," Aunt Maggie said, "but I was just getting used to having company. It's going to be right lonely once Laurie Anne and Richard go back to Massachusetts."

"Not necessarily," I said, looking pointedly at Augustus. He looked back at me, and then at Aunt Maggie like he was thinking. She looked at him, then at me like she wondered what I meant. I wanted to say something, but resisted as hard as I could. I didn't want to push either of them into a situation they didn't want.

Augustus finally said, "Actually, Aunt Maggie, I was thinking I could start going with you."

Despite what she'd just said, Aunt Maggie bristled. "I've been doing fine for years—I don't know that I need any help now."

"It's me that needs help," he said. "I want to learn the business."

She looked dubious, so I pointed out, "Augustus spent a lot of time at the flea markets in Germany, and you saw how good he is at selling."

"You're not so bad at selling yourself, Laurie Anne. Augustus, you know I work long hours—the flea market is open every weekend. And I spend a lot of time at auctions and going to the thrift stores. You won't be able to go out all the time."

"That's all right," he said.

"And it's *my* business. You'll have to do like I say."

"Yes, ma'am."

"It's not much money. I make enough for me, but I don't know that we can make enough to support you, too."

"I've got some money saved up to keep me going until we see if we can build up the business. If that gives out, I'll get a part-time job someplace where I won't have to work weekends."

She looked at him for a long time, but finally said, "I suppose we can give it a try and see how it works out."

Augustus broke out in the biggest grin I'd seen on his face since he'd been back in Byerly. "Thank you, Aunt Maggie. I won't let you down."

I could see that he wanted to shake her hand or hug her or something, but he wasn't sure if he should. Aunt Maggie must have seen it, too, because she said, "All right, go ahead and hug me." She gave a big sigh as he did it, but I don't think she minded as much as she let on. In fact, I think she was pretty pleased with the whole situation.

Naturally, Aunt Nora started to cry, but that didn't stop her from running off to tell Uncle Buddy, Aunt Daphine, Aunt Nellie, and anybody else she could find.

Once she was out of earshot, Aunt Maggie said, "Augustus, I didn't want to say anything in front of your mama, but I'm telling you right now that I don't want you high on the job."

Augustus, Richard, and I nearly choked. Then Augustus said, "I didn't know you knew," at the same time I was saying, "I didn't tell her."

"Nobody told me. I know reefer when I smell it. You youngsters may have been born in the sixties, but I lived through them."

Richard laughed so hard I thought he was going to bust a gusset.

There was one more piece of good news that night. The Burnettes were expecting a new arrival. No, Vasti wasn't pregnant, though anybody could tell from how worn out Arthur looked that it wasn't from lack of trying. It was Aunt Maggie who was getting a little one.

It turned out that Rusty had slipped out one last time before Bender had him fixed. The result of that final adventure was a pregnant golden retriever. After the way Rusty had helped save her, Aunt Maggie figured the least she could do was take one of the puppies. Between Augustus and the puppy, loneliness was going to be the least of Aunt Maggie's problems.

Later on, as Richard and I sat watching the family enjoy the party, I said, "It hasn't been such a bad vacation, after all."

" 'All's well that ends well.' "

I didn't say a word. I just grinned.

After a minute, he realized what he'd said. "No! I blew it! With only one week, two days, and twelve hours to go."

I patted him on the shoulder consolingly. "Don't feel too bad. You did your best."

Then he perked up. "You know what they say. 'What's gone and what's past help should be past grief.' *The Winter's Tale*, Act III, Scene 2." He proceeded to quote me as many Shakespearean quotes as he could come up with. I guess he figured that since he'd already lost the bet, he might as well have fun. As for me, it's a good thing I couldn't get a word in edgewise, or I might have confessed that I'd missed the Shakespeare, too.

Please turn the page for an exciting sneak peek of

Toni L.P. Kelner's newest

Laura Fleming mystery

DEATH OF A DAMN YANKEE

now on sale wherever hardcover mysteries are sold!

Chapter 1

Richard was still asleep when I woke up. I thought I'd heard the phone ring, and I stumbled downstairs to answer it, but Aunt Maggie had gotten there ahead of me. I looked at the clock. It was a little after nine o'clock, which meant that Aunt Maggie would normally have already been making the rounds of the thrift stores, and I wondered if there was something wrong. Since she was mostly listening, I couldn't tell who she was talking to, so I got a glass and some water from the faucet, rummaged around to see if there was anything in the refrigerator I could eat for breakfast, and waited for her to get off the phone.

Finally she said, "I appreciate your letting me know, Tavis. I'll talk to you later."

"What are you still doing here?" I asked, stifling a yawn as she hung up. "No thrift stores open today?"

"I sent Augustus to make the rounds without me because I was planning to go to the union meeting with Saunders this morning."

"I'd forgotten about that. When's the meeting?"

"There isn't going to be any meeting, at least not with Marshall Saunders."

"They're withdrawing their bid for the mill?" I asked,

selfishly hoping that they had so I wouldn't have to worry about them anymore.

"Marshall is dead, Laurie Anne."

I guess I blinked, but I don't think I did anything else for a few seconds. I know I didn't speak, because so many questions were trying to crowd their way out that I couldn't decide which one to ask first.

Aunt Maggie said, "You know that old warehouse out by the train tracks, the one where they used to store shipments for the mill before they started shipping by truck? They found him in there. What was left of him, anyway. The place burned to the ground last night, and he was inside. Tavis said they put the fire out last night, but it wasn't until this morning that they realized he was in there."

"Marshall wasn't the one setting the fires, was he?" I asked, almost hoping he had been. It was terrible of me, but it was better than thinking Linwood could have done it.

Aunt Maggie snorted. "Not unless he set the fire and then tied himself up."

My stomach rolled. Aunt Edna had only been worried about somebody being hurt by accident. Neither she nor I had even considered murder. I remembered how angry Linwood was about the proposed changes at the mill. Could he be angry enough to kill?

Aunt Maggie leaned over and touched my arm. "Are you all right, Laurie Anne? You look like you just saw a ghost. I thought you only met Marshall the other day."

"I'm fine," I said, knowing that I couldn't explain the truth without mentioning Aunt Edna and Linwood. "It's just hard to imagine Marshall dead."

"People die every day, Laurie Anne," Aunt Maggie said. "One time I was talking to a friend of mine, and she left my house to go to the grocery store and got hit by a car not ten minutes later. It throws you, but it does happen."

I was a little leery of asking the next question, but I tried to make it sound casual. "Do they have any idea who did it?"

"Not that Tavis knew of. I imagine Junior will be keeping busy with this one."

"How is the murder going to affect the buyout? Is Mrs. Saunders going to go through with it?"

"Nobody's sure yet. I think that even Big Bill has enough sense not to ask a brand-new widow a question like that, but I hope she says something soon. Tavis says he's going to see what he can find out and get back to me. I'm going to see if I can catch up with Augustus." She got up and gathered her pocketbook, but stopped at the kitchen door to look at me. "Are you *sure* you're all right?"

"I'm fine." It was a lie, but it satisfied her, and she left.

I sat at the kitchen table while too many thoughts ran through my head. First was the shock of somebody I'd just met dying, especially since I'd liked him. Second was the idea that my cousin might have been involved. And third was what Junior had talked about: coincidences. The day after Richard and I showed up to investigate Marshall and his wife, he was murdered. What with the problems with Linwood and not being able to get in touch with Burt, we hadn't done much yet—certainly nothing that could have pushed somebody to murder Marshall—but it was a big enough coincidence that I couldn't help but feel guilty.

Eventually, Richard came downstairs, rubbing his eyes. "Good morning," he said cheerfully.

I didn't answer.

"No sausage biscuits?" he asked.

The thought of well-done meat made my stomach roll again. "I'm not hungry."

He sat down across from me and studied my face. "What's wrong?"

"Marshall Saunders was murdered last night."

"Good God! What happened?"

"He was burned to death," I said and told him what Aunt Maggie had told me.

"Do you think Linwood did it?" he asked once I was finished.

"I just don't know, Richard." Suspecting Linwood of arson was one thing; suspecting him of murder was something horribly different. Then I remembered something. "He couldn't have!" I said. "He was at Aunt Edna's house last night."

"You're right," he said, sounding as relieved as I was. "Let's call Aunt Edna and give her the good news."

Unfortunately, there was no answer at Aunt Edna's house.

"What about Burt?" Richard said when I hung up the phone.

"I'm sure he knows about Marshall already."

"Don't you think we should find out if he still wants us to investigate?"

"I hadn't thought of that." I tried Burt at the mill and at home again and left messages at both places. "No luck," I said, "but surely he'll call us sometime today."

Realizing that Linwood was off the hook had given me my appetite back, but there still wasn't anything to eat in the house, so Richard and I took turns in the shower and were about ready to head for Hardee's when we heard Aunt Edna at the front door.

"Thank goodness y'all are here!" she said, rushing into

the kitchen. "I tried to call, but the line was busy, so I came on over. Have y'all heard about Marshall Saunders?"

I nodded. "Tavis Montgomery called Aunt Maggie and told her about it."

"Then it's true!" She burst into tears.

"Aunt Edna?" I said, mystified by her reaction. "This is good news, isn't it? Not about Saunders being dead, of course, but at least it clears Linwood. He was with you last night, so he couldn't have set the fire."

Aunt Edna started crying even harder, and I got that sick feeling in my stomach again. "Linwood *was* with you last night, wasn't he?"

"No, Laurie Anne, he wasn't." She made a visible effort to pull herself together. "Linwood, Sue, and the kids did come to my house for dinner last night, just like they were supposed to, and things went real well at first. Caleb was really working hard to kind of bring Linwood out of his shell—playing with the kids, and talking to Sue about cars because he knows they've been looking at minivans—and it was going so well. Linwood didn't talk much, but at least he wasn't saying ugly things the way he has before."

"Then what?" I asked.

"We ate dinner, and the kids were cranking homemade ice cream when Caleb said, 'Linwood, I've been seeing your mother for quite a while now—I think it's pretty obvious how I feel about her. I want you to know that I'm going to ask Edna to marry me, but I want your blessing first.' "

Aunt Edna's eyes shone as she remembered Caleb's words, but then they teared up again. "Laurie Anne, I swear that was the first I'd heard of it. Oh, we'd talked about marriage, but I didn't know Caleb was going to say anything to Linwood like that."

"How did Linwood react?" I asked.

"It was awful. He said there was no way in hell that he'd let me marry Caleb. And that Caleb had no right to come sniffing around me the way he had been—that everybody knew he was only after one thing." Aunt Edna snorted. "As if a good-looking man like Caleb couldn't get *that* anyplace he wanted it. Sue was trying to hush him up in front of the children, but then Linwood turned on me. I know he didn't mean it, but—" She paused to wipe her eyes again, and I reached over to take her hand and squeeze it gently. "He said that I should be ashamed of myself for running around with Caleb, that I was being disrespectful of Loman's memory." She shook her head. "Everybody knows what he did to me. He doesn't deserve any respect. But still, I've tried to do the right thing. Loman had been dead over a year before I started seeing Caleb. Don't I have a right to be happy?"

"Of course you do," I said firmly. "There's not one thing wrong with your seeing anybody you want to."

"I told Linwood that, but he said that if I married Caleb, I'd be no better than . . . no better than a whore!"

"He said that?" I said, aghast. I'd known Linwood was mighty messed up, but him saying that to his own mama shocked me worse than the idea of him burning down buildings.

Aunt Edna looked down at her hands as if she were ashamed, and I went from being shocked to being furious at Linwood for making her feel that way.

"I had to hold Caleb back, as you might imagine," Aunt Edna said.

I nodded, thinking what Richard would have done in that situation. My husband isn't a violent man, but he can be when it comes to people he loves.

"Then I told Linwood that he had no business talking to Caleb or me that way, and that maybe he was a grown man, but while he was in my house, he darned well better watch his mouth. He started to say something about it being his daddy's house, but I told him it was *my* house and *my* life and who I decide to spend my time with is *my* business. And moreover, if and when I decide to get married again, that's my business, too."

Now her eyes were flashing, and I remembered stories Aunt Nora had told me about Aunt Edna as a young woman, how she was the spirited one in the family. The spirit was still there, even after her years of being browbeaten by Uncle Loman, and when it came out, it was something to behold. Then she seemed to deflate as she remembered the next part.

"Linwood got real still, the same way Loman used to when he got mad. It wasn't Loman yelling that you had to worry about—it was when he was quiet that you knew it was bad. Then he stood up and walked out the front door. A minute later, we heard the station wagon start up. He just drove off, with Sue and the kids sitting right there."

"What time was it?" I asked.

"Early enough for him to have set the fire, if that's what you're asking. Caleb kept apologizing for springing it on me and Linwood that way, and Sue didn't say much of anything other than to tell us that she and the kids needed a ride home. The poor kids didn't know what to think—I felt so bad for them having to see and hear that. Of course, being kids, they still wanted their ice cream, so it was probably an hour or more before we finally got ready to go, but I figured it was just as well because Linwood needed some time alone. Caleb wanted to come with us, but I told him to go on home because I thought I should talk to Linwood by myself. I had

Sue in the front seat with me, so I saw her face when we got to their house and the station wagon wasn't there. She looked scared, Laurie Anne, and she wouldn't say a word. She just took the kids inside.

"After that, I couldn't seem to make myself go home. I kept hearing what Linwood had said about it being Loman's house. So I went to the church and got Reverend Glass to let me in so I could sit and think things through. It was close to midnight before I finally left there, and when I drove back by Linwood's house, he still wasn't home. This morning Nora called to tell me about Marshall Saunders being dead. I tried to call Sue and Linwood, but they didn't answer, and when I went to their house, I saw Junior Norton's squad car in the driveway."

"Did she arrest him?" I asked.

"No, but she wanted to know where he'd been last night. Sue swore that he'd been with her and the kids the whole time."

"Even though he hadn't been," Richard said.

"I was so glad the kids weren't in the room to hear their mother lie that way, but the thing is, if Junior had asked me, I'd have lied, too. I've never lied to the police before, but maybe not telling her the truth is the same thing."

I patted her hand. "I'd probably have done the same thing. What else did Junior say?"

"She asked Linwood about gasoline. I guess she'd checked around town and found out that Sid Honeywell has sold Linwood gasoline in a can several times these past few months. Linwood said he needed it for the lawn mower."

"Oh Lord," I said, remembering how high the grass had been at Linwood and Sue's house. "What did Junior say to that?"

"There wasn't much she could say, but after she left Sue and Linwood's house, I saw her going up the drive to the neighbor's place. I know she's going to try to find out if anybody saw him coming or going last night. Maybe he was lucky and nobody was looking out the window. I don't know because I wasn't there long enough to see if she came back."

"Why not? What did Linwood do?"

She sighed so deeply it hurt to hear it. "As soon as Junior was gone, he looked at me so hateful and said, 'This is *my* house.' I tried to talk to him, but he wouldn't listen, and Sue said that she thought I should go."

"Oh, Aunt Edna, you know he's just mad—he'll get over it."

"I hope so, Laurie Anne. But no matter what, there are two things I decided while I was at the church last night. First off, I can't marry Caleb if it's going to ruin things between me and Linwood. I love Caleb, Laurie Anne, and I don't think I'll ever stop loving him, but I can't stand the idea of losing Linwood. I'd be miserable if I went ahead and married Caleb, and it would just sour our relationship." I started to object, but she said, "I know what you're thinking: that I ought not let Linwood keep me from what I want. But I don't want to lose my boy. He's the only child I could ever have—I had to have a hysterectomy when he was just a little thing—and he and his children are the world to me. You'll know what I mean someday."

She was right. Until I had a child of my own, there was no way I could understand how the possible loss of one would affect me. I already knew I'd lie to the police for Linwood—I didn't know what lengths I'd go to to protect a child.

"I decided something else, too," Aunt Edna said. "You

two and I have never talked about religion, but there are some things I believe. One of those is that a person has to redeem himself when he sins. Murder puts a blot on a man's soul, one that stays there until he repents. If Linwood killed that man, he's got to admit it and ask for forgiveness. If he doesn't, he'll be damned for all eternity." She took a ragged breath. "I won't have that, Laurie Anne. I asked y'all before to find out if he was setting those fires so we could stop him ourselves, but it's too late for that. If Linwood didn't do it, I don't want him taking the blame for it, but if he did, he's got to go to jail and redeem himself, even if that means my losing him forever. I'd rather lose him than have him lose his soul.

"Laurie Anne, I know y'all don't want to be responsible for sending your own cousin to jail. It should be my responsibility, and I'd do it if I could, but I don't know how. So I'm asking you two to help me save my boy's soul."

It should have sounded melodramatic—people just don't talk about redemption and saving souls that way—but I knew Aunt Edna meant every word of it. She was willing to forgo her own happiness with Caleb, but she wouldn't risk her son's eternal soul for anything. Could I live with myself if I didn't take a risk to help her?

I repeated what I'd told her before. "We'll do what we can, Aunt Edna. That's a promise."

ABOUT THE AUTHOR

Toni L.P. Kelner lives with her family in Massachusetts. She is the author of six Laura Fleming mysteries. She loves to hear from her readers and you may write to her c/o Kensington Books. Please include a self-addressed stamped envelope if you wish a response.